Belladonna

Belladonna

MARY FINN

CANDLEWICK PRESS

Copyright © 2011 by Mary Finn

First edition 2011

Library of Congress Cataloging-in-Publication Data

Finn, Mary.
Belladonna / Mary Finn. — 1st U.S. ed.
p. cm.
Summary: In 1757 England, clever but unschooled Thomas Rose helps the spirited Ling seek Belladonna, the horse she rode in the circus, and in their quest they meet painter George Stubbs who euthanizes animals to study their anatomy, but he assures them her horse is safe at a nearby estate.
ISBN 978-0-7636-5106-0
[1. Interpersonal relations — Fiction. 2. Lost and found possessions — Fiction. 3. Horses — Fiction. 4. Stubbs, George, 1724–1806 — Fiction. 5. Great Britain — History — George II, 1727–1760 — Fiction.] I. Title.
PZ7.F49744Bel 2011
[Fic] — dc22   2010038707

11 12 13 14 15 16 BVG 10 9 8 7 6 5 4 3 2 1

Printed in Berryville, VA, U.S.A.

This book was typeset in Baskerville.

Candlewick Press
99 Dover Street
Somerville, Massachusetts 02144

visit us at www.candlewick.com

For Daniel

O, she doth teach the torches to burn bright!

—Romeo and Juliet

This Book

I AM THOMAS ROSE, originally of Horkstow in the county of Lincoln.

I am sixteen years of age now, but I write of what happened last year. The summer of 1757 was when all the strangeness began.

At the time I saw only an end, not a beginning, only bad circumstance and not a sniff of adventure. But it was that end and that circumstance that returned me from the town of Brigg to my own village in the month of August.

If I had not come, I would never have been able to set down this story in pen and ink, as a writer does. Worse, I would never have met the remarkable people who were there, one in particular.

Part One

Swan Song

ON THE LAST SCHOOL DAY of my life, I didn't even make it as far as the Grammar. So perhaps the day before was truly the last, but I do not remember that one.

I was late again because my friends the swans kept their own good time for breakfast. I wasn't the only one who fed the birds, but that day I was alone on the bridge. There was just my face, and what my sister calls my teasel mop, looking back up at me from the water, and then a white cloud broke me into bits, and three gray cloud puffs followed fast from under the arches. A second white kept its distance.

The female nudged the babies if they lagged, but she was as sweet about it as if her beak were only a soft feather, like the rest of her. She was the pen. The father was the cob, the master swan.

Why does the mother swan deserve such a cruel name?

I aimed the pieces of crust as best I could toward the young grays, who bent and twined their necks like ropes. They thought the swan god was dropping bread from the sky.

Then I saw old Waterworth the writing master on the town side of the bridge, turning left, making his way from the early inn to the schoolhouse. I knew the man by the hobble, not the face. If he'd come over the bridge and seen me there with my bread for birds, there'd have been the devil to pay, though the man wasn't the worst of them.

He was bad enough, all the same.

When I thought about the day ahead, my stomach hardened into a knot. I felt for the sharp nib that stuck out like a canker from the Latin primer in my bag of books. I loved the length of a charcoal or a crayon in my hand, but I hated ink as if it were poison.

"Old Nick dips his pen in Thomas Rose's inkwell."

Once a day a master would say that, or something like, and then the boys from the town joined the fun. *"Ink on his fingers, ink on his hooves. Blotch, splotch, gollygotch."* They kept their own song for the yard.

"Tom foole may go to school, but ne'er will he be taught there."

We'd be up then and hammering blows, my two fists against ten or twelve of theirs, and even though I was a head taller than any of my mockers, I often had to help myself to whatever made a handy weapon, or be pulped on the spot.

Only the last Friday, my grandfather had been billed, yet again. A snipe of a boy from the lower form ran into the shop bearing a summons from the Grammar, and my poor old gloverman forefather had to down his needles and leathers and threads and go to learn why he was persecuted so.

He came back white as lint.

"They said to me, 'For the wanton destruction of a desk, a property of the school, one guinea down, sir, for the wrong done, and also for our insurance if Master Rose is to continue, but we advise against it.' They said you were as unteachable as a rabbit plucked by its ears from the marketplace. They said you fight the best boys of this town. What will I tell your mother, Thomas?"

I said nothing. What was there to say she didn't already know?

Old Waterworth had vanished. A cart clopped over the bridge, taking it easy. If it had been facing for home, I would have jumped on the back and tried my chances right then, but it was heading east, through the town.

Back on the bridge, the nib was worked free of its shaft at last, and I flicked the useless thing out over the water. It fell as soundlessly as a piece of bread, but unlike bread, it sank.

My swans paid no heed to the tiny plop of the nib, but when I wheeled the bag of books over my head like a slingshot, they scattered, even before it had hit the water. They were mute, poor things, so their shock was all in their wings and feet. That was badly done by me, to heart-scald the birds like that. I should have crossed to the other side of the bridge to get rid of my chains.

Anyway, the bag had sunk all right, down to the bottom-most part of Brigg, taking with it all my chances in this world, for sure.

All I had to do now was bid my grandfather thank-you and farewell, gather up what lay under my bed, and beg a passage home, or walk the ten or so miles. My mother must be told the truth, nothing less. Maybe at last she'd believe I'd never count for anything. My father was already primed to swallow that news, though I knew how proud he had been of his son. Thomas Rose, the scholar, learning his Latin in Brigg! But now he'd know, black for white, that all the fine pictures I see in my head are worse than nothing, because they can't escape out of me into the world.

Who'd ever look at what I put down on a page?

In this way, I left school behind me forever.

The Girl with
Geometry in Her Legs

I SHALL BLOW OVER the squalls that followed.

The next day of note in my sorry life was several weeks later.

I'd left my father's work in the late afternoon and taken the road to where I believed I'd find something to interest me. I thought it only fair to give warning by kicking a clod ahead of me, but the thing didn't rise, only broke into dust. There was no damp in heaven or earth in the weeks since I'd come home to the village. My father said I had brought drought and bad news, both.

Anger sat around our house like a guest that wouldn't leave, and lightning cracked the skies outside without bringing rain.

But the girl was there.

This was the third day I'd spotted her, huddled in the road ditch that ran between Horkstow and the water.

Each day there was less of her. She was like a clever ground-nesting bird the way she had learned to settle herself deeper down into that tangle of ditch. She was much the same color as one of those birds too, brown and dull. There was only one bit of her that was bold.

Whoever she was, she was smart enough to cover her dress with fat dock leaves, but today, just like the other days, it was the red flash of her kerchief that gave her away. How could she know there were never berries so bright in that hedgerow?

I stopped as if to show that my boots hurt me, and her red top dipped down deeper into the green lattice of weeds. *A sly move, girl, but no use to you,* I thought.

I looked back along the road.

Ahead, as far as the lane, there was nobody, and then there was nobody again all the way as far as Ottleys' barn, where Tim Peck and his dog, Pox, were shifting cows for afternoon milking. Man and dog were the size of bees, the beasts big as brown soft-blown moths. I had to squint harder for the other direction, but yes, there it blew, the dust of Fulk the Ragman's cart, as it headed for Horkstow.

"Who are you?" I called out, standing right above her hiding place. "Don't you know Seth Catchpole will do for you if he finds you breaking open his fine hedge?"

I meant the words as a joke to the girl, not a threat. But my voice came out rough, and likely as belly-curdling as old Seth's own. There was just no telling what sounds I'd make from one open mouth to the next. My speech might go high as a fiddle or growl as it just had. My companions at Brigg Grammar had noticed this very well, though they were little better.

"Go away, you fool. I am busy."

That hiss from the ditch sent a spit onto my boots.

"Busy at what?"

"Leave it, will you, moonhead."

All I had to do was lean over and part the elderberry branches she'd pulled over herself. The dark leaves and baby fruits peeled away from her face like barley silk coming off nibs of grain. The smell of honeysuckle rose, even now, even as late as August.

"Won't leave me be, pig? I have a something sharp here for your ribs if you're thinking more of it."

She was crouched down like a milking girl on her hunkers, but she was small anyway, maybe even as small as my sister, Nan, who was only ten. There was more age than Nan's, though, in her pale fierce face and in the slight swell under her ragged cotton bodice. The hair scraped back into the red kerchief was black, black as a plum. Plums were about the right size of her eyes too, huge dark things, poisonous.

She made sure I could see the blade in her left hand, a sharp one, with a handle the color of goose legs.

Well, I thought, *best be mannerly.*

"If I thought you were using the hedge for your business, I wouldn't bother you."

That was my steady voice and only the luck of a moment, but I continued so.

"But you were here yesterday and the day before too, at right this time. So —"

"So, what is that to you?" she sniped back at me. "Are you this Mr. Catchpole's constable? When you saw nothing of me, I saw *you,* head up head down like a sniff dog, on your way to that old gray church in the village. Are you the priest's baby, then?"

Baybay, she said.

I know I turned red as her headpiece when she said that. It was true that the church was my bolt-hole since I'd come home. She had that spotted right. The old man there left me alone to my pencils and papers, and the cool light space was a blessing over my head. None of that was this girl's affair. She was the stranger here, and it was far fitter for her to answer questions, not ask them. Besides, I was sure I'd seen her first.

She laughed instead, before I could speak. "No, you're not a sniff dog. They are low to the ground. You're a great tall lolloping thing, you are. Yes, I know what it is you make me think. It is *giraffe*!"

What that last word meant I would not ask. She talked so strange, anyway — what did she know?

"Why don't you stand up onto the road, and let's see what *you* are, then?"

Lucky me. Even a turnpike man might envy that strong voice, not a quaver in it.

The girl stretched her neck upward, and without any heed of me, she rolled her head on it easily, a red flower turning on a slender stalk. She lifted her arms to each side the way a fisher bird holds his wings to dry them, though her left fingers kept tight hold of the blade all the while. Then she took one long step out of the ditch and stood in front of me.

All in all, the work of a neat cat, easy done and perfect.

She bowed low then, mocking again. But when she moved that one foot behind her, she made a geometry all her own. It was a beautiful thing.

Now that it was right under my nose, I could see that her red kerchief was made of a fine stuff, perhaps a silk.

There were little holes punched along its border, and the color caught the light and shimmered. Stolen, for sure, because the rest of her clothes were straggly, a proper beggar's outfit.

She looked straight up at me when she spoke.

"My name is Ling, and you can help me. If you will. That which I search for is only a man's name, so it is nothing much to trouble you."

The Brown Man with the Brown Horse

WHAT SORT OF a name was *Ling*? And what sort of talk did the girl have, for that matter? *That which I search for.* She'd made a strange mess out of saying "nothing" too.

"Did you say Ling?" I asked. "I never heard a female called that, not in these parts, anyway. Are you all the way from Grimsby, then? Are you from fisherfolk?"

I had no wish to twist her. But she had just called me something odd, and if I knew anything, what she'd called me was probably worse than a fish. I was well pleased to see I could redden *her* cheeks.

"My proper name is Hélène, but everyone around here is too stupid to say it right, a French name like that. All they know is Ling. And Ling is a name for the heather flower, anyway, not the fish, fool."

The plum eyes glared, daring me to take it further.

Then I surprised myself. I bowed back to her, and it was not all playact either, though I give my word that I had never done such a thing in my life. Small as she was, there was something about her that pulled a person up, something rare. It didn't matter the poor clothes she wore or the daft name she said was hers; she had an air to suit her grace.

"Thomas Rose, at your service. What do you want to know, then?"

The bow amused her, I could see, but then the black brows met again.

"That old brick cottage down the lane ahead—one can just see it down in the dip. Who lives there?"

One?

I looked where she was pointing, but I knew I had no fit answer for her, and that irked me.

"I can't tell you his name. He's not there much, anyway, they say. Someone from up north is all I've heard. Could be York, maybe. He's not a working man. I've not seen him yet. I'm only this way sometimes. More since—"

"He *is* there," she cut in. "I was told he was the person who has her, and that was only Saturday past."

The person who what?

Suddenly she grabbed my wrist and pulled me hard, down with her, back again into the ditch where she'd just been. In that touch I felt her spirit, a hunted thing searching for safe ground.

"He is coming now again," she muttered. "But that's not my Belladonna he has. Hush till he goes past."

She put her finger to her lips then, as if there was need when nobody was near. Quickly, she draped the leafy elder limbs around us both. A thorn spray scraped my neck, and I felt the blood trickle and stick while we sat. What chance was there that a horseman on the road would not spot the two of us from his high perch? It wouldn't matter if we were quiet as young hares in a field.

There was a sugar scent off the blossoms and it could have been sweet there, peaceful even. But this Ling was every bit as mardy as she was quick. When I leaned forward to peek, she yanked me back, in a fury.

"Easy, easy," I said. There I was, fool enough to play her whispering game. "You may be the lucky sort who can see far like a fowler can. Well, I'm not. Whatever you see now is only the size of a tick to me. And it certainly won't see or hear us yet, not by a long shot."

Her answer was a thump on my thigh, but I didn't mind that touch, not one bit. We sat back down then, dressed in our pieces of hedge and ditch, until we heard the hooves. First the beat alone, then the heavy sound of the metal hitting home. That was an old horse surely, slow, all *clinkum-clankum* in its loose harness.

As the man and his horse passed our hiding place, we were shielded from sight by the poor beast herself, for her master was walking the far side of her. Only his legs and head were on view, dressed alike in brown. He wore leather splatterdashes below his knees and a leather skullcap pulled down over a full, pale face. He was middle-yeared.

The mare was a small dark roan, spavin-legged. Mange was eating away the coat over her quarters, and her tail was only a few gray wisps. But she whirrupped as she passed us, then slowed. Perhaps she knew there were watchers down in the green ditch. The man murmured something to her, soft, then clicked his teeth like a carter and jingled her bit. They moved on at a slower pace.

Ling sucked in air as if it were water but said nothing. Nor did I. Like mice behind a wall, we sat under our weeds and listened to the man and the mare go their clattery way as far as the turn for the cottage. Once they reached it, the grass took the harshness out of the mare's gait. Her steps grew quiet and finally went silent.

"Well, there you have him," I said to her. "A brown man with a brown horse. Perhaps that's his name, after all. Mr. Brown."

I had an urge to stretch my arms out to the sides the way she had done before, but that would be foolish, like a thing our Nan would do. So I clambered out of the ditch — a proper Harry-long-legs I looked, surely — but she was up there before me, stamping a foot in fury.

"What does he want with that poor old thing? What has he done with my beautiful Belladonna? I'll kill the dirty Dane that sold her; I'll kill him for that and for all the times he cheated my mother and me."

Those huge eyes she had were looking, not at me but away, over the distance of field and marsh meadow that rolled smooth down to the estuary, and not seeing that either. They had a dangerous sheen on them, her black plum eyes, and I knew I could not bear it if she wept. If it brought my father roaring at me again for being late, I had to wait her story out, even if there was as little to be done for her as for the mare gone by.

"Ling, who is Belladonna?" I asked. "Or the dirty Dane?"

Belladonna

SHE WAS SILENT so long, I thought she'd never answer, but then her words came pouring, like stopped water bursting through.

I should record it here that Ling told her stories in a way different from anyone I knew. Even a bear would listen to her and believe she was dripping honey down his throat. I have done my best with the words she told me then, and afterward, to make them into proper tales. Though I can never do her justice, I hope I show how different a body and spirit she was from me. It was no wonder she had two names. She might have had six.

"I was called Hélène then, as I told you, but my *maman* had a rare name, very beautiful. Zéphyrine. I think there are not so many Zéphyrines in England."

For a moment I thought she was making a joke, but her face was tight.

"She was named for the west wind, and she was as warm and kind as that gentle wind. She danced like the wind too — so graceful she was, Thomas."

She pointed at her eyes. "You see these? So black? Zéphyrine's were blue as hyacinths. Otherwise I look like her. If you met her, you would think she was my big sister."

She shook herself, suddenly, like a dog that comes out of the river and throws the weight of water off himself. "My clever *maman,* she taught me how to dance, and every night we went out in front of the lights. We had such beautiful costumes. We were the sun, the moon, the stars! Oh, Thomas, Maman had such long legs! When she moved *en pointe* across the stage, all the faces turned, like sunflowers following the sun. I was the little sunflower, her baby *tournesol,* so they clapped me too."

I was sitting in a ditch not far from the Humber waters, but as Ling continued her story, I might as well have been standing in front of that wooden stage topped with its sky of baby angels, my head turning with the rest of the crowd. But then her words shoved me into the arena instead. That was a much rougher place, where the torches spat green and red sparks, and the wood pollen flew up to dust the bare legs of the dancers, or their lace stockings, if they had them.

Best of all were the great parks outside the city, where, she said, the trees were cut into long green arrow tips, or even into the shapes of birds or bears.

"Thomas," Ling said, "I promise you this. In the parks, the naked statues danced too, for delight, even though their skin was made of marble!"

I blushed to hear that. Was it the statues that whispered, or was it the people? When Ling spoke, I could nearly understand them. *"Merveilleuse, la petite. La petite, c'est Hélène? Oui, comme nous, elle adore les fêtes galantes."*

Ah, *les fêtes galantes.* Those were the parties in the parks. I guessed that even before she let me know what the words meant.

"At night the parks were lit by flaming torches held up by hands of stone. When we went there first, I thought those hands turned too, to follow us, just like the heads."

But my tour of France was over. Ling's voice suddenly turned hard as a flint. She told me that her baby brother, Sebastien, had been born and had died, when he was not even the small size or the pink color of one of the stage angels. When he was buried, Zéphyrine put away the lace and the ribbons and the dancing shoes. No longer was there a stage, nor parks. Not even the arena was open to them. Zéphyrine had lost the key to everything.

It was Hélène who stopped them from starving then.

"We lived in a cellar on the rue du Bac. It was horrible there, but if you could run past the guards on the bridge, you came to the king's city gardens, the palace gardens. I knew how to slip through the railings and steal the bread the fat *monsieur* left out for the birds. It was safer to steal that than try to steal anything at the market. I knew a boy who lost a thumb to a knife in the market."

Ling bit her lip, but it was not for the poor boy's thumb. It was for the trick of the *monsieur*, who, one morning, hid himself behind a statue, all the better to watch his little feathery guests at their breakfast. For all that he was old and fat, he took a temper and laid hands on Hélène when he saw her stooping from crumb to crumb.

"What harm was it if a girl took his bread instead of a pigeon?"

What harm indeed? But the man had spun her around all the same and shaken her pickings from her hands and her bib.

"Then he saw my face and he cried out, *'La petite Zéphyrine! C'est impossible.'* Then it was clap hands and bring fresh bread and creamy milk for *la belle*, quick, quick, *vite, vite.*"

For, stranger than strange, it was this same fat *monsieur* who had discovered Zéphyrine on the streets, when she was not much older than Hélène.

"He was *Monsieur Essentiel,* because it was he who drew up the lists of dancers and actors, Pierrots and Columbines, who performed for the king and the court. And that day he watched me as if I were one of his pigeons, waiting until I sucked the last crumb from his silver spoon. Then he asked me if I could ride a horse. What do you think I said, Thomas?"

I lifted my hands as if they held reins and clicked my tongue. But Ling did not laugh as I hoped she would.

"Oh, *ma foi,* Thomas! I said yes. And I had never been even on the back of a mule then! But it sounded so good, what he was talking about. I wanted to be part of it. What else was there for Maman and me?"

"Part of what?" I asked.

"He told me that a man from Denmark was making a troupe of dancers and acrobats, even some of the *saltimbanques à la turque,* who wear the funny pantaloons. But you had to be able to do your act on the back of a horse. And you had to be young, because the lords and ladies liked that best. So there would be nothing for poor Zéphyrine. I would have to keep her with whatever I earned, he told me."

She leaned forward, and I thought I saw a shiver run down her spine under the gown. "But, oh, Thomas. The day I went to the great *place* where he told me to go, you must believe my knees were rattling together like dice made from bones! My heart was beating like poor little Sebastien's in his last fever."

I found it hard to believe that Ling's knees ever knocked. That was my trick, surely. But when she turned, her eyes were huge again, and she told me what she saw that day. So many fine horses, looped together. So many children busy with them, like little cavalrymen. A tall fair man dressed in black, thin as the whip he carried and cracked, which made a noise like gunshot.

"All I knew was that none of these horses had a back broad enough for me to dance on and kick my legs as high as the angels. I could see that, like I saw the sun. I nearly turned around to walk back to the city, but instead I gave the man the letter the *monsieur* had given me."

The man was the leader of the troupe, the *maestro*. He read the beautiful handwriting of the *monsieur*'s letter while his fingers traced the swells of the fat wax seal.

Then, as if he had sucked her worst fear out of her mind, he led Hélène to the smallest horse of all, the prettiest too, a pure-white beast with a tail the color of barley.

"He said to me, 'Belladonna can count. She keeps time like no other horse. That is why she is best for dancers.' That was good, I thought, Thomas, but then he laughed and said that Belladonna could tell a cheat quicker than he could. He lashed the whip from the top of the air to the flat of the ground, and the whole place turned silent."

I could see this man, the Dane. I knew his teeth were small and smooth, as if he filed them whenever he was not cracking his whip. His eyes were cold as the river that ran past the king's palace.

Ling laughed. "But I saw what he didn't see, Thomas. I saw that although the little white horse had beautiful eyes, all the time what they do is follow our hands, his and mine. She wanted our hands to give her something. She was hungry. He did not care enough to see that, but I did."

Along with his letter, the *monsieur* had supplied a freshly baked bread roll. Hélène broke it in two and held the larger piece out to Belladonna, who took it, delicately, between her black lips. Her teeth ground the sweet white bread into crumbs.

"When the bread was gone, this man, all he said to me was, *'Dansez, maintenant.'* That was his joke. He told me I could dance, as if he were the ant and I was the *cigale.* Do you know what that is, the insect that sings in the grass for all the summer?"

"Grasshopper?"

She nodded. "*Alors,* the grasshopper. *Peut-être que c'est lui.* But I cared nothing about his coldness, *rien.* I had no fear left, because Belladonna's warm breath on my neck and my arms when she nuzzled me, it felt like love on my skin, Thomas."

Spider Dust

LING PAUSED AFTER she had spoken about the love of the horse, as if to tease me, but I was up to her trick. She thought my eyes were closed, but I could see the sly look she was giving me. We were in the ditch again, the two of us, our backs hard against the brimming of old Catchpole's summer wheat.

She thought my eyes would open when no further words came from her. I waited a bit and then let them open, slowly, as if she held strings to work the lids. My eyes are blue, doubtless not the same shade as this Zéphyrine's, nor like any flower, either. But from my mother to the old women in the village, females have always told me my eyes are too large and fine for a boy to own. They say my lashes are as black and long as a girl's. Then they shake their heads, mourning my brows, which meet across the nose in a dark ugly line.

Hers made two perfect arcs, save when she scowled.

"Well, what happened next?" I asked her. "For all that, you were never on a horse! How did you trick that man and do your dance on the back of one?"

I needed a picture in my head of her doing whatever it was she said she did on the back of a white horse. Her words had not taken me that far.

But she was no help. She said simply, "You see, Belladonna loved me from that moment, Thomas."

She said my name wrong, without the *s. Tohmah.* I let it go, for I liked the way it sounded.

"And it was not just for the bread," she said. "It was because I noticed what she needed. So she did the same for me; she knew what to do when the time came. She stood there for me when I danced, as if she were a beautiful table fixed to the floor, not a horse." She laughed. "Besides, the *monsieur* made sure that morning to give me a certain powder for my shoes! In the theater we call it *poudre d'araignée.*"

She made a claw of her hand then and made a dash for my leg as if she would scratch it or stroke it. That made me shift along right enough. Was she mad, after all, the ditch girl?

"That means spider dust, you see," she said. "We call it that because spiders coat their little ropes with a sticky stuff to catch their flies. We catch people but we don't stick them, no, we stick ourselves instead! We make the people to gasp at the magic we do. They never see the ropes we use, or our sticky feet."

She laughed, but straightaway she was serious again. "Thomas, I promise you, I am a good dancer too, *la meilleure, enfin*. If I tumble, it looks like a step of my dance. After a week, he told me I was the best dancer he had, and he would know, that thief."

Her little heart-face filled with blood, but I knew it was with anger, not shame, as is usually my story.

"This Dane, who was the master," I said. "Where is he now? How did you come to England?"

She held up her spider hand again, but it was solemn now, like a schoolmaster's hand with chalk in it. Or a stick.

"It doesn't matter now how we came. It was before this silly war—oh, is that what you are thinking? That I am a spy?" She laughed but I felt only confusion, because I had thought no such thing.

"Oh, I would be a very good spy, Thomas. But no. Things got mean and hard in France, that was enough.

The English love horses, he said. So we came. We were lucky to come when we did, for soon after, along it came, this war. France and England who hate each other so much that they must fight all the time, fools."

She shook her head. Then her hands were on the move again as she measured space between one limb of elder and another.

"The first year we went by the long, straight road from Canterbury — look, that is where I am, *here* — to York in the north, by you, *there*. So many towns and such a long way to go, with all the fairs we could want. Thomas, they had never seen anything as good as us!"

She shook her head at the wonder of it. It was not really a boast, not the way she said it.

"The next year the Dane said we would stay near Newmarket Races, for the good money, but there was trouble when the king came, your king, for he did not like us. Since then it has been Cambridge and Nottingham and Lincoln for us, in a ring. Smaller ways we made. We got smaller too, our little troupe."

She made circles in the air, circles that became less, then stopped. There was silence then, and not even a shout in the distance to break it.

Truth was, I wished she would begin the story of French Hélène again and bring that other world back into my dull one. I wanted to see again the green and red fire sparks, and the angels, the statues that danced in the park, the king's palace by the river and the king's *monsieur*, the black warhorse and the little white one with a tail like barley.

Belladonna.

But I had the good fortune then to look toward the village, and there was Harkin the Clock, striding past the stone granary set proud beyond the last house. It was his hour to head for his home facing the sandbanks, for his evening meal of boiled duck and barley-water.

If so, that was Bessie Pell going the road behind him, as sure as mud made bricks. The Clock would say nothing about me, but if Bessie were to see Thomas Rose with a strange hussy in the ditch, his life would be cut open and left out like gizzards for the dog.

I struggled out of the ditch for the second time that afternoon, and this time the tingle of blood flowing to my feet was a torture. I had to be moving home before Bessie Pell got a proper gawp over this way. But first I had to know about Belladonna. Then maybe I could do something for Ling.

I reached out a hand to help her safely over the nettles. Hers was no larger than Nan's, and I wondered whether she could master a horse as she'd said.

"And then? What brought you here to Horkstow, Hélène?"

There, I'd said it. Hélène. Fool. She looked surprised but didn't thump me again, as I thought she might.

"Better call me Ling. Even Maman learned to do that when we came here. It is best not to be French now, you know."

She looked quickly away, toward the estuary again, but of course with her sharp eyes she'd seen that odd pair, Bessie and the Clock, barreling along from the village. She missed nothing, that one. *Priest's baybay*, indeed.

When she answered, her words tumbled out.

"Last month when my *maman*—when she was—"

She took a deep breath. "When she was *malade*. When she was not well, Thomas. That was the time I went to look for something she had lost, something we had all lost. It was then that the Dane took my Belladonna to the horse fair at Brigg and sold her. He told me I would be able to dance on any horse in London if I chose to. But I'll not dance again in my life until I get Belladonna back. Your Mr. Brown bought her; they were able to tell me that when I came to Brigg. And the worst thing, Thomas, do you know what that is?"

She was looking directly at the middle buttons of my shirt now, not at my face, so I reckoned the tears were only just held back.

"That man we saw, *him*." She jerked her head in the direction of the lane. "The people in Brigg called him the horse butcher of Horkstow. *Le boucher de ton village*."

Roses Come Out
of the Rise

IT WAS A CLOSE CALL, after all that, making sure
Bessie Pell had no news to spread around like muck.

Ling took off down the lane, heading for a little
copse of willows set well past the brown man's cottage.
She told me that was where she'd spent the previous
night, wrapped up and dry enough.

"I lifted a loaf that was cooling on the brown man's
windowsill yesterday, and I have some sour apples, so
I've enough to get by," she called out. "But perhaps
you would bring me a piece of ham hock tomorrow,

Thomas, or even a marrowbone? I'll wait there till you come in the morning."

In the morning? Lord's nest of sparrows, what did this mad girl know of anything, or of what the likes of me might manage so early?

Her voice grew fainter as she came within sound and sight of the cottage. But when she turned, she did an odd thing. She pitched her voice, curling it like a ball so that it reached me, clear and sharp.

"Unless I find Belladonna before then. If that happens, Thomas, *je quitterai mon petit campement.* I will be gone."

Even as I looked after her, she *was* gone. To ground again, like the lark. But, of course, the reason she had disappeared from my sight so smartly was right to hand, hanging there like robber's guilt, the red kerchief snagged on a thorn. Carefully I lifted the piece of silk free and stuffed it into my pocket.

Bessie Pell looked hard at me when I greeted her on the road. "Did I not see you in company right now, young Thomas Rose?"

"That was a fowler from the shore across the water, Bessie. A dwarfy fellow asking about our Horkstow ducks, as if they were any business of his. I told him what was what. I told him the biggest ducks from all around were yours."

Bessie Pell had a tongue like a furze fire, but with his other hand, God had given her squint eyes weaker even than my own. She squawked now to hear of such blabbermouthing.

The Clock had stopped too, briefly, but he said nothing and passed on. He never spoke unless to answer. This tall bony man turned up every morning to split and saw wood for my father. He could make music with a saw or an adze, but few could remember when he had strung more than three or four words together. His nickname was part of his strangeness, though nobody used it to his face. They said that even if you had no timepiece you had the Clock, because he came and went every day by the sun.

We lived a quarter mile or so beyond the far side of the village, where the road headed straight for Saxby All Saints and after that for Bonby and Worlaby. The Low Villages lay between the ridge of the wolds and the rich flats of the river meadows. They were strung close together like beads on a chain. Nobody knew why, not even John Rose, my father, the wheelwright who'd lived there all his life.

When my older brother, Hugh, and I were little, and Nan just a baby, on fine Sundays our father would take us in the light dray cart he kept then, following the swell of the wolds as far as the road took us.

"Roses come out of the rise," he'd say, pointing toward the ridge crowned with tall lime trees. "That's why you boys will grow tall in your time. But our Nan came out of a hole in the hill like a badger."

Though he'd not grown so tall, Hugh had been working alongside Father for two years now, and those two were both so full of love for working wood that my mother called them the block and the chip.

But it was I who was the spit of Father. We wore the same dark eyebrow over our nose and the same long tow-colored hair tucked behind our ears. I was still only fourteen that summer, but already I was as tall and long-limbed as he. Some might find height a good property, but I swear it had many ills, not least that it was a bully draw. And there were girls who tittered when they passed me on the road, saying they could hear my knees and hip bones groaning out loud, for all they had to carry.

Nan came running now, hearing the squeak of the wicket gate, with Chap the spaniel following her, nosing all he could reach of the smells that were stuck with the weeds to my boots and legs.

"I kept some of the taties for you," Nan said. "Mother said you'd not get any tonight for you're come so late. They're under your bed. But you must bring the bowl down again before the morning, or she'll miss it. I did all the clearing."

"I'll wash first," I said. "You're a good one, Nancy Rose. Did I ever tell you that before?"

Nan went pink with pleasure. "Yes, you did! And so you'll make me a song?"

"They'll sing your song on the streets of Lincoln one day soon," I told her. "And at every fair from York to Canterbury."

Nan had her old slate piece with her, stuck into the pocket of her pinny. When she wasn't at her tasks, or grooming Ox the pony or poor Chap and his spaniel ears, she was sitting down somewhere scraping away on that black slab. I thought suddenly of my nib and my books rotting at the bottom of the Ancholme River. Why hadn't I kept them for Nan, who could make proper use of them?

The truth was, her quickness with books ran me through like a knife, even though I loved her for it too, as I loved her dark-rust bonnet of hair. Our Nan lacked even the ghost of a curl.

"Tell me the words, Tom, I'll write them, and then you can make the tune up when I go to bed."

"I'll splash first, all right?"

I went to the water barrel that stood by the door, where Father's smooth downpipes fed it from the house gutters, and dipped my head in, holding my nose, letting the coolness soak into my skin. I felt for the scrape on my neck and washed the scab that had formed, gently, so it didn't break.

"Did they tickle you?" Nan asked, peering into the barrel, her nose wrinkled. "I'd never do that." She hated the red worms that lived in the rainwater.

"Where is Mother, then? And Father?"

"Mother is away to poor Widow Brice with a jelly. Father is up the road to see what he can see. Maybe he saw you."

If my luck were to hold, he had not.

Home

OUR HOUSE HAD TURNED its back to the road long ago, but some people still called it the Sulk House. The door faced the yard instead, where my mother fattened her bright gillyflowers all summer, their pinks and whites and purples growing tall against the walls of the house and the outbuildings. Swallows and martins came back to the yard every spring to build their mud nests, and my mother never raised a brush to smash them down, as most women did.

"The poor creatures must set up family somewhere, just like us," she'd say.

The door of the shop was well bolted now, but the birds dived and circled in and out of every other space. Over the shop, the wheel sign I made last year was swinging on its bolt, squeaky as an old weather vane. Every time there was a hard wind, my mother swore she'd go up the ladder herself and unhook it with her hoe. But it was still there, my bold red wheel. Red for Rose.

"I'll go and eat your taties now," I said to Nan. "And then I'll tell you the first words of your song."

Pots and plates were stacked neatly on the kitchen shelves; the long table was wiped and scrubbed, the floor swept of any crumbs. There was no cheese left in the open larder, and my mother's lock was hard and fast on the closed one. There was nothing a body might eat, except for four green apples ripening on the windowsill.

Ling would have to dream on about her ham hock, then. She had more to thank the Lord for this night than I had, with her stolen loaf and her apples.

The room Hugh and I shared was more a space than a room, and we reached it by narrow ladder. It swelled out above the road, making a bump on the flat front of our house. Under the bed was Nan's bowl, with a good enough mess of potatoes and cream, green onions mixed through. A thick slice of gammon sat on top, as long as my hand.

My trickster of a sister hadn't told me about the gammon, bless her. And her hand hadn't reached far enough in to find my paper sheets and charcoal, rolled tight into my cap.

I ate everything except a fair half share of the meat, which I brought downstairs with the bowl. I'd wrap that in a twist of linen to bring to Ling. And her kerchief. I felt for the silk in my pocket. Yes.

"I have the words now," I said to Nan. "And I thank you for my supper, kind lady. Do you want to hear your song, Nan? It goes like this."

I sang while I scrubbed the bowl in the dirt water.

> *"Oh, Nan, she is a fairy*
> *As quick as any goat.*
> *She's clever as the king's own queen*
> *But prettier than oats.*

> *She tells the news and feeds the poor,*
> *She rides the pony Ox,*
> *And every lass the village owns*
> *Will run away in flocks*

> *From Nan the queen, who's not so tall,*
> *Not today at least,*
> *But when Nan grows up, she'll rule us all*
> *And treat us all to feasts."*

I grabbed Nan's slate and took down a wooden spoon to beat the time out on it, and together we sang my nonsense again, scrambling the last words all out of time.

"So, you're idle all day and idle again now, boy."

There I was, caught foolish-handed and flush-faced. I laid down the spoon and tried to press the slate into Nan's hands, but she'd already crossed them across her chest, stiff, as if they were stone hands carved on a tomb. She stood there in front of me, on guard, until I pushed her toward the settle.

"Father, I'm sorry to have missed our supper, but the Reverend asked me to come back and practice the bells with him."

That was not entirely a lie. That good man had said as much to me, only not this day.

"You're behind in that too, then? Couldn't grasp your letters, can't grasp the rope firm and proper. I heard no bells today."

Father sat down, heavily, on the settle and pulled Nan to him.

"My girl."

I hated to see the pucker in Nan's face as she tried to reckon who had the right of it. She uncrossed her hands at last and nestled into the crook of Father's arm.

"I'm sorry, Father," I said. "I'll plane for you tomorrow. Or anything else you want me to do. I just have to go down to the river early to do a job for the church. I'll be back before anyone's up."

He grunted. "Did you get your supper, then? No, better don't tell me. Nobody sings so glad happy on an empty belly, as you were at just now."

He reached above his head to the shelf where his books were piled up, high as the copper pitcher sitting alongside them. He felt until he had what he wanted and eased it, carefully, from the others.

"Read a little for me, poppet. I'm too weary now to throw my own eyes on the book. I'll show you where to begin."

Father closed his eyes after Nan found the page he pointed to. As always, she read in a clear high voice, the way a thrush might read. I watched the shifts her eyes made, so tiny, less than pulse beats. What did I miss on the page that this little noodle sister of mine could treat with so easily? I knew the worth of every word she spoke, but let the world dress them up in black type and a paper face and they are lost to me.

I could have caught Nan's face, though, with my pencil, in my own special book. Nobody knew that.

Nan didn't stumble once, not even when the barn owl shouted above, very close. When she'd finished, I got up and went to the candle shelf, picked out the great tallow and the rushlights, and put them on the table.

"I'll go for Mother, then," I said. "It'll be rising dark soon."

All These Good Things

I HAVE A GOOD MEMORY. When I was outside, I could say off the words Nan had read, as easily as another person might the Lord's Prayer. The passage was not new to me, nor to my father, nor even to our clever Nan. All of us so different, yet each loved Mr. Defoe's story of the traitorous ducks of Lincolnshire who flew to Germany and Holland to tell the ducks in those countries to come to England because . . .

> *The English ducks live much better than they do in those cold climates; that they have open lakes, and sea shores*

full of food, the tides flowing freely into every creek . . .
that the lands are full of food, the stubbles yielding con-
stant supplies of corn . . . that 'tis not once in a wild
duck's age, that they have any long frosts or deep snows,
and that when they have, yet the sea is never frozen, or the
shores void of food; and that if they will please but to go
with them into England, they shall share with them in all
these good things.

Of course it was not only ducks that betrayed their
fellows. Humans too might be tricked into leaving good
homes if the right words were used to snare them. I
knew that much, even though at the time I speak of
I had not traveled far in any direction. I wondered how
Ling was, this hour of dusk. Was she wrapped already in
her canvas on the copse floor?

"Thomas. Are you come for me?"

There was my good mother, stepping out from Jane
Brice's gate, her basket crooked on one arm, her ker-
chief and apron like drifts of mayflower in the dim light.
She smiled as I came close, and I felt easy.

"Did Nan feed you well enough tonight, then?"

I was ready to plead my sister innocent, but then I
saw Mother had only mischief in her, and so I nodded.

"She was like a cow with her calf, so I let her be," my
mother said. "I played the scold so that she got braver
and braver, running hither and yon with her bowl. She

would have fed Christ's own multitudes with her five taties and her piece of ham."

She took my arm and linked it in hers.

"There was no need for you to come for me, Tom. Poor old Jane, though. You'll not see her out at her hives again. She has the ague bad and won't last the week."

A small gust whipped past as we walked back. It blew from the southwest, coming over the marshy carrs, and with it came the scent of water. The night was cooler than day had promised. It spoke of autumn. Eastward too, the makings of a moon stood ready to swim across the sky.

"Harvest's moon will be swelling soon," my mother said, eyeing it. "Hugh's down by the river now, doubtless, casting his lines. Fish for tomorrow if we're lucky."

A party of girls from Bonby swept past us, spilling out greetings that turned to giggles as they grew distant.

"Good night, tall Tom!" one of them called behind. "You should come along the road with us for a bit of fun."

There was more laughter and I bloomed hot in the face, even in the dark.

"Someone has an eye for you," Mother said, amused, "but you'll find she's that brave only in company and where her face won't be seen."

When we lifted the gate latch, Tassie the silver-striped cat stalked from the small kennel I'd made for her and the dog to share. It was gabled like a church, and the two of them shared it every night, like good Christians. Tassie went ahead of us into the yard, holding her tail stiff as a baton, and when I bent to scratch her head, her velvet nose mapped the traces of gammon on my hand.

Mother stayed me with a touch. Her voice was changed.

"Thomas. Before we go in. Have you any answer yet to your grandfather's offer? Today he sent word again to know if you'd go back and learn the gloving with him, but the only body in the house was Hugh. The message made little sense to him, but thank the Lord he spoke to me first about it, not to your father."

My heart pounded then, as if I'd run that minute all the way from the estuary shore.

"No, Mother. Give me to the end of harvest, will you? There'll surely be enough work around for me till then to keep Father from throwing me out on the road."

Her gray eyes stayed on my face so long, I knew she was searching for a weakness to press. But suddenly the weakness was all hers. I could hear the shake in her voice.

"Thomas, I cannot ever forget what that schoolmaster said about you last month. So vicious his words were. How could he say my brave clever boy is unteachable as a rabbit? I think there is a sickness in your eyes; if only we had means enough to take you to a doctor for it.

In Lincoln, or maybe if we went all the way to York . . ."
Her voice tailed off.

I put a finger to her mouth. "Hush, Mother. Don't vex yourself. We'll sleep on it, and very soon it'll be no hard bones to any of us."

But that was a lie. When Hugh wormed into the bed beside me later on, all damp and cold and cheery, full of triumph for his catch, I gave him only a grunt and pretended I was slipping into first sleep.

Yes, it was true there was the matter of my eyes, which must always squint tight to see far, but that was not it. I mightn't be able to tell an oak from an elm where they stand on the rise, but I had no bother seeing every black spike and white egg laid out on a page. The problem was that they made less sense to me than ants on their journeys.

I did not want to go and live again with Grandfather in Brigg, not even under the new notion they were cobbling together. No Grammar School this time, but a pilgrimage to become Thomas Rose, glover, after years of learning to cut and stitch tinier than the fairies' cobbler ever did, and dealing with uppish townspeople all the while. No. Even our dear mother had run as fast as she could away from that trade.

I turned my back on Hugh and thought of how I would wake early and go and find the girl waiting for me in the clearing. If she hadn't been a dream, that is, cooked up by the heat of the day and the shimmer on the water.

Together we would find the white horse Belladonna—of course I would fight for her if I had to—and Ling would tell me more of her stories. Only this time I'd be in them, alongside her. I would have earned that prize.

No rabbit from Brigg had ever sat in a ditch with a girl like her—I was sure of that.

The Duck Egg

LING HAD SLEPT LATE. Or perhaps I was earlier than I knew.

There was still silver light across the sky when I found where she was lying, wrapped up. She was a brown curl, a cocoon with a black top of silky hair, and I thought what a star butterfly this girl would hatch into. She'd have wings of a color no one had ever seen in the air above Horkstow. My fingers tingled.

I didn't come unnoticed, however. Her dark eyes were open, and she yawned a greeting at me in language

I didn't catch. A leaf or some such thing had left its trace on her left cheek.

"I'm cold," she croaked. "Have you brought meat?"

I laid the gammon at the turn of her knees.

"Where's your stolen loaf, then?" I asked her. "We had none baked this early in my house."

"All gone," she said. "I gave what was left to the foxes."

"The foxes!"

"A mama *renard* and her three little ones. They came in here when the night was just leaving. They looked so hungry, Thomas, and afterward they played for me as if this space was a stage and I their crowd. Besides, I knew you would bring me something."

My stomach growled like bagpipes. But I said nothing, for it was almost a food to see her. And a spice, too, those French words she dropped into her speech, so smart that even I could understand them. *Renard.*

She sat up and struggled out of her canvas cover and then hugged it tight around her shoulders like a shawl. She reached for the ham and devoured it, licking her fingers when every scrap was gone.

She sighed with pleasure. "I have not eaten meat in a month, you know. Now, wait here. There is a stream that way and I will be back."

When she returned, her face and her hair were freshly wet, and the leaf mark had faded. She bent her head and grasped the dripping lengths of hair, dark now as blackberries, caught them up into a tail, then a knot, and tied it with a green ribbon.

"You lost this."

"Oh, Thomas! I was desolate after it. It was my mother's gift. Thank you."

She fastened the red kerchief neatly around her top-knot and did a little bob for me. "Quite the lady, am I not?"

She came forward then, with her hands hanging open and loose, and suddenly lifted one of them to my left ear. That startled me, for she had all the moves of the herb woman that some called a witch. I had my own hand up to ward her off, but she laughed and held out her cupped palms.

"So this is what you keep under your roof, Thomas!"

There it sat, a duck's egg, moist as her own cheek, clean as the morning sky.

"How did you do that?"

It had been an impossible thing!

She opened my hands, placed the egg inside, and closed them over.

"Don't fret. I left her three for herself. This one was dropped only this morning. It's full of meat and will make you a good breakfast. Then you will not grudge my little foxes their bread."

We left the copse then and walked across a sedgy stretch of meadow until we reached the lane. The sun was a fat gold watch face just rising over the wolds. I looked back, and there were our shadows marching along behind, flat on their backs. Hers had a small top-knot like the one my mother's sweet loaves wore.

For no reason, I began to tell her about my years in Brigg, in the classroom where the air was dead, for all the grand high ceiling.

"They didn't send Hugh to school because all he wanted was my father's work. Mother said I was the quickest child to speech she had ever known."

More full of music than a lark, too, she'd said, and with more fancies in my head than any peddler kept in his pack. For all that, I'd been sent off to Brigg with no letters, a skill that caused no pain to Hugh or Nan.

"It was like sending a soldier to battle without his kit. They had a song about me in the yard within a week."

They beat time with their measuring sticks on my back: *"Thomas Rose's back, bony and stupid like a knacker's ass."*

My anger was a dirty yeast inside, still. I looked at the half face that was all I could see of Ling. "You had your spider dust when you turned up with the horse folk," I said, "but I had nothing. I was a head over them all, even at ten years of age, but when I looked down at a page, all the letters would twist as if they were fishes trapped tail-up in the mud. Latin or English, it made no difference. And when I made my own letters, the writing master said the devil had picked me out to take down his words."

We were stopped. She had pulled up our little marching parade. She put her hands up to my face, delicate fingers moving on my jawbones, reaching my mouth. Thistledown. I could hardly breathe.

"Many a *monsieur* can read, Thomas, but cannot think. I like the way you talk, because it tells me how you see the world. You like things to fit well and to be fair, and you have this"—she tapped first my forehead then my chest—"a head to match your heart. I know about your heart already, because you are here with me now, even though your belly wants bread." She gave me a poke. "Also, you are hungry for what I say."

All I could say was only lame. "Oh, you find me hungry, all right, Ling."

But I glowed inside. How had she come to have such ideas of me? What had I ever told her that was fair or fit? Surely all the choice talk had been hers? And, clever miss, she had made sure to say as much just now.

It was no time for thinking, for our task was before us. We could see the brown man's house just ahead, two floors of rough stonework huddled behind a wall.

"What are you going to do here, Ling?" I asked. "If

you go close and the man catches sight of you, he'll fair guess who grabbed his bread. Who baked that loaf for him, anyway?"

She shrugged. "That is not important. Look, do you see any horse about? I do not. Where is the horse he was leading yesterday? Does this man ask a horse into his home as if it was a guest come to supper?"

I had no answer for her.

"First of all, I go to every window and I look. It is early; he will still be in his bed. Truly, it is so. You wait at the wall, Thomas. Be my good eyes and ears."

There was no proper garden to the house, just a patch behind the wall where the meadow grass had been scythed a day or so before. Where it still stood, the grass was taller than ripe barley, with hundreds of red poppies scattered through, corn cockles pink as babies, and the egg yellow of bedstraw and buttercups. At the end of the sloping meadow, a little outhouse stood. I'd always heard it was used as a smokehouse for fish and eels. From somewhere in the meadow came the harsh call of a corncrake.

Crrraaaakke. Crrraaaakke.

The cottage door had a top and bottom in two parts and hung crooked and loose in the door space. Some of the casing had been removed, so that the door did not breach the gap as it should. When the winter easterlies came blowing, this place would let in rain and rats along with the cold. Could the brown man really have taken the poor spavined horse inside with him?

Ling had skitted off to the back of the house while I was figuring the door, but now she came around again. A shake of the head and then she was at the left-hand window, which was set too high for someone her size. I watched as she found some bricks and began to lay them one on top of the other. *She'll knock them out from under when she stands on top,* I thought. But of course she didn't; she made a picture, neat as ever. Elbows on the sill, skirt for triangle, her two skinny bare ankles poking from under it.

She seemed to be wiping the glass clean, which was surely needed, for even where I stood, I could see that the other window, the right-hand one, was filthy enough to make my mother spin. Nonetheless, I could make out the oddest thing hanging down behind the glass. Was it a sword? That would be something to see.

The Horror

I LEFT MY PLACE by the wall and moved toward that window, but Ling must have heard me, for she turned and beckoned me over.

"*Regarde,* Thomas," she whispered. She could reach my ear now, perched on her pile of bricks. Her breath tickled. "It is his parlor; the horse is in there and so is he, and he is feeding the poor thing some grog mash. He cannot be too bad, then. My Belladonna loves that more than anything! It makes her laugh; I swear it."

I was careful to keep my head as low as possible in front of the small square that she had tried to wipe clean.

It was just as she said. There was little furniture in the room, and what there was had been placed against the walls. A chair, a small table, a chest with shelves on top. The hearthstone had a ring set into it, and it was to this the roan mare was tethered. One hoof was resting and it was only half ironed, if as much. The creature had not been shod in an age. The man had his back turned to the window and was stroking the mare's neck and withers with one hand, while the other held an oat pan to her mouth. How did Ling know it held a grog mash?

As if he felt stranger's eyes on his back, the man turned his head slightly, but I ducked quicker.

"Did you see?"

I nodded, but there were the dark eyes, pleading for more. "Ling, come over to the other window."

That year I had learned that when you whisper, you can have full control of your voice. But a man can't whisper forever in real life.

"Our friend inside nearly caught me just now," I told her. "Anyway, I saw something that I want to take a look at, over there, and then we should be gone from here. Unless you have the notion to burst in there right now and ask him where your horse is."

She stiffened at that, but came with me past the gap-boarded door over to the second window. This time it was I who did the mop work, making a peering space best I could, for most of the murk was on the inside. I put my eye to the glass.

It was suddenly, then, as if I were back in the school-room, faced with a printed page and its puzzle of marks. Nothing in front of my eyes made sense. How could I read this sight for Ling?

The thing I'd seen from the distance was not a sword but a great knife, bent like the beginnings of a sickle, then stretched straight in its end. The blade was silver but blackened with stains. That one hung like a warning behind the window glass, but over on the table set square in the center of the room lay rows of other knives. Some had shapes I could hardly describe, and they came in lengths from a finger to as long as my arm. There was a handsaw also, and a band saw, and even my eyes could make out a number of fat curved needles, readied with some kind of rough thread. Three buckets stood underneath the table, a taller churn in front.

If this was the man's kitchen, it seemed bigger than the other room. Another mystery was the iron beam that crossed the ceiling along the width of the room. It looked like a huge fire crane that had been ripped from its proper place and set up there. Hooks hung from it. The floor underneath was strewn with fresh straw, but the straw sat on top of dark stains that had soaked into the floor like spilled ink.

"What is it, Thomas?"

Her voice had a hard crust on it. How long had I been looking at the horror inside?

"Come away, Ling."

I grasped her arm, but she planted her small feet, like a jenny mule, into the earth, so I had no leverage on her.

"Tell me, Thomas. Is Belladonna in that room? Is she laid out dead?"

I shook my head.

"No, but you must not look, Ling. I think the man might indeed be what you called him yesterday."

Ling's eyes left me then, though she still faced forward. They died. It gave me the coldest feeling, seeing the light in her beautiful eyes snuffed, just like that, just like the life in a candle. My words had done that.

I reached again for her arm, but she grabbed mine instead, sprang from where she stood, and walked up the arm to my shoulders. She sat astride them, no heavier than Nan, and kneed me on the neck as if I were a horse.

"Turn. I must see what you saw."

I could only obey. I bent so that she could gaze into the killing room. I waited for her to cry out, but she did not. She rubbed more of the window clean and leaned forward and pressed her nose against the glass. She turned me then to face outward, and before I could lower her, she slipped from my shoulders and stood beside me.

"*Le diable! Je vais le tuer, je vais le tuer.* Thomas, I'm going to kill that devil man before he murders that other poor horse too."

But she didn't move. Tears ran down her face, free as raindrops on a pane of glass, but she made no sobs, made no sound at all. All over, she was shaking, as if she had the same ague that was carrying old Jane Brice away from this world.

The Anatomy Lesson

LING TOLD ME she could not remember how old baby Sebastien had been when he died. Four weeks? Five? She was never sure, but she remembered the day her mother had a fresh hope that he might be saved. That was the day I heard about as we stood on the road above the lane. I was only a hand's width from her, but she was as lonely as a thorn tree in the middle of a field.

"We were walking to find the hospital under the great dome. Sebastien was wrapped so well in his warm blanket that I could not see him. He had black curls, Thomas, black as wet coals! It was very cold that day, even though it was already spring. One of Maman's admirers had given her the name of a famous doctor. He said we would find the hospital easily because you could see its dome all the way from the river."

I had never seen a dome, but I could see this one, a hard green sun rising above the narrow streets of the city. Paris. I wondered if Zéphyrine's admirer was the father of the baby with the curls. If so, why had he not accompanied them?

"They were unkind to Maman at the hospital. They said the famous doctor would have nothing to do with babies unless they were dead, because he was an *anatomiste*. I do not know the English for this."

I shook my head. She spat the word out again and moved her hands, pushing it away from her. "But I stamped my foot down and said we would not leave. I told them we had a letter, even though we did not, only the name of the doctor. So in the end, they had to send us along the corridor to his room."

I'd believe they had to, if Ling had flashed her eyes at them. As she told it to me, I could see the long corridor, paved with tiles of black and white, like a game board. There was a room at the end, its door open as had been promised to them.

"That room, Thomas, you could not believe it! I thought we had walked into the arena again, because of all the men who were looking down at us."

There were wooden seats rising in banks and young men sitting on them, leaning forward, keen as hounds. What did they think when they saw Hélène and Zéphyrine standing at the bottom of the well, in the hub of the room?

"The doctor, the famous doctor, was standing at the table in front of everybody. He was bald as an egg and had a long robe like a monk. He had a dead rabbit in front of him and I thought he was saying the Holy Mass over *le pauvre lapin,* for the way he held his hands over the fur."

I had never been at a Mass, but I could see the bald man at work, his hands rising and falling.

"There was a *squelette*—you know this word, all the bones?"

I nodded. "Skeleton."

She made a face. "*Oui.* It was hanging in a box on the table. It is small, maybe a cat or another rabbit, I think. There were glass jars that seemed to be full of olives, only these were not olives but something else. I could smell them, sweet and sick. There was a bundle on the table too, wrapped in a blanket, just as Sebastien was, so well I could not see his curls."

She took a breath. Then she told me about the different knives the bald man had on the table, all different sizes, and I thought of the window I had led her to. That kitchen.

"Of course, the doctor turned to look at us because all the young men were looking. He asked Maman if we were lost. She said we were not, but that we had a baby for him to make better. The men laughed so it was like a hot wind, and the doctor became cross, but not with us, only with them. He made the noise of a lion at them, but he told Maman we should take a seat and wait for him to finish his class."

Ha! I thought. Even a bald man dressed like a monk could fall for Zéphyrine's eyes.

"Maman began to climb the steps at the side so we might sit down. But I kept looking back, Thomas. I was like the poor lady in the Bible story who looked back when she should not have. I forget her name."

I wanted to tell her how that story made Nan so cross, because the lady *had* no name. She was only Lot's wife and then a pillar of salt. But it was not the right time.

It was because she had looked back that Ling saw the man spread the rabbit's white stomach flat, as if he was going to take a smoothing iron to the soft fur. Instead he reached for one of the hanging knives and plunged it into the poor creature's belly, as if he were the devil itself carving up his dinner.

"But there was no blood, Thomas! No blood! And then the man became a fiend, right in front of our eyes. He spoke such words you have never heard in your life. I remember some of them. I could never forget them."

"Adductor, viscera, femoralis." She whispered the black words.

"So, that was the end. I grabbed Maman and pulled her down the steps and out the door. Out into the air, away from that devil and his room."

They ran along the tiled corridor and out into the cobbled street, where carts and carriages clattered past, ignorant of such monstrous things and of men who had sold their soul to the devil.

"You see, Thomas," Ling said. Her jaw was set and there was a hard note in her voice, as if there were metal in her mouth. "I saved Sebastien that time, even though it was of no consequence in the end."

White Horses Are
Called Gray

WHO HAS EVER heard a sadder story?

I could never leave Ling by the side of the road now. That would make me just another person to betray her, like the Dane, whatever kind of rogue he was, or the man below with his dreadful kitchen. He didn't know her, but he had cut out her spirit with his knives just as surely as if it were flesh.

But what could I do to repair the damage?

The sun had his full face now, and the day would be warm, for sure. People were already on the move into the fields. Father had said our shop would be busy.

Ling raised her hand as if to say I shouldn't bother with her. There wasn't a scrap of color in her face, except where the tears had left dirty streaks. She made to wipe them but dropped her hand to her skirt instead.

Only then did I remember the blade with the goose-foot handle, which she must have hidden somewhere under her clothes. I knew now it was the last gift the *monsieur* gave her before her company took to the roads and that its strange handle was made of coral, a growth of the sea.

But, as ever, she was ahead of me. She looked at me full with her sore eyes.

"You think I will do something foolish now, don't you? All I will do is ask that man what it was he did to Belladonna inside his hell kitchen and why he did it, Thomas. I want to hear it from his own lips, when he must talk to my face, not like now when you make me run away."

"We will go back there together, then."

I prayed we would reach the house before the man began his butcher business. Strange, but it was Ling who slowed the pace as we went back down the lane. She clutched her skirt in her hand like a field girl.

"We would have heard a cry, Thomas. We would, yes?"

I took her poor hand and was still holding it when

we came to the door of the cottage. I used my other fist to rap on the boards, but the wood was so holed and eaten that it had all the sounding of damp plaster. I called out.

"Ho, inside there, sir. Can we speak to you?"

We heard the scrape of a chair and steps across the flagstones inside. The door pushed outward, not inward, but of course, that arrangement had to be for the horse. I knew then nobody would do so much for only one horse.

He was a big man who filled the door so well that he had to bend his head a little to save it from a bump. He was broad in the face and had a chest and arms to match, like Fossel, the pork butcherman in Brigg. But I found his dark eyes shrewd and his mouth soft, a strange mix in a man like that.

"What can you pair be looking for at this hour of the day? Who sent you here?"

Like Ling's, his voice came from somewhere else. He might even have been one of those passing gentlemen who came looking for my grandfather's best gloves. That was not what I had expected.

Ling whipped her hand out of my clasp and held it out, but high, as if the man should do something with it. Instead he stared until she dropped it to her side. I wanted to slap his face for slighting her.

"Monsieur," she said, "I believe that you may have knowledge of a something that belongs to me. A beautiful white mare with a tail as gold as barley."

"Gray," the man corrected her. "In England white horses are called gray. In France they keep their true color. What does that tell us, *mademoiselle?* That the French tell no lies? Or that the English are blind?"

If he expected an answer from Ling, he didn't get one, but she kept her eyes stuck to his face. From within we heard the poor roan shake herself and whirrup. The man let out a long breath.

"Come in and see for yourselves what it is I have."

He went ahead of us into the room with the knives, where he'd moved the mare. No matter where I placed myself, there was no keeping Ling's sight away from it. The poor beast's eyes were drooping and bloodshot, and she still held her half-shod hoof clear of the floor. There was a faint smell of horse dung in the room, but I saw no trace of any fresh dirt. Perhaps it was an old smell.

"Are you going to kill that mare?"

Ling had changed her voice to sound more proper, more English, though anyone with half an ear would know she was not so. Her voice was too interesting. Perhaps she did it because the man had mocked her with the fancy title he gave her, but, better than I, at least he'd recognized that she was French and not from Grimsby.

"I intend to, yes, *mademoiselle,* as soon as I see the backs of you and your friend. Already, you see, my clever potion has worked on the beast so that she will never know what smote her. If there is a horse heaven, I hope she will be attended there with the good memory of grog, rather than the whip under which she spent her life. But you had better be fast about your errand. I have no more of it to give her, and I must begin the work."

"Why do you do this? Did you kill my Belladonna too? Who was so beautiful?"

I squeezed her hand. *Do not cry, Ling. Not here.*

The mare opened her eyes, and the man saw that small change too. He raised his arms to let us know there was nothing more to say, that we must go. His forehead was creasing. We were an irk to him. If Ling saw any of this, she did not care. She stepped forward to the man's chest and made to prod him with a finger, but he caught it.

"Did you kill Belladonna? Why do you murder horses? Are you a devil like the doctor who would have killed my brother?"

She spat on the floor.

The man let Ling go and then laid his hand on my back, to move me back the way we had entered. I shrugged off his touch and took Ling's hand again. It was cold and dry, as if blood were draining from it.

"I must do my business straight," the butcher said. He spoke to me only. "I will not be cruel, and you will aid me in that by taking the girl away at once. I cannot talk about these matters to her now, whatever her story may be. If you have anything further to ask me, come tonight to the low house at the end of the meadow behind us."

It was as if a bailiff had done the job, so fast were we outside the door. There was no point in blundering back in, nor in staying on the patch of grass outside. Which of us wished to see or hear what would happen next?

In many ways the man had spoken sense. But why had he not answered yes or no for Belladonna?

Ox

"COME TO MY father's house until evening time,"
I said to Ling.

There it was again, my fool boy-man's voice, skit-
tering like jackstones thrown across a schoolroom floor.
But my croak would bother me no longer if only it made
her smile. Better to share her at home with everybody
than have her go back alone to the copse where the cold
stream ran. I felt for the duck egg, smooth and perfect in
my pocket.

She made no answer, just hung her head down onto
her chest.

"If I didn't have a sister, I'd let you steal our pony. Our pony, Ox, that's older than I am and fat as a tick. My sister, Nan, swears he talks to her."

She raised her head at that. "You have a pony? I did not take you for a horseman, Thomas."

"No, you took me for something else — what was the thing you called me yesterday?"

Her eyebrows rose. "What thing?"

"You said it was something tall. Something that lopes along?"

But she didn't seem to remember what she had said, and her eyes turned dull again.

Yet, whether she wanted to or not, we were now walking toward the village, and that was surely something won. I slowed my stride to suit her sluggish one. A wagon trundled past with two men up and two others walking alongside, heading for the day's mow. They called out to us, and I knew their eyes were taking in all they could of the girl they had no name for. It was no matter. She was with me.

St. Maurice's bell for six hours rang out clear from the square tower. Harkin the Clock passed us without a word, stepping urgently, his arms held tight against his sides, as if they were bolted. He looked like one of the family of peg dolls that Hugh had carved for Nan when she was little.

"We must hurry," I said to her. "That man in front of us, the Clock we call him, he's my father's sawyer. Every morning my father and my brother wait inside to hear him raise the gate latch, and then they're out into the yard to open up before you can say billy-o."

She said nothing to that, but her step picked up and kept steady. When we came close to our good old sulky house, I pointed to where my room swelled out over the road.

"That's it, Ling. Our house. That's where I sleep, in the bump. The shop's at the back, across the yard. My father's the only master wheelwright between here and Brigg, or here and Barton. We get every kind of job coming along to us."

Who'd have thought I would trumpet all this out? I sounded like a proper guildsman's boy. But there was nothing coming back from her, not as much as a shrug, and yet a company like hers, with all its wagons and carts, couldn't be strangers to my father's trade. Surely even French wagons had to have their wheels repaired.

"Look, we can stop by the kitchen and my mother will find you a task in return for some dinner later on, if that's a worry to you."

She set her feet down flat and shook her head, furious.

"I will take back my duck egg from you to give to her

before I do that. I sing for my supper, Thomas, or I dance for it, but I am not so low yet that I must wipe or scrub like a dirty slop girl."

I put my hands up to make peace. What wrong thing had I said that was worth such a passion?

"Then I'll show you the paddock where Ox is. You can wait there and Nan will be out soon to tend him and milk the cow too. You'll like Nan. And she'll want to hear about all the dancing and the tricks. The statues in the parks. Just don't tell her about—you know what."

With Nan around, my mother would find out about Ling soon enough. That is, if she hadn't already spotted her from the high window as we made our way along the road.

If Mother were to put her eye on Ling, she'd be safe. For today at least. It wasn't only house martins who came to our house for their home comforts.

Hands to the Wheel

THE WORKSHOP DOOR groaned like a dog when I pushed it open. For all that the door kept the morning sun locked out, inside all was light. My father had set windows high up at the other end of the shop, and the floor was buttered with pale wood shavings.

"Thomas?" He didn't sound too vexed.

"Yes, I'm returned, Father."

All I could see of him were his head and shoulders, because he was down in the pit, planing the nave of the new wheel for Bramley's lime cart, readying it for its iron casing. Hugh was above him, clutching two fat spokes, arm wrestling them into the spoke-dog's grasp. His face was strained, and no wonder. The short spokes always pulled hardest, as if they were fighting for their freedom.

My father and my brother speak in those terms. They believe that a wheel has a live mind of its own and that some wheels are wayward, just as some people are. Perhaps they're right. I prefer what moves my mind. That's what my hands would wrestle with, if only they could.

"Will I try it for you?" I asked Hugh, but he only snorted. Nobody should imagine, however, that my brother is mean-mouthed, for he is the gentlest of us three. At birth I got his full share of temper in addition to my own.

"Get the felloes ready for me, Tom," he said. "I have these nearly mastered."

I reached for the neat pile of felloes, the curved arches of ash wood that would grasp the spokes tight inside them and form the rim of the wheel. The wood was smooth as a weathered bone. That was all Hugh's work. My brother could now turn his hands to almost everything that Father did.

And I? I could saw well enough, and plane and paint. I could carry a load of timber as well as anybody else, fetch the right tools for a job, sweep like a stable boy. But my heart does not turn over for a fine wheel.

I had tried to explain this to my father last Christmas, but it hadn't turned out well. Perhaps it might have, if my schoolwork had been better.

"The things I love to make have different patterns, Father," I told him. "They begin in my head, like a puzzle. But nobody can do better than a wheel, because it's perfect already."

Father said that was only gimcrack talk. "Why not be content, then, to do what's perfect, boy?" he'd huffed. "Are you God that you will try to make something new in the world?"

All the same, he'd admired the steep-gabled house I built for the dog and cat.

"If you would only apply craft like that to your books, Thomas, you'd go far."

Now, ever since I'd run away from my schooling in Brigg, Father was like a pot on the boil, fixing to dunk me rightly into his full wrath. It was risky not to be in the workshop at sparrow-fart every morning, sweet to do whatever was asked. We all knew it would boil up soon enough, but meantime we tiptoed around that pot of anger.

Hugh slipped each felloe on, a crown for every pair of spokes, until the wheel made a perfect disc. Father heaved himself out of the pit and brushed his front clear of the elm shavings that clung to his shirt and breeches.

"Get me the sledgehammer, Tom," he said.

The tools hung on rows of nails driven into the plaster, neat as cups on a dresser. I lifted the heavy hammer from its perch, and when I handed it to him, I put the question.

"Father, do you know anything about the man who's taken the house just above Ottleys' place? The place that has the smokehouse down at the end of the field?"

Father turned the wheel, checking how well Hugh had fitted the felloes, tapping firmly on each with the hammer. From the paddock behind the shop, we could hear the steady sawing of the Clock. I wondered how Ling was faring out there. The Clock would say nothing to her, I'd wager, not even if she tried to pull a dozen duck eggs out of his ear.

"Do you, Father?"

"I do."

Hugh looked puzzled, as well he might, because not even on Christmas Twelfth Night, not for a joke, would Father ever be so short with him. With me he played a different game. To gain more, I had to offer something.

"I met a girl who's fetching to find her horse. It was stolen from her, and the man I'm talking about bought it at Brigg last week. But she's grieved, because there's no sign of the beast around Horkstow."

"She's right to be mardy about it so, Tom."

Very dry, Father sounded. He was standing on an old stump step, his eyes fixed to the rear of the shop, his hands reaching blind for a coil of rope.

"But that's no call for her to be doing what she's doing on the back of poor old Ox right now."

What?

I had to go toe up then to see what he was looking at through the windows. He had the better view, but still there was no mistaking what was to be seen in our little paddock.

Fat Ox, whose best pace these days was a slow trot, was cantering in a tight circle. Ling was on his back, standing ramrod straight, holding his tether rope in one hand, as if it had the makings for a proper bit and reins. Maybe there was something to that, for our old bay pony was holding his head as high as a carriage horse.

Ling faced outward for each orbit she made, and she held her free hand proud, and up in the air, as her body moved with the pace of the hooves. But her face was completely still on top of all the movement, like a mask. I could not make out her eyes.

Oh, lord, she was graceful now. Full of grace.

At the hub of the circle, as if he and his saw were the nave and axle, and Ling and horse the rim, spinning, the Clock continued his steady to-and-fro work, not bothered enough to raise his head. Had she slipped the spider dust on her shoes? Where was Nan? I couldn't see her, but she was shrieking away to the treetops.

"Go, Ox! Fly, boy!"

I looked at Father and lifted my shoulders to him. What could I say?

Hugh stood beside me to look and then gave his gaspy laugh. "That one'll be dancing on Betsy the cow next. She must have given old Ox some root mix to have him going so hard."

Father headed for the door.

"If we lose a day's milk out of Betsy in all this caper, Tom, that'll be another charge to your sheet, mark what I say. Now, get the fagots stacked up outside and then go tell Jack Proctor we're ready when he is."

"Father?"

"What is it?" He was nettled.

"Will you tell me, though, about this man? Tell me what you know before you say a word to the girl about it. And go easy with her. Please. There's no harm in her."

There must have been some keenness in my voice, because he turned back and answered me plain. "The man's name is Stubbs. They say he makes pictures for the Nelthorpes. Pictures for covering the walls in the big rooms they have up in Barton. Spends his time now with a brush and colors, but before this the story goes he used to work as a skin stripper. Owned a leatherworks somewhere out north or west, and there's money in that. He's not been spending much of it around, though, and no one's best pleased about that."

He turned and pushed the door of the shop open. Now we could hear the saw louder, its harsh biting insect noise, and under it the soft even clip of Ox's hooves hitting the dirt, *butter-and-eggs, butter-and-eggs.*

"All else I know is he's been picking up horses here and about, and that's nigh all anyone knows, except that what he brings away with him is not good horseflesh. That is the matter that has everyone foxed. That and the long-haired woman he has."

Singing for Supper

AT TABLE, Ling was not at all shy or fearful. She sat on the bench between Nan and me, and her head turned this way and that as she talked. Her voice was high and bright. She had never shown so much of her teeth to the world before, either, small, even pearl teeth, with one missing on the side by me. Except for the teeth, she put me in mind of the colored showy birds at the fair, the kind kept in hanging cages to sing tunes.

Since we'd sat down, everybody wanted a piece of Ling's song, even Hugh, who was usually no great maker of talk himself. Only Father and I kept ourselves apart.

On the table were the last of the old potatoes, creamed and salted and served with new turnip greens, along with cuts of the fish Hugh had landed last evening, a big tench. Mother filled a jug with milk and gave small beer to Father and Hugh. The Clock drank nothing in company and ate only bread, but even so, there were only four mugs on the table. Had Ling not been counted in? I fretted about that because I'd handed her duck egg over when I came in, small due though it was.

"Do you want some beer, Tom?" Mother asked.

I shook my head and poured a mug of milk for Ling. "We can share it," I said to her. But she took the mug without a word, drank the lot down, and then pushed it forward for more.

"See how thirsty I am, Thomas. Can you wait for yours? This milk is so creamy. I've never had better."

Perhaps Betsy had been taken under Ling's spell, too. Father had made Ling water the cow and stroke her, while he felt her udders for any stiffness and strain. After all, he said, what might a good milker have made of all the morning's antics? Only when he was satisfied did he let Nan milk her in the normal way.

Anyway, Ling's thirst was hardly a marvel, because she hadn't drawn a breath. She'd filled our ears since we'd sat down with stories of the fairs her company had come upon, on their great journey from the north down to Canterbury. She'd said nothing about her life in Paris, nor even that she was French. Nor had she told the story of her mother — except that she had one — nor the poor baby Sebastien.

Could none of them hear that her voice was strange? That it could never be an English voice?

Perhaps they couldn't, for just like one of those prattling jackdaws or the green-feathered birds in cages, Ling turned out a proper little mimic. That was a trick she hadn't practiced on me yet. Except for that one time with the man Stubbs this morning, she had been pleased enough to sound true French, or at least like a rare thing, whenever she opened her mouth.

But now when she spoke to me, or to Mother or Father about me, I was "Tom" and "Thomas." She gave me my *s*, like everybody else in the world did.

Nan couldn't hear enough of the horses, and the dogs that wore red ruffs and walked on two legs. Hugh wanted news of the hard high roads between the big towns, and the fine-wheeled carriages that raced on them. Mother asked first about the holy city of Canterbury, but then all her questions were about the people in the company, the poor hardworking children and how they lived and ate, day to day.

Ling painted a fine picture of Belladonna and her tricks, but she said nothing about the sale of the same white mare at Brigg last week, nor a word of the king turning sour on her company at Newmarket. *That* would have been something for Mother to share with the gossips.

She must keep the bad stories for me alone.

Then Father leaned back in his chair and broke into all the bright chat. "Young mistress Ling," he said. "My son tells me you are in search of that very white horse you have danced out on our dinner table for us today. Will you tell us more of that errand? Is she your own mare?"

Ling's cheeks went crimson as paint. Lord, had I done the wrong thing, telling the tale?

"No, sir," she answered. "I cannot say she is mine, not exactly. All the horses belonged to Carl the Dane, the man I told you of, the leader of our company. But I am the only one to ride her these years past. She looks to my care as if I were her mother or her sister. She will have only me on top."

"Well, now," said Father. His tone was gentle enough to set my neck prickling. "If I said to Nan here—and mind I do *not* say it, Nan—that the time was come for our Ox to go to his peaceful end, for he might be in pain, then I would leave no fence standing between saying that and making it happen. And . . ."

"But he said nothing, sir," Ling interrupted, "and there was nothing in Belladonna that was at all hurt or poorly. She has only eight or nine years, and I have taken such good care of her all the time we have been with the company. *Sans cesse, monsieur!*"

Well! Now she had entered the war, with her French speech for guns. My mother shot me a look but Father carried on as if he hadn't noticed any word spoken out of place.

"So you say. But if it is true that the mare was bought at Brigg last week by our lately come villager, Mr. Stubbs, then my hearing is that that gentleman buys only horses that are next or nigh to eternity, animals that are spent. They call him a butcher, you know, though it passes my understanding, all that is said around on this matter."

He looked at Ling, hard. She stared back, so there was a pair of them playing stags. The huge eyes gave away nothing, but she was turned as white again as she had been outside the butcherman's house that morning.

"I have heard that said, yes, sir," she whispered.

"So, I will tell you this, my girl. If the mare was not yours and was sold, you have no claim at all on her, whatever the rest of your story may be. But I have always hated a twist in a thing, and what I cannot get right in my head here is that a sound horse be sold to a man who buys only the worst and, more, that no sign of her be noised around."

He set his mug down. "Girl, no one in these villages

has seen your Belladonna, for there would be word of such a beast, and I would hear it as likely as anybody else. And here now is the man who will tell you I am talking truth."

There was no doubting whose were the heavy boot steps on the doorsill. Up went the latch and Jack Proctor the smith tramped into the kitchen, rubbing his hands on the black leather apron that was his outer skin for six days of the week. Only on Sundays did it come off. Mother readied a plate for him.

"You'll have a bite to eat, Jack?" she asked.

"Bitten and eaten an hour since, Susan. You've Bramley's wheels ready, John? Fire's likely hot and all, now."

"Sit awhile, Jack. This young slip here is called Ling, and she's run away from the fair, best I can reckon what she says, all for her little mare being sold to our Mr. Stubbs at Brigg last week. A white mare with a barley-colored tail and fine gams under her. Not poorly, she says, and so not his usual kind. Now, what can you tell the lass?"

Proctor screwed up his face, as black with smoke as a crow's suit.

"He's like to be making paintings of the mare, then, if she's the eyeable kind."

I heard Ling draw in the smallest gasp.

"They tell me that's what he's doing plenty of up at the Nelthorpe place, painting horseflesh for her fancy-ship. Painting her dogs too, like they were kings and queens."

Ling made a steeple with her hands, as if she were praying. Then she took them apart and put them neatly in her lap and stared ahead, at nobody.

Jack had not finished. "Listen to me, John. Your Tom might be able to land work in that same place now, making frames for the pictures that Mr. Stubbs paints."

So, it was my turn to have news. My heart gave a lurch, as if it had been pushed over an edge.

"I hear there are that many to be put together," Jack continued, "and then gilded after, that the man up there can't keep pace. I'll drop the word if you wish it."

To escape the glover's needles that Grandfather was sharpening for me! To do fine work in wood and earn shillings for it! I looked quickly toward Father and then away, for there was no answer there.

Jack spat on the floor. "But the horses the man buys himself, well, that's another story and not one for this table."

He turned to Nan. "Well, young Nancy Rose, have you found anything new for me under the sun today?"

Nan had a good answer for once. "I was the one who found Ling in the paddock this morning, and she told Ox he could dance, and he did, Jack, he did! I'm going to learn how to make him do it, and then I can go away with the fair too."

Nan prattled on, and I could feel Ling grow restless beside me. I knew she wanted to be away, to brew up something with the fresh news she had now, but I couldn't leave until the wheel shoes were done, and perhaps not even then, if Father had another piece of work in mind for me. He surely would now, if only to be contrary.

My stomach was turning over like a churn. When I looked up, Jack's eyes were on me. Had he the right story about the picture work? I'd never yet made a frame, but surely all that needed to be done was squaring-off work and perhaps some carve piece for prettiness. That would be no hardship to me, and I would be out in the world.

More than that, if there was any truth in the rest of Jack's tale, I might be the one to find Belladonna after all.

Danelaw

"YOU SEEM MUCH HAPPIER when there are other people around," I said to Ling.

She looked at me as if I had hit her, or called her a cutpurse or worse. I was only saying what I saw. Since we'd left my house, there'd been very few words coming my way. Perhaps I had played my part and now she knew what there was to be known about Stubbs. Perhaps I was too gloomy for her.

We were on our way to the house of death, just as we had come from it so early in the morning. Now it was milking time, or just past it, and most people were at home, though there was plenty of light and height still in the sky. My day hadn't been so very charged after all. After the shoeing, some cart shafts needed planing, and a brace of thole pins had to be cleaned and oiled. Then Father gave me a brush and paint to cover the new wheels, while he and Hugh and the Clock took off to look at some fresh oak timbers laid out for selling in a field near Elsham. He'd said nothing further about Ling or about the framing work, and nor had I.

There left only Jack Proctor, who came sniffing around me with his own itch to find out more about Stubbs. "I'll settle the matter of the mare for the girl quicker than you will, Tom," he said.

I looked over to where Ling sat on a mounting stone, waiting for me. She must have heard him, for she ran a finger across her throat and then stood up and stamped across to the gate.

"This is something she must do for herself, Jack," I bid to warn him off. "It's a long story and I'll tell it to you someday."

For answer, Jack had dipped his steamy turnip of a face into the water barrel. When it came out, it had two things to say. Only one had been welcome.

"Tell Mr. Stubbs, then, if he needs a shoeing or such a works, I'm his man. And you, Tom," he said, lowering his voice, as if he, the man of iron, was about to tell me the secret of turning gold, "take it tidy with that lass.

There are home folks and there are rambling folks, and one lot can harm the other as soon as look at them— take it from me."

Jack Proctor to talk about such things, who'd never had a woman across his doorsill! I hadn't known whether to lash out or to laugh, but I'd buttoned my lip.

Just as Ling was doing now.

"When I was sitting at your dinner table, Thomas," she answered at last, speaking slowly, "it was as if I was in the arena during a performance. I had to smile and talk and pretend my life is good and easy. Nobody wants to see a pout face. That is the first rule for the performer."

I shrugged.

"Listen!" she said. "When I joined the troupe, Maman was like a ghost. I told you this." She swallowed. "Even so, she remembered to tell me I must smile for the Dane, just as the two of us used to smile for all the gentlemen who came to see us dance. We showed our teeth even when we were tired or when we had *la grippe*."

"Is that like *grip*?" I asked. "Like this?" I reached for her wrist and held it, but did not press as hard as I would if I held Nan's. It seemed so fragile.

She wrinkled her nose at me. "Silly Thomas. When you have *la grippe*, you are ill; you make the shivers."

"Oh." I felt stupid and let her hand drop. We walked on without a word, until she started up again.

"The first day we joined the wagons, the Dane brought me to his big basket of costumes. First I thought it was full of arms and legs that were chopped, cut off, but, *non,* they were little uniforms, with soldiers' stripes and gold *épaulettes.* We were a cavalry, he said, as good as the king's. There were animals' heads too, made of wood and canvas, and velvet suits like skins, to make bears and birds, frogs and lions. Even *la cigale,* your grasshopper, remember? He told me the lords and ladies loved to see the fables. That was true. They would make the noise of the goose and clap their hands, but they never saw themselves in the stories."

I tried to honk, but it sounded more pig than goose.

She laughed. "He told me I would be a very good *cigale,* but he saw well I was not a good rider. He said Augustin would teach me how to ride so I become part of the horse. In return, he said I must teach the other children how to make the beautiful arabesque, the *fouetté,* the curtsy, the *pirouette.*"

"Who was Augustin?"

"*Lui?* He was the boy who had looked after Belladonna until then. He was to get a new horse, even though he was still small, like me. That day Augustin hated me because Belladonna loved me already. I thought he would put poison in my bread, only that he knew I shared it with Belladonna."

"Who else was there?" I asked.

She opened her fingers and began to count. "We were thirteen in Paris, but only seven when we came here, to England. The best riders were Sylvie, Gaston, Augustin, and me. We had Kirsten too, with the white hair. She could twist herself into knots, because her bones were soft as a cat's. The Dane was her uncle."

She told me how, that first day, the Dane had fixed her with his water-cold eyes and told her he would find out what her troubles were.

"He said he didn't care about them, but that when I was in front of an audience, I must wear a smile that would deceive the devil himself into baring his fangs. Imagine telling *me* such a thing, Thomas! I told him Maman had taught me that when I was a baby."

She sniffed. But I was light inside. It had cost me some heart to ask Ling why she was gladder when others were there to hear her talk.

She touched my wrist bone, just a feather touch to slow me down. A woman was coming toward us, likely from Ottleys' farm. She walked swiftly and was tall and spare, except for an odd bunchy bag she wore around her middle.

"That is no village woman from here," Ling whispered. "Do you think she might know Mr. Stubbs?"

What had Father said, something about a long-haired

woman? I'd forgotten that, and even leery Jack Proctor had said nothing of it.

"Likely," I answered.

But as she drew close, I was surprised how young the woman was, surely not many years older than I was. The wool shawl she wore over her chest left her hair free, and she wore no kerchief or bonnet. The black hair hung loose and straight, and her skin was dark like a fieldworker's. She was handsome.

She greeted us and made to turn down the lane, but Ling ran forward and stopped her.

"*Madame*, please."

The woman smiled at the strange title. "You're not from here, then, no more than I am," she said to Ling. She looked hard at me, and I couldn't remember when a woman's eyes came near the same level as my own. That was how tall she was.

"I saw you this morning, did I not, staring through the windows of our place below?"

I gawped at her. How could she have seen me? There'd been no one abroad so early.

"You took my bread, then, didn't you? And look at me, sir, when you answer that."

Ling got there first. "No, *madame*, this boy Thomas would not steal as much as a blade of grass from a cow. I took your bread last evening, because I was starving. But, look, I have one for you now in return. That's why we are come here — and to talk to Mr. Stubbs in a proper way."

She was holding out her gift, one of Mother's rye loaves. For the life of me I couldn't decide whether it, too, was stolen, or whether my mother had packed the bread for Ling when she left our house.

I reckoned the odds on both were about equal.

Ling's God

THE SMOKEHOUSE at the bottom of the field had a slant view of Stubbs's house. That was how I'd been spied earlier. Ling had done all the good peep work at the back windows and hadn't been spotted. My usual luck.

The woman—Mary Spencer was the name she gave—led us now along a trodden path toward the shed, with its one small open window.

"We live down here in the one room because George needs the whole place above for his work," she told us. "And for what that is, you know, it's not a fair or a clean place for a body to be stationed for any length of time. Nor to sleep, either. I help him most days, and I have to go down to the beck afterward to soak myself, for I find that even a barrelful of water on its own will not wash it off."

His *work*? I could think only of the knives I'd seen and the poor mare at her last breakfast. A butcher did a fair and honest job for all folks to see — *that* was work.

Ling's face was pinched and pale. No smile for the devil there.

By the door there were hens scrabbling and gossiping inside a wicker crate. Mary Spencer shook her head at it. "I've lost one to the fox already," she said, "and she was outside for no longer than it took me to rinse a few cloths."

Well, the same fox had got the woman's bread that morning too, without even having to snout for it, thanks to Ling's charity. There was no sill to the small window. Perhaps that was why the woman had left her loaf to cool at the house by the top of the field.

She waved us inside the room and immediately sat herself down on a chair near the door.

"I'm weary out," she said. "I've walked from the shore with these shells for George. He's mad for cockles, winkles, or anything that crawls into a shell." She laid her big bag down with a clatter.

The room was perhaps half the size of my mother's

kitchen, though it seemed smaller again because the ceiling was so low. There were rough beams running straight across, with gobbets of dirty fleece stuffed in wherever there were gaps. The walls had no plaster, just the rough stonework. It was surely not a room for a man who spoke as smartly as Stubbs did.

Yet there was a life here. A bed against the far wall was neatly dressed with blankets; a broad-brimmed hat sat on the pillow; a sheepskin warmed the floor. A narrow truckle bed under the window had bolsters stiff as rocks at each end. There was a set of shelves with crockery; hooks were knocked into the stonework to bear clothes; buckets stood in a row. I admired the finely made table that had books and papers stacked into one corner. A plain jug sat in the center, stuffed with meadow flowers and grasses.

It was not just the books that set the place apart from any cottage in the village, however. Never before had I seen a smoke oven, though from time to time Father brought home an eel with crisped gold skin. This brick oven sat in the middle of the space, raised from the floor by a couple of steps. It wore its iron chimney pipe like a tall hat.

But it was what was propped against the oven that was remarkable. I'd not had much truck with pictures of any kind in my life. There was what hung on church walls, or the colored glass pictures in church windows.

There were the silly fashion plates my grandfather sometimes hung above his glass counter come Easter-bonnet
time. Lord knows, there was all I blacked onto paper
myself, my daft bits and pieces. But these! I'd never seen
the like.

In each drawing there was a horse, striding as if it
would move out of its paper world into the real one.
It led with the right foreleg, and its rear left hoof was
caught on the clop. Though it wore its ears back, there
was nothing fretful about it. It might have been stepping
out toward its mother or its mate. But the horse had
plenty to worry it, because in every next drawing it lost
more of itself. Its flesh began to disappear.

Still the animal marched on, even when its legs
were opened up to show that its knees and ankles were
only hinges made of bone. I thought of the cairns of
pebbles Hugh and I used to pile up outside the kitchen
door when we were little lads. So, whenever he made a
horse, God did no more work than children do.

In the last picture, the horse's face was a mask,
and its ribs were clinkered like the timbers of a boat. But
it was not sorry for what had happened to it — oh, no, it
did not care. It marched on.

I had hardly moved all the time I was examining the
paper horses. But Ling had. She stood in front of one
drawing, then another, and then started over again. She
walked around the four sides of that oven like a Papist

doing worship. Of course, she *was* a Papist, for the French were so, I knew that. Yet to eye her as she moved past each picture, it was simpler to believe that Ling's god was a horse.

She was silent.

It was Mary Spencer who broke the stillness. From her stool she had a view through the small window. "Here comes George and so now you can put your question to him, young Ling. But what on earth is it he has clasped?"

Ha, Ha!

THE LATCH LIFTED, the door was pushed in, and with a stoop to his head, the horse butcher came into the room. His hands were cupped around something small.

"Oh, George, cast off your shirt outside as I tell you to, and take this one." Mary Spencer threw a garment toward the door. "There are young folk inside that say you asked them here, and you are like to give them scandal. Besides, it ain't good for any of us and our health, nor for you either, in this heat."

Without a word, the man picked up the fresh cloth and off out with him again, still bearing whatever he had in his fists. But his woman was right. His shirt arms were covered in blood, brown and red blood, old and new. He had the stench of blood on him too, which stayed after him in the dry air. What must the other house smell like now?

I moved closer to Ling, who was still facing the drawings, her neck thrust just a bit forward. That neck was the weakest thing in the room. In Horkstow. In England. In France. It could never bear the worst news. If it were the case that the butcher had already done away with Belladonna, Ling's poor neck would never hold her head up high again.

I could not bear it. "Where has he gone to?" I shouted at the woman. "He has business here with us."

She gave glare back to mine, fair and equal. I had shaken Mary Spencer, but there was no stir from Ling. Had she even turned when Stubbs came in?

This time he managed the door silently, for it was a shock to see him suddenly standing again in the room, with a clean shirt on. He stood in front of the woman and opened his hands to her.

"Look what I found lost and wandering down the lane just now, Mary. We'll keep him to grow into your very own companion, I think."

What the idiot man had was a brown puppy that fit in his huge hands like a nut in a shell. He set it down onto the earth floor and it staggered forward a little.

Then it sat plump onto its hind legs and sounded the smallest bark you ever heard.

Mary Spencer laughed.

"And do you know, it bears a sign to show that it is meant for us, my dear," Stubbs said. He lifted its hind paws and pointed at something. "Look at the extra dewclaw this one has, soft as an infant's toenail."

It was no bother to me to break into all this sweet music and joy.

"Mr. Stubbs?"

"Yes, George." Mary Spencer pointed first at me, then at Ling. "These two young folks have an errand with you. Hear them out. The girl's brought good neighborly rye bread for us. It's the boy you must watch out for. He's that cross, like a bag of weasels."

She thought herself well revenged on me, but Stubbs didn't smile. He bowed his head to me.

"For all that you are in my house, I'll not offer you my hand in peace, young man, for reasons you may best imagine. Though I wash myself after my work as well as it may be done. How may I assist you?"

Before I could answer, Ling stepped forward. Her skin was tight against her cheekbones and she was pale.

"You heard me well enough this morning, Monsieur Stubbs, before you began your cruel work."

"*Bien sûr, mademoiselle. Continuez, en anglais ou en français, comme vous voulez.*"

"I will speak in English, Mr. Stubbs, because my friend Thomas must hear what you say. I know that a week ago you bought my little white mare, Belladonna, who was taken from me in a cruel trick. I wish more than all the world to have her back, and I ask you now to help me in this. Can you do this?"

"Tell me more about this mare, *mademoiselle*, so I can best understand you."

She let out a long breath like a sigh. "She is a little smaller than the dark mare you killed with your knives. But my Belladonna was as fine and fit as any horse can be. She had no aches or swells anywhere, and she is clean and white, not gray like you said but whiter than snow, all over, except for her tail, which is long and thick and the color of barley."

She turned and pointed at the drawings. "She wore her ears like this one, always back but not in a passion. I think she found she could hear things better this way. She liked to hear me talk. Always her ears moved."

Poor Ling, steady so long, now had a crack in her voice. I wanted to take her hand, but to do so would weaken her, so I did not.

Nobody could have reckoned for what Stubbs said next. He sounded just like one of the preachers who turn up on the streets of Brigg with their heads aflame. He sang his words out just like one of those roamers.

"*He swalloweth the ground with fierceness and rage. . . .*

He saith among the trumpets, Ha, ha." He had the cheek to look sharp at Ling. "The horse that will say *Ha, ha* to the trumpets of war is a very fine beast, do you not agree, my dear?"

Mary Spencer clicked her tongue at him, as if he were a child.

"Oh, George, for goodness' sake. Give the girl a truthful answer, not your doomy old Job's talk. Don't you see how the poor thing frets?"

The man cleared his throat and nodded. "Yes, Mary, you are right, as always."

He opened his hands then, as if doing that much made him an honest man. "My dear girl, whose name I do not know, you describe your mare very well. Those are the very qualities for which I bought her to be breeding stock for my employer. That is Lady Nelthorpe of Barton. There was another reason, and I'm sure you'll agree with me here."

I would not like to have had Ling's eyes fixed on me as they were on him, but he breezed on, that unfeeling man.

"Apart from her good looks, the mare seemed an uncommonly well-trained beast. You see, the lady has been in difficulties this last while, finding a decent mount for her young son. She . . ."

Ling would not hear him out. "But, *monsieur,* she was *mine.* You had no right. She was stolen from me."

Surely, everyone must hear the tears in her voice. Her fists were balled up now, though whether to hit him or to boost her own spirit, I couldn't guess. The red silk had slipped down her back, and its string stretched across her throat like a slash of blood.

"Sir," I said, desperate enough to be mannerly to him, "it is as Ling says. The man you bought him from was nothing but a common thief."

"And, if so, he should be hanged for it, doubtless," said Stubbs.

The man was smug and stupid as an ox in clover, and Ling was twitching at her skirt again, like a mad person with an itch. Again I thought of her coral-handled blade, though this time I longed to hold it in my own hand.

"You see, I buy only what I have proof of title for," Stubbs said, slow as he liked. "Or else, as you have witnessed already, I buy what nobody on earth requires further."

I looked at Ling. Proof of title? What could that mean? The wretched man had said nothing about his so-called work or why he did it, but there he stood talking about the law as if he were the best citizen in the country.

"What about that pup you just took from the road outside?" I shouted. "Do you have a *title* for that too?"

He looked puzzled more than angry, but I knew I'd

roasted my chances of any work that might be going. At least my voice had held firm.

The pup was curled up where it had last reached, asleep, its underparts rising and falling like a baby bellows. Mary Spencer picked it up and walked to the bed, where she laid it down as tenderly as if it were a human infant. She even placed a pillow down so that the small thing would not roll off.

"Enough," she said. It was me she addressed. "Young man, you should take your leave now, and take your temper too, and return to your home."

She turned her head to him. "The wheelwright's place, George." Then back to me. "Your friend is welcome to spend the night here with us. I can make her comfortable, believe it or not, and she will be safe. I can feed her, with all our thanks for her good rye loaf. And George will make better sense of all this on the morrow. Now, go."

The Barley Mow

THERE WERE BLACK CLOUDS over the villages the next day, but these were not the kind that live in the sky and skim across water like swans.

No, my father was entirely right about the barley mow and all the fuss and busyness that came in its train. He called us boys at first light, when the earliest carts began their trundle to the fields stretching between Horkstow and Elsham cross. There was already such heat abroad that the casement window in our room had swelled itself into a sulk along with the house. I tried to open it to see if anyone was abroad on the road, but it wouldn't budge without a hammer's blow.

"Leave it be, Tom," said Father. "That heat is set to stay like a fever until sundown. The yard will be hopping with wains, like a dog with fleas. There'll be no chance for mooning around, nor fishing either."

So, even my dutiful brother was ticked off! There was more when we tripped down barefoot to the kitchen, where there was no breakfast, only a bad smell.

"Yesterday's milk has turned, and it's too early for Betsy to oblige us. Bring bread and water with you and get your boots on; you know better than to dawdle, both of you."

What we had to do all that day long was the kind of wheelcraft not even Hugh could enjoy much. Poultice and bandage work, Father called it, though every year it brought good money. No farmer wants to lose a day's waining because of an axle break or a cranky wheel.

I was like a collar-choked hound that scrapes to be away, though for once my work was needed and no one was out to mock me. But I didn't want to be anywhere but by Ling's side. I had delivered her to strangers, after all, and who knew what they were really like? Ling was so small in her person and yet so fierce. What if a man like Stubbs thought she was a French spy after all? He might hand her over, for that would be a way to get rid of her and her claim.

People said there were regulars and naval men in Barton and along the Humber who might be summoned with a blast of a whistle if some foreign whatnot or other was spotted. I'd never paid heed to such nonsense before. Perhaps it was not nonsense. But as long as I didn't know how Ling was, I fretted, and as long as I fretted, my mind cooked plots into puddings, so that I knew even less. Whenever I could, I went to the gate to see if by chance she was on the road, waiting for me. She was not.

The first cloud came over around midday. Nan came running into the shop, crying about it. "Humphrey Pell's draft horse is pushed under and crushed to bits!"

Some fool had whipped the wain down off the wold at a lick, and for that bad work the great horse was killed. It took ten men to unload the wain, drag it past the groaning animal, and pull it into the yard for mending. The front wheels were twisted so that they dangled out of kilter like the arms of a poor soldier I saw once begging in Brigg.

Nan cried for the rest of the day, and the horse lay where it had fallen, until Pell himself was seen above the hedge, coming with a face on him to shoot it.

The second cloud was all my own, and it waited until later in the day to show its face. No one had expected Jane Brice to live out the week, but the heat took the poor thing away in the afternoon, while Mother was visiting her. When she came back from the cottage with the news, there was another task for me.

"Tom, you'll carry down old Jane's stock of honey. I'll not keep it myself; I'll give it out to whoever needs it, but it can't be left there while the place is empty and all manner of people are on the road. Your father still needs Hugh, but you can be spared. Look there."

She pointed. "Mr. Harkin made up the coffin as soon as he knew Jane would fail. Wait on your going until they take her away from her house. The poor thing can't be left there in this heat."

Did my mother persuade the Clock to make coffins now? I hadn't seen the plain oak box in the shop, but now it stood ready right under the signboard, planed and waxed to a gleam.

"He even asked me for some of Jane's beeswax for it," Mother said. "He's a proper craftsman, Tom."

I boiled inside, and I boiled again as I waited. I'd set a plan to catch Ling early in the dusk and hear what she had learned about Belladonna and what it was the butcherman did with his horseflesh. But what could I do?

Nan came with me to carry the smallest crocks down, though she wasn't much help and was still inclined to sniff. We barely spoke, though I told her we had walked a hundred miles for sure in our journeys back and forth with the honey. She made no song out of that, as she would have done another day.

At last all the honey crocks stood in the coolest part of the kitchen. There were sixteen of them. Who'd have thought there were so many bees at work in Horkstow? Mother covered each crock with a jug muslin against the wasps. "It's never the bees that come looking for it, only those thieves," she said. "You might swat a few for me, Tom."

"I'm that sticky I need a proper wash," I said to her. "I'm going to the river."

Her brows shot up but she said nothing.

I might as well have walked Nan's hundred miles after all, so sore were my feet, when at last I reached the smokehouse. Even without a breeze I could smell the ebbed sands of the estuary, and under that scent, the slightly bitter smell of the Ancholme. I took off my boots to walk through the meadow grass. It tickled but was still warm, not the cool touch underfoot I'd wanted.

Behind me all the way was the moon, fatter by a day, though still only a shrimp. The stars gave better light. But nothing was needed when Ling came to the door. Joy blazed in her face.

"Mary saw you coming. I thought you would come before now. Oh, Thomas, I have such news. For you and for me. *Nous sommes les enfants du paradis.*"

Paradise

Of course *PARADIS* was the French word for paradise. I should have guessed as much. No lesser place would do for my Ling.

She was headed there in the next day or so, and I would join her — oh, it would be perhaps a little later; she could not be certain when. I'd get my wings when I'd learned everything the butcherman could teach me.

"Yes, Thomas, I know it is so strange what I say, *incroyable* too, but he will teach you what you need to go far in the world. He knows people. You will see."

It was difficult to slow her down and find any sense in what she said. Perhaps it might have been better after all to have had Mary Spencer's cool eye on us rather than be lying flat in the meadow with the timothy grasses pressed into pillows underneath our heads. But even if we had not chosen to be outside alone, Mary would have pushed Ling over the doorsill.

"Shhh!" she whispered. "George is fast asleep. Go away from here and be quiet when you return. I'll leave the door off the latch."

Now Ling's eyes were skipping from one thing to another, everything under the moon, and whatever she caught she had to make into something else.

"Do you see the *hibou*? The owl? There, like a little shirt that has sleeves too long. That bird is good luck for us. Did you see the chimneys of the big house up on the road? I walked across the sharp blade of a rooftop once, just like that one, like a *funambule* on his rope, because Augustin dared me to."

I had never danced in all my life, but perhaps this mad whirl was what a dance with a girl felt like. I had no steps for it, so what I made was all my own. I stood up and straightaway sank down on one knee in front of her. She sat up to look, and I pretended to sweep a big hat from my head. I laid it at her feet.

"Please, my lady, tell me first the news of the beautiful Belladonna. Or else I must arrest you and bring you to your old enemy, His Majesty King George of England, and show you for a spy."

She laughed and tried to kick me, but I caught her foot. "Take care with the feather of my hat, dear lady. It is the fashion of our court."

Now she was the sober one. "Sit by me and listen, Thomas. It is very important, *très* important, and you are being silly."

Her smile was worth the scold. I put on a good-boy face and sat beside her again.

Belladonna had been the first of us to arrive into paradise, it seemed. She now had a stable of her own, as much oats as she could eat, and grooms to scratch away her smallest itch.

"This milady is so pleased with her she treats her like the princess she is. But the boy has wooden legs. He cannot make her—"

"Wooden legs?"

"You must know this condition, Thomas! You have wooden legs when you cannot make a horse do what is proper. Like when you are drunk, you have a wooden head."

"Oh."

"That is my Belladonna in her heaven. Next there is me! Monsieur Stubbs is going to bring me to the lady's house, which is so very big, and there I will be the teacher of the boy. For the way he must ride a horse, not for proper lessons, though of course I can teach him to speak French too. If he wishes."

She waved a switch of grass to one side and then to the other.

"He will go to school in another place soon, but because his legs are so bad on a horse, he cannot yet go out with the hunt. The lady is ashamed of this because his father is dead, and so he must learn to be the great master."

She made a face. "My Belladonna has never gone with a hunt. I do not know if she will like *la chasse*. I will teach the boy better things. I will teach him to fly, believe me. I will take Belladonna away if she is unhappy, but she will be so happy to see me now. Look there, Thomas — our owl is back!"

The lady lived in Barton, and it seemed our Mr. Stubbs did more than buy new horses for her. It was just as Jack Proctor had reckoned. He painted the horses she had, and her dogs too.

"He has put even this lady into a picture, though she is quite old, and now he paints the boy, because his name is John *le baronnet* Nelthorpe. An important *monsieur*." Who had wooden legs for all his fine name.

"Now, Thomas, this is the difficult thing for me, to explain what this person Stubbs does. I do not like it. I hate it, but I have seen it."

She drummed her heels against the earth. Her feet

were silver and her thin toes made a straight line, all save the little ones, which were curled over themselves like the smallest winkles left by the tide. If they were Nan's, I'd tickle them.

I slipped a grass like a thread between one little toe and its neighbor and tied it with as fancy a knot as I could manage. First she giggled. Then she nudged me.

"I am trying to be serious, Thomas. I will tell you now what happened here today. I will tell you what I know, but it was not so easy to learn it. That man makes me go to the killing house with him before he will tell me all this about the boy and the lady and how I can be with my Belladonna again."

She blew out a sound, *puh.*

"He made me see, but first he beat me, Thomas. I hate to tell you that."

I felt something had jumped into my gut and clawed it. The man did that and was lying asleep now like a baby! I made to get up, but she stopped me.

"No, silly boy, not beat with a stick, not like you at your school, poor you. I mean like in a game. He beat me like Gaston always beats our big Antoine when they take up their *rapières* to fight in the arena. You see, Gaston knows how to make the best parry. And so does Monsieur Stubbs."

À Outrance

A *PARRY*? What on earth was that?

Ling put her thumb on my lip. "Listen, Thomas. I will tell you how it was when you left." She smiled. "When Mary sent you away."

Ling told me that after I'd banged the door of the smokehouse behind me, there was silence for a while. The man and the woman busied themselves separately, she with the food, he with his pencils and papers. Ling stared at the drawings that faced her.

"So cruel, so strange, but beautiful. *Comme ils étaient beaux!* I cannot say why they were beautiful," she said.

I could have told her it was because they were true. But I said nothing.

The same Mary Spencer who thought so little of me had drawn up a third stool to the table and placed a small bowl of steamed cockles in front of Ling.

"She had a larger bowl and then there was a proper *bassine* for the big *monsieur*. Thomas, I had to hold my stomach not to laugh, because the table is now spread just as in the story of the three *ours*, the bears who lived in the castle with their bowls of different sizes. And I was the crafty fox come among them, and they did not know it!"

That did not mean she was happy to eat with the man who had traded away her horse, but she had no choice in that matter. What she could do was talk.

"Thomas, you know that words are the *armes*? They are the weapons for the small clever person who will always beat the cruel giant in a fight *à outrance*, to the death."

I shrugged. I was neither small nor clever nor cruel. Perhaps I was a giant. But it was true that words were weapons. I knew that much.

Ling narrowed her eyes. "I point at the drawing that cuts away most of the horse, so he looks like a boat. A broken boat." I nodded. I remembered it. I remembered all of them.

"I say to him, 'Monsieur Stubbs, how is it that you

were able to hold the animal altogether in one piece? A butcher must make cuts in order to hang his meat. You must be very strong.' I think, this way his head will grow big and he will talk."

But the man said nothing, only rooted away in his great bowl to see if he had a full cockle remaining. When he spoke at last, he ignored Ling's question.

"Instead he asks me if I know there is a city in the north of Italy where the horses race every summer in a great square. I say to him *rien*, nothing. What do I care about his city in Italy? Then he said that the horses there are kings for that special day, because the young men dress them up in bright colors before they gallop out. He said each *quartier* has its own badge and colors. Some wear the caterpillar, some the snail or the eagle. He said sometimes the horses die after the race, and sometimes the men die too, because it is so fierce. He told me he was in this city once, and they call the race the *palio*."

"English races are not like that," I said. "Do they have races like that in France?"

Ling closed her eyes.

"I think of the sun, and it is different," she said. "Once, long ago, we went away from the city, far to the south. A *monsieur* invited us to perform our fables. It was so warm there, Thomas! Belladonna was like a flower in the sun. We had all the cherries and white raspberries we could eat, and the white wine was cold as water in a well."

She opened her eyes. "You would like the sun, Thomas. You would go brown there, your arms and your face, but your eyes would be as blue as the sky."

That was enough to darken my cheek on the spot, but she rushed on.

"So I said to him that white horses love the sun because of Pegasus, who flew close to it with his wings, but that does not mean they are happy to die too soon. When men are cruel."

But if Ling thought she would wound Stubbs, it seemed she had the wrong man, because he pushed away his bowl and leaned across the table.

"He is like the man who wrestles with his big arms. Do you know what he said, Thomas? He said that if he ever finds Pegasus, it will be his duty to cut away his wings to see how they worked. Then he says, 'But I would get on his back first!' So I tell him he will never get his wish."

It seemed the big bear did not mind what Ling said to him, however.

"He laughed! Then he asks me if I have ever seen an Arabian horse, and I think of our Basil and I say I have. He tells me the Arab horses are born out of the south wind."

I snickered. First a horse with wings, and now there was a wind that could breed a king's horses! Even Mr. Defoe, who told stories, kept his tale to the ducks everyone could see all the year round.

Ling's voice had become a whisper.

"Thomas, I told you my mother was named for the west wind," she said. "*Zéphyrine.* How did he know that? And I never heard that story about the Arabian horses, but at once I tell him I would not swap my Belladonna for any of them. I said she must miss me so much, and I knew she dreams of me, because she comes to me each night."

Ling bit her lip. "That was my mistake, Thomas. I told him too much. That is why he won. He kept silent but I spoke what is in my heart."

So she attacked him again. Another parry.

"I say to him, 'Monsieur, why do you not draw what is alive in front of you? Is it because to do that is more difficult for you, because it moves?' I told him I saw a devil in a hospital one time, cutting up a rabbit. I asked him why he did that when it was dead."

"What did he say?" I asked.

"He said I must look at his drawings and find the one that captures the body and the soul of my Belladonna. If I will pick that one out and then go with him to his butcher house, he might have a proposal for me."

She sighed. "And he did. For me, and now for you, too."

There was silence when Ling finished telling me this, nothing to hear except the small sounds of the earth shrinking at last into coolness. The owl had glided away home. I remembered lying in bed with Hugh when we were small, listening to noises we had no names for, fearful. It was Mother, the town girl but the glover's daughter, who told us that the night became still only after the fox pulled on his black gloves and stockings to go hunting.

"But what did you see when you went with him? Was the mare . . . ?"

She pressed my lips shut as she had done the day before when I spoke of my school.

"Thomas, I will not tell you what I saw, because you must see it with your own eyes."

"But why must I look at it, Ling, if you have, and if Belladonna is safe? Making frames is the work the man needs, and that I can do. That's what Jack said."

"See, I am become like him, like *Barbe bleue*," she said. "Bluebeard the wife killer."

She rushed on before I could ask what she meant.

"That Stubbs, he is not a man who tells you what a thing is; he *shows* you. He left all his drawings there"— she pointed toward the smokehouse—"and did not bring even a crayon to the house. When I ask why, he says his first pencil is the knife. Then he shows me what he does."

She banged her heels against the ground again, and I heard her swallow hard.

"It is all blood that does not flow, eyes that cannot see, legs that flop loose like Polichinelle's in a puppet show. And a smell like a battlefield of corpses covered in old fish."

She sang that dark talk out like a rhyme Nan would sing. All these names. Bluebeard. Polichinelle. Pegasus. Who *were* they?

"So, after all that, and when still I do not kill him with my blade, we come back to have our bread and cheese with Mary. Then I tell him that you are very clever like him, that you draw too. You told me this."

"*What* did you say to him?"

"You heard what I said. You see, Thomas, his work, the *anatomie* he calls it, it is very hard on him and on poor Mary. I could see that. He did not say it but I could see it. He needs a strong man to help. But the man must understand what it is, this work; he cannot be just a country *boeuf,* a stupid ox fellow. That is when I tell him about you."

She was suddenly on her feet, her hand reaching for mine, to pull me up.

"So, I must prepare you now how you should talk to Monsieur George Stubbs. After all, he has formed an opinion of me that is not so bad, you know. I think I know what is best to be said."

She rested her black head against my heart for a moment, and I had no speech for her.

If all lessons could be like that, what geniuses all we boys would be!

The Bell

THE NEXT DAY had the same shape to it, hot by dawn and busy as market day, and I knew better than to say to Father what was in my head. But, midmorning, when I saw my mother taking the big pitcher to the spring across the road, I left my timbers and ran to help her.

Her eyebrows climbed high to see me. "You must have been washed cleaner than a trout when you came in last night, Tom. I fell asleep it was so late."

"Mother, I have something you must hear."

It came out in a rush. I told her about Stubbs and his need of a helper.

"Remember how Jack said they might need some-one up in Barton to make frames for the man's pictures? Likely he's right, but this job is something else, and it's right here in Horkstow. I just want to talk to this man, that's all I ask. It may be worth nothing, but maybe Ling is right; perhaps this might bring me to the kind of work I can do. He draws, Mother. Pictures that you would hardly believe."

Over in the paddock, the Clock's sawing never faltered, no more than Mother's eyes did. They held steady on me, even when the Reverend's wife passed on the road below and greeted us.

"She'll move on, you'll find," she said at last. "That white horse is not a matter that can be made up to her good in the end, you know, a penniless stranger girl like that. She'll have to go back with her own folk, whoever they are. I hold nothing against gypsies or their like, you know that, Tom, but the people at Barton will see through her."

Why had Mother turned to Ling's story? Why did she say *gypsy*?

"Mother, I'm not talking of the girl here. Look, you don't want me to go to Grandfather's shop. I know it and you know it, that it's not for him or for me. And Father knows in his bones I'll never make a master wright like Hugh will. I can't be what *you* want either, because books and writing down are lost to me. There *is* something that

I can do right, though, I know there is. I can make my own works with my own skill; I know I can. I just have to find a way to learn more."

After a moment she nodded, but there was a tight line to her mouth that promised nothing. "We might all think better on it, Thomas, maybe, if we could hear the man himself speak and know that it was not some jape of yours."

I had to hold my peace, though I flamed to hear my own mother say that. Her habit was to call all her geese swans, even me. But when we came into the yard, she took the pitcher from me and pushed me gently toward the shop.

"Big houses. Oh, Thomas, hold your fire. When he's in his blackest moods, all your father can see is you being a rabbit catcher in the finish. He fears for you, who are so like him. But all I can see is my clever boy used up and trodden on because of his strangeness to the books." She lowered her voice. "Even if you had to go to Brigg and work with your grandfather, you could make your way out of there with proper papers when your time was served. You would be your own man."

Mother got a part of her wish before day's end.

We had all gathered to see Pell's new horse led in to take away the remastered wain. He was high-stepping and black and such a giant that he sent poor Chap running. Jack Proctor walked around him, singing his praises.

"Ask what he's called, Nan," I said, to humor her.

But she shook her head. "The one they killed was called Percival. I liked that name, Percival Pell. They didn't even bury him, Tom, just chopped him up and hauled him away. I'm going to put a stone where he fell with his name on it, just like the ones in the churchyard."

She sniffed and turned away. Another time, Nan would have been up close beside the men, making sure they matched each harness strap to the right buckle. She'd stroke the horse between its huge eyes, blow her warm breath into its nose, and tuck a sprig of elder behind the head straps to keep flies away.

As Pell's men made ready to lead horse and wain out of the yard, one of the church bells rang out. It was the high treble bell, and it made a right giddy roll before tailing off as quick as it had begun, like a songbird caught by a cat.

"Hark at *that*," Father said. "That bell knows we've done a good job, or else Lime Harry went to the ale shop early and fell into the bell tower on his way home."

Only a small while after the bell sounded, another horse clopped into the yard, this time a stout gray cob with a docked tail. Stubbs was up! For all his bulk he made a neat enough seat, but it was clear he was flustered. Behind him, grinning like a goblin, was Ling. Her legs were astride the cob like a man's, but Nan rode Ox like that and nobody made any question of it.

I stood there, stupid, trying to dust down my arms and legs, but the sawdust still caulked my nostrils and stuck under my nails, and my neck itched with it as if I had the mange. I knew my mother's eyes were on me for the least thing I'd try now.

Father stepped forward to take the bridle. "Can we help you, Mr. Stubbs? Though maybe it's Jack here you have need of. Is it for shoes?"

"I won't dismount, Mr. Rose, begging your pardon," Stubbs said. "I came to ask if you would send this boy"—he pointed at me—"to my place in two days, when I'll be back from Barton. I may have some work for him, if that is agreeable to you and if he is agreeable to me. I hear he is between appointments."

Now it was my father who looked stupid, his single eyebrow twitching like a hundred-legs turned over in the soil. Mother spoke up.

"Tom has already spoken to me about this, John. I think it is all right if he tries the work for Mr. Stubbs. Bart Ottley might be able to stand in for Tom if you're still pressed as hard as today."

I stared at her. How had she fixed that much together since we had spoken? And how had she come up with

Bart Ottley, the whiniest lad in the parish? He'd not stick the dust.

"I'll talk with my wife, sir," said Father. "If I find a proper reason I should send my son to you, he'll be there as you say. He must be found fit for something."

I glowered inside to hear Father say that in front of Ling, never mind in front of the man who might take me, but it was no time for making a quarrel of it.

Stubbs merely nodded and turned the cob around. Ling stared straight ahead at his back as they left the yard, her face grave as a dame teacher now and her skirt pulled down as low as she could fix it over her knees. Mother would notice that. Still, I wished Ling had said something to me, if only by the smallest sign. She could have mouthed some French word and only I would have known the shape of it.

Tohmah.

When would I see her again if she was to be in Barton all the time? For the first time, that struck me hard. As I saw it, Jack's plan of making frames was much the better one, for then I might be working alongside Ling. I wanted to run after them, but it was too late.

Work slackened at last, and the Clock took himself off for home, his face scratched across with pain because his usual hours were all out of pattern. The swallows swooped lower for their food as the heat of the fire fell away underneath them. The banging and clattering of the shop died down too. But there were still shouts coming from the fields and screeches of laughter behind the hedges.

Jack was back from a stroll, slapping his leg.

"Did you get the girl's message, lad?" he said to me, cackling like an old gossip. He reached for the cup, but instead of drinking he poured the water over his head. If she were there to see it, Mother would chide him for not walking over to the rainwater barrel to take his splash. I looked around. Father was at the gate, looking up and down. Hugh was returning hammers, saws, and chisels to their nails on the wall.

"What message was that, Jack?" I asked, close to a whisper.

"The bell."

I stared at him.

"It was her. Your girl. I just had the story from that Mary Spencer."

I flushed. It was not fair what Jack was doing, gregging me like that, like a fish trapped in a water hole. I dipped the mug into the water and poured. The liquid ran down my face, but it was warm as blood.

"You're not right, Jack."

"Oh, indeed I am. That was the fancy way the girl wanted to let you know she was away, off in triumph to Barton with the horse butcherman. No whispered messages for that one, only hop down and into the church and get a bell to do the job! Old Reverend Dunn and the digger man shooed her out like a rat when they laid hands on her."

He laughed. "The butcherman wouldn't let her run off, though. He made her do her bobs and say her sorrys. It was only then that he made it his mind to call here. Mary Spencer said it was to see if the Roses were as ungovernable as the one he had on the horse behind him. He said he'd not deal with two wildcats in the same county."

Creation

IF LING'S GOD was a horse, what was mine?

I looked up at the stone face set high on the column across from me. Would it open its mouth in horror to have such a thought running loose in the church? If it did I'd be out of there, and quicker than Ling.

A slant of late sun came through the windows, left of the altar, where the light always looked pale and rinsed. Mother said it was hallowed. My back was firm against one of the round pillars, and the stone felt smooth and cool like a fresh linen.

I looked around. None of the four faces set into the church pillars had paid the smallest heed to my blasphemy. Not the king, nor the curly top, not the savage bearded man just above his head, and certainly not the saucy fellow opposite. I supposed they had their proper names, but I'd never asked the Reverend what they might be.

I took my notebook out of the bag.

In these pages was the only help I'd had through the years at Brigg. I never brought the book to school, for that would be as good as putting my head on a block for the ax. If Grandfather's housekeeper, Martha, had ever troubled herself to sweep under my bed all the time I lodged with him, she might have found it, but what would Martha have seen if she'd opened it up?

Scribbles only, and scrawls, for my book was a creation all to itself. Only I could make sense of it, though there were some who might recognize the faces of my four stone gospel men. I was the god of this book.

I traced the bat map with my fingers.

I'd caught the creature in one of the yard sheds and had taken it down to the Ancholme in a pot. I dabbed fresh lime on its belly before setting it loose so it flew, white underneath. I followed that tiny ghost as long as I could, going up to my waist in water to track its zigzag flight. On the map I drew, each turn the bat had made became a point like a star. Here they were, on the page, the stars of the bat's world. I had joined them up, putting in lines and arrows for directions. I was ten when I drew that one.

Here were three pages of my dictionary. If she'd peeked, Martha would have seen only mouths, hundreds of them that might have frightened her wits away. For, instead of the letters I could not read, I drew lips, teeth, tongue, all busy making words. But it was too troublesome to make more than thirty or so of them. I knew a printer would do it better and easier, if he were told what each mouth was saying. I could still read the mouth shapes for "sword," "Christmas," "Nancy," "Horkstow."

I smiled to see my child's plan to stuff my boots with pebbles for weight and place a long hollow reed in my mouth for breathing. I'd believed it possible to walk underwater on a riverbed, or even the sea. I'd yet to try that one.

Here was the frog skeleton I'd found buried by the doorsill of a ruin near the river. Someone had surely buried it alive to bring luck to the household. The thing was so perfectly like a frog, even without its flesh, that I had wept for it. That sketch could be shown to Stubbs and perhaps the one of the barrows, too.

One day last summer, Father and I walked to see the old barrows, a distance from Horkstow, high up on the wold. That was a place where spirits walked out at special times of the year, Father said, but I doubt he believed it. I had tried to picture the barrow humps as a bird might, in flight over them. I'd played with their shapes, turning them over this way and that in my head before drawing them. Only a bird could tell if I'd pictured it right.

I stood and made my way to the bell tower. There was less light here, and what there was fell from high up, from where the bells hung. The ropes were tied neatly at the wall. All save one. Imagine a rope that can make you smile! I touched it to my mouth, then tidied it back to its nail.

I wanted to make a map for Ling. I would picture all the moves she had made until she came to Horkstow, just as I had followed the bat's flight years ago. The stage, the parks. The cellar and the palace. Paris to Canterbury to York. Then the circles, always getting smaller.

But she was gone from my sight for now, and besides, anything the likes of me could make with a pencil was only foolish.

·:Part Two:·

The Blood School

DOOMY OLD STUBBS had a way with him. That I would grant.

He'd won Ling over half the way, and that was no easy matter, considering how he spent his time. Even though she'd drummed her heels and made her bulldog face, she'd found some worth in what he did. Something about him had taken Father's fancy too. And there was Mary Spencer, who seemed to love her man, for all that he was stocky in the belly and well older than she. Nobody in the village knew whether the two were man and wife, for she answered only to Spencer, not Stubbs.

The morning I reported to their door, Mary walked with the two of us across the field to the farmhouse. She kissed the man on his cheek, without even a blush, and turned back down the lane toward the village, with the puppy frisking at her heels. She had given it the name Zachary.

"See how you've saved me from my slave's toil, Thomas!" were her parting words. They'd been no comfort, though we'd made our peace, she and I.

Stubbs pushed open the door. "Prepare yourself, Thomas," he said.

But only a grave digger, or a soldier at war, perhaps, could believe this smell. Or the sights inside. A proper butcher would be run out of town if he were to keep such a thing behind his door.

Blood that does not flow, eyes that cannot see. . . . And a smell like a battlefield of corpses covered in old fish.

Stubbs reached above the door and took down a small tub.

"Wax, with tincture of lavender mixed in," he said. He showed me how to dab a snifter of the soft stuff inside my nostrils. "Not too much of it, lad," he warned. "We need to have our proper senses too, to keep ourselves safe from contagion."

Contagion! I didn't know what that was, but it was here in this ugly room, I was sure of it.

The poor dead roan was now trussed along its back-bone to the hooks that dangled from the mysterious iron bar in the kitchen. This acted like a crane, Stubbs said, to pull the creature's body backward and forward for him as he needed. "Else the carcass, being so heavy, can pull a man's back out of its center and twist him for good."

The *carcass*. There it was, ghastly, full on, with its four legs seeming to stand. Only they did not, being a good two inches from the floor and settled onto a wide plank. There they rested without any force in them, like the legs of a child's rag dolly. *Legs that flop loose like Polichinelle's in a puppet show.*

The animal was already rotting, was as evil-smelling as an old sheep fallen in the meadows, and there was more of it on show than I ever wanted to see. It was opened up completely at the neck, and its veins bulged.

"Now, Thomas, shall we begin our lesson? First I'll tell, then you'll ask your questions, and in that way we shall learn where we stand."

On the morning Ling and I first called on him, Stubbs had cut the animal's throat quickly, and as its blood ran, he saved it in buckets. "That's how my Mary's potatoes are the best fed in the whole kingdom. You'll have some for your mother."

I'd heave them into the river first.

That day Stubbs had already begun the next step in his work. "I stuffed the empty veins and arteries with tallow fat. You know, Thomas, that part of the operation is quite like the making of a pig's pudding. Quite enjoyable in its way. Only I must do it backward, pushing stuff back in, not pressing it out." He squeezed a place to show what he meant.

"Next you must take away the innards, just as you must do with any animal for the pot. I have no interest in them. Then you have to flay the skin. That's as easy as peeling an apple, though I daresay you won't think it as pleasant a task."

I sneaked a look. Poor Polichinelle still had her skin on, best I could tell.

After those preparations came the stripping and layering of membranes, muscles, tendons, and cartilage, right down to the bone. Finally the bones themselves must be named and numbered for the drawings.

"When the time comes, I will call these names out to you as if they were boys' names on the school roll call. You'll find when you touch the bones that each sits sweetly into its slot. Your father would admire the fit they make, Thomas."

Call these names out to you. There was my job over, then, before we'd even rightly begun. At last I knew where I stood, and it was fast outside the door, where the winds blew.

"I cannot read or write, sir," I said, and though I tried to be hard, I had to swallow at the shame of saying this. "Is that a block to you?"

The man's eyebrows jumped up, then settled back to themselves. "I'm buying your muscle and your understanding, Thomas," he said after a pause. "I can educate you where it matters. You are quick in spirit or you'd hardly be here. That *mademoiselle* would not have bothered singing your praises to me if she found you lacking."

I went dark to hear that, and straightaway, so he wouldn't linger on my face, I shoved my notebook into his hands, open on the frog. Then I began with my own questions, as he'd said. He answered each one as he slowly turned over the pages of the notebook.

It would take five or six weeks to finish the job on hand. That was the *anatomy*, and he'd finish his drawings from it as we worked. This time he wanted to stay with the animal's head and no other part. "You see," he said, "by now I know a horse's legs as if I had four of them under me to gallop with."

As well as the hauling and the bloody work, there'd be other tasks for me to make myself useful. Papers, chalks, and inks must be prepared. And, yes, it was true indeed, perhaps at the end of it all, there might be some work making good wooden frames in Barton. If the man there was not up to the full task, and if I was able. But there was no need for me to trouble myself with Barton just yet.

No?

As for where he kept his own cob, that good beast had a stall at Ottleys' farm. Heavens above, he'd not dream of setting his poor Walnuts out of his skin by keeping him closer at hand to this killing place! "Don't you know horses are the world's worriers, Thomas?"

He smiled when he said that, this man who gave them so much to worry about.

Then I gobbled my question about Ling and Belladonna so fast that he didn't hear it right, and I had to ask again. He slapped his leg when he answered me.

"That was a rare sight, as touching as anything you would see in the York playhouse. When the girl got up on the animal's back, I thought I was looking at a centaur."

When I asked what that was, he said it was a fairy beast that was half horse half human. I barely stayed myself from asking him what Pegasus was.

"Yes, your friend Ling's pretty ways of riding impressed all she met at Baysgarth House. Though they had their doubts about her origins, and who would not? We cobbled a sort of a story up between us, she and I."

I could well imagine who had the most part in *that* stitching.

"However, it's best she doesn't become too fond

again of the mare, for there is no fixity to the arrangement nor to how long she can stay. She should apply herself to matters of instruction, and perhaps at the end of it all, she'll find a settlement somewhere."

Well, for all you think you know, you do not know the mademoiselle *at all,* I thought, but I said nothing.

Giraffe

WE SETTLED DOWN to the work.

There was just no guessing what Stubbs might say next. He talked enough for two men, three if they were men close with their words, like my father. However, listening and answering took my mind away from what my hands did, which was no bad thing.

He prattled about a tavern in the port of Liverpool when he was young, he said, where a pair of monkeys dressed in bonnets and skirts walked among the drinkers on their hind legs, their hands out for pennies, like human beggars. Then off with him to some place near

London where all kinds of creation skipped around as if it were the Garden of Eden. I pricked my ears when he spoke of some of these.

"There were great spotted cats—mind, those ones were kept in cages—that could outrun racing horses and tear wolves apart as if they were mice. But the beauty of the long-necked giraffes, Thomas! They're tall as wind-mills and graze from the trees with soft blue tongues. Their eyes are as big as saucers."

Giraffe! That was the word Ling had spoken the first day, the creature I put her in mind of, she'd said. Tall as a windmill. I said its name over, several times. Did such creatures live in France?

"Let our poor beast down, now. Favor that side. See where too much fat sticks like butter in her great jugular? Squeeze, boy, as if it were a sausage in your hands."

We fixed the tackle so that the horse's body might be held more upright, and Stubbs secured the head with wires so that it didn't wag. Then he took me to look at the knives laid out behind us on the kitchen table. He picked each one up and gave it a name. He made me choose the different blades, over and over, until he was sure that when he spoke a name I'd bring him the right one.

"When your father says 'adze,' I'd say you do not bring him a chisel. Not twice, anyway, if I was any judge of the man."

Now I felt a little wiser about the work we were

beginning, but still I had to look away the first time Stubbs took the fine knife he called a scalpel to the forehead of the horse. There was no blood left to run, but still it seemed an insult to slice the animal like that. The man did it so well, the curls of skin dropped like wood shavings into his hands.

"Take these for the bucket. I'll burn them afterward."

He handed me the cutaways. They were neither cold nor warm, neither dry nor wet. They felt like nothing that could ever have been alive.

"I came here when the fields were in their winter stubble, Thomas, and this poor roan is my third cadaver. Do you know what that word means? It's a corpse that doctors learn their trade from." He steadied the head under his fingers. "And now quack-man George Stubbs is going to learn the lessons of the head of this noble animal. The answer, you know, to the old jest, 'Why the long face, Mr. Horse?'"

He laughed, but that loosed a fresh waft from the corpse, and I had to reach to dab another drop of the lavender into my nostrils.

"Stay your hand, boy," he warned. "You must accustom yourself. Today, the smell is nothing; take my word for it."

Already I was breathing so hard through my mouth that I could feel my ribs rising and falling like a bellows.

"Why do you do it, Mr. Stubbs?" I burst out. "If you want to know how a horse works, is it not better to copy it when it is well and kicking and looking its best?"

The dark eyes were steady on me. "No, Thomas, it is not. Sadly. We will talk more about this, but I believe the boy who drew such a fine skeleton into his own book already knows this for himself. The best secrets are kept under the skin."

He wiped the scalpel on a rag and sighed. "We have done enough and our best today, and you have conducted yourself well for a first outing. After all, I grew up with the skin trade and you did not. I believe we can do good business together, Thomas."

He smiled. And curse me for a fool, I couldn't help it that I smiled back, though I didn't know why I felt proud of what I had done today in this blood-and-bone room. All this time I might have been breathing in the goodness of fresh wood and the clove scent of my mother's gillyflowers whenever I stepped out into the air. But the man was right. There were lessons for me here, though I didn't yet know what they might be.

Stubbs reached again above the door and took down a thick yellow square. Was it wax?

"Take this good piece of Barton soap home with you, Thomas," he said. "Wash your hands and nails well every day you are here, and tell me if ever you cut yourself, for then you'll need to salve it with the vinegar I keep. The forces of putrefaction are like besiegers that seek out the smallest surface open to them."

I was outside the door when Stubbs called me back.

"I won't require you here tomorrow," he said. "I have an engagement with a master of the hunt that cannot be turned away, though it eats into my time. We'll begin again our anatomy the day following."

On the Road

THE BOY fingered the rough cloth of the blue coat with the brass buttons. If only the coat might cover his head and his legs at the same time, he would be invisible. The master could not call on him if he was not to be seen.

But it was no use. All his tugging could not bring the coat both up and down at the same time. And now that he looked toward the floor again, he could see that his boots had turned into hooves. Well, that would be certain cause for a beating. He could smell the onions on the master's breath, sour, coming close.

He put his left hoof down on the boards. It made no sound.
Why, then, the whip that slashed across his back now, like a knife
with teeth?

I sat up, bursting out of my dream, my heart wild. Hugh
slept on, bunched up like a child. I watched him breathe,
each breath a small whiffle, and grew calm.

Today my brother was sixteen. Not until October,
when I'd be fifteen, would there stand only a year's
number between us again. For all her clever slate work,
Nan could not fit this sum right. "Hugh was one year
older than you yesterday, and now he is two," she'd say
each year. "That is *stupid*, Thomas."

It might be Hugh's birthday, but this day belonged
to me. It was my very own gift, and the beauty was
that nobody knew anything of it. My family thought I
belonged to Mr. Stubbs all day.

I stretched my legs and rolled out of the bed. Our
small window faced east, toward the rise, but outside
only a pearly gray light showed, as if the sun were still
dreaming of the moon.

I'd slept in my clothes. Now I picked up my boots
and pulled the door open from where I'd set it last night,
a spill of elm stuck under it. The ladder made a small
creak. I padded across the kitchen. Last night Mother
had picked the first of the season's green apples to make
a pie for Hugh's birthday. Had she locked it away?

No! For our mother knew there was no soul in her house so bad as to cut into that pie until we'd cheer Hugh's fortune at supper time. I felt my robber's stomach turn as I carved out a large piece of the pie as cleanly as I could. Surely the worst she would make of it was to think Stubbs didn't feed his hardworking boy well enough while she fed our best meat and gravy to my stand-in, Bart Ottley.

I took a handful of oatmeal from its jar and trickled it onto the center of the kitchen table so that it formed an *X.* If mice did not nibble it, at least it would say something. *Sorry, Mother. Love, Thomas.* Four words in one letter — not bad.

I could make quite a few letters, but I always stood them singly. It was that which had driven the writing master most demented.

"All you make is spinster letters, Master Rose. Where are their mates, lumpkin? What is a word made of but letters that marry and breed!"

I lifted the latch and tied up my boots in the yard. It was still so early that neither cat nor dog stuck a nose from the kennel. I stepped over our small wicket gate and headed for the church and then the turn northeastward for Barton.

It wasn't a walk I knew well. Barton lies much closer to Horkstow, but because of Grandfather's shop, we Roses took our business to Brigg whenever we had need of town. When we were smaller and Ox could take us all, squashed like sacks into the belly of the small cart, we'd spent many fair days in Brigg. That was long ago, before I had lost all my taste for that town.

This climbing road, with all its ridges and ruts, was best suited for a rider. Father said it was the oldest trail around, and it was easy to believe that. Near the top, by Beacon Hill, there were some tidy farmhouses set low into the hillside, their bricks clean of weeds and ivy. Nobody stirred.

Once I crested the hill, I turned north. When at last I could see the Humber, I felt easy. There it was, a giant ribbon of water, glinting all shades of silver. The lighter parts pulsed toward the sea, while darker stripes showed where the tides tried to drive the river back again.

A stonechat landed on a furze bush just feet away. It didn't move as I passed but scolded me, the cheeky speck, round eyes staring, bold as brass. Its black cap quivered as if it were a real hat, separate from the tiny body. The bird was the spit of Ling the first time I'd seen her!

I began my descent toward Barton.

Where did Baysgarth House lie? I thought it best to head for the market area, for if this town was like Brigg, that was where the morning would start. Perhaps someone there might tell me something useful.

The Market

As I came into the marketplace, the first of the morning's wagons rumbled past me, loaded with greasy sacks. A skinny boy about Ling's age was standing on his own, shifting from one foot to the other, hugging himself, although there wasn't the smallest breeze about to chill him. At his bare feet was a large jug. I guessed he'd been sent for milk.

The fellow had foxy hair cut straight and short over his forehead. He had the speckled pale skin that all copper heads have, but his arms were rosy enough for all they were thin. His clothes were poor and smelled damp

and dirty. He stared at everything in the street in front
of him except me, until there was nothing else he could
do but face up to me.

"Do you know the Nelthorpe place?" I asked.
"Baysgarth Hall?"

"What do you want to know that for? Are you from
over there? Your voice is right strange." He was pointing to where the river must lie, so over there must mean
across the Humber. Well, he had cloth ears, then, two
of them. Even when my voice shot skew-ways I knew
I didn't sound like a man from the north.

"Never mind," I answered him. "I'll find it myself."

I stepped away and watched the wagoner lower
his sides so the sacks could be lifted down. A few more
sleepy-looking boys were on the streets now, lugging
baskets, or clutching rods to make up the market stalls.
More carts arrived and with them a powerful smell of
dung. A man with a sack and shovel ran to collect what
had been dropped. Women called out to one another as
they set up for trade.

Soon I could smell hot meat pies close by. Pork, or
maybe rabbit. If only I had a penny or two, Hugh's apple
pie might wait its turn for longer. A man walked past with
three round yellow cheeses on his head. When I squinted,
I could make a saint of him, just stepped down from a
church glass, his halo golden, golden, golden. But if he
were a proper saint, he'd give me some of his cheese.

It was a sight's worth, all this market hustle. Everyone seemed too busy to stop, or else too strange to ask my way from. Even as I looked for a face with answers on it, I was shoved in the ribs by a great basket of silver herring. Seawater spilled over my boots when the basket was hoisted up on its end to show the catch off. A man shouted something at me, but the words made no sense. I might as well be in France, the speech was so rum.

Then I saw the two men. They were standing outside the market inn, dressed in loose breeches and sack jackets, but all their best work was watching me. I was sure they were not constables, but their look was too mean for my liking. Did I have no right to be at the market, then, even if I had no money? I pulled down my jacket, which was too short, and moved away from the leaky basket of fish, but when I looked back, the two men were still staring.

"I'll take you there, then."

The foxy boy was beside me again, but perkier now his errand was done. He lifted his hands, and I saw the jug held a fat waxy honeycomb, oozing gold. He swung it under my nose and then covered it fast again.

"This is the honey off the wolds, the furze blossom kind. But it goes so fast in the market—you have to be here first light and then get away fast in case a body takes it from you. My gram gets it because she's dying and she might as well. Where are you from, then?"

"Horkstow."

"But that's no place at all!" The boy's face fell so far, it was comical. "And you looked like someone come from outside, the height of you, like a soldier or something. Or a sailor maybe. I see plenty of *them* where I live, down near the water."

He sighed and shifted the jug under an armpit. "I'll show you the gates of the big house you're wanting. Are you going to work there?"

"Maybe. What do you know of it?"

"Oh, not much, just the lady there takes all the rents she can find. My gram says her boy is spoiled worse than a duke. They say he needs a man's hand or he'll treat the people rotten when he's of an age."

That was Ling's prince with the wooden legs. "And where do you work?" I asked him.

The boy's face blazed. "I have to look after my gram till she dies. I do this and that now, but after she goes, I'll work proper. I'm good with horses. I have one, and all."

I didn't believe a word of it but said nothing. If only there were a wedge of bread handy to spread with that honey! I thought of poor dead Jane Brice and her hives. "There's honey better than that in Horkstow," I told him. "My mother would let you have some." Then I bit down on my lip. Mother must never be told I came to Barton. But the boy had nothing to say to my kind offer, anyway, thinking as little of my village as he did. He took a coughing fit, and I let him be.

The street we were walking now climbed a little, and I could see two tall brick gate piers ahead of them at the top. "Is that it?" I pointed. "Baysgarth?"

He nodded. "What's your name, then?" I asked.

"Ezra," he said fast. "Ezra Quickfall." Then he turned on me like a savage. "But you don't care, going to the big house for work and not giving me a proper word about anything, for all I tell you."

That was all it was, then. Attention was wanted. Our Nan could be just the same when the mood took her. I cleared my throat. "Look, I don't know if there's any work there for me. Really, I'm come looking for a friend, and she's only here a day or so yet, so likely you won't know anything of her. She's a horse rider and she came here with a painting man."

"The painting man? The whole town knows about *him*! They say he can paint the hounds so they all look like themselves, every one of them different."

He beat his fingers on the jug as if it were a drum. But it wasn't Stubbs he was interested in after all. "Is she your girl, then, the horse girl? What sort of a girl is that? What's her name? What's your name?"

That was a sore pinch, all right. If only his first words were true, I'd gladly answer a hundred daft questions. "I'd never say that about her," I said, "that she's my girl. But the name she goes for here is Ling. And I'm Thomas Rose, Master Quickfall."

Young Ezra went pink to be greeted like that. He stretched out one of his bony arms, pointing. "There you are, then, Thomas Rose. There's your Baysgarth House. In there through those gates, you'll find all their fine horses lined up like the king's men. I've seen them. I've been in often enough when nobody saw me. Such fields of grass they have, it's like a country for horses!"

His voice had such a longing in it that I felt there was more to him than he told me, for all that he was full of chatter. He had to take a deep gulp before he could speak again.

"There you go," he said. "But maybe I'll fare after you quick enough if my gram dies. I've never seen a horse girl before. I didn't know there were any of them in the world."

I saluted him then, just for the trick of it, but got nothing back except the two begging eyes, green as gooseberries. When the silly stick of a fellow didn't move off as he should, I turned my back on him and walked through the gates toward the wide brick spread of Baysgarth.

Master Wooden Legs

I WAS BUSY when the shout came.

"Hey! You there, tall fellow! Get out here where I can see you, now, sir! Or I'll let Cromwell go for your throat!"

I turned so quickly, the loose brick I'd been levering out of the stable wall came out as suddenly as a baby tooth. It landed full sore on my right foot, then bounced onto the bag beside it.

My heart was thumping, but it was fury, not fear, that had it going. That was a rich boy's voice, but his words were a gamekeeper's, and the kind that will raise any man's blood. I bent to pick up my bag. Hugh's pie was surely in crumbs now.

But the closer I came to the owner of the voice, the more I wanted to laugh. The young chap standing at the top of the path was a credit to somebody, that was for sure. He wore button-down breeches over tight-skin white stockings, and his black buckled shoes were likely taking their first walk. However, it was the top end of him that was the real marvel. His fine topcoat wasn't enough on its own, it seemed, for there was a long velvet jacket underneath, and lace growing like flowers out of every outpost. Buttons as big as dilly-cakes marched down the front of both coat and jacket. A girl would have been proud of the bleached ringlets he had flopping loose over his collar.

Who'd have thought such a fancy creature lived and breathed, and so close to Horkstow?

He was pretending to pull hard on a dog's collar. But the racing dog inside the collar wasn't about to jump at my throat within the next year or two. It was rolling its eyes toward the paddock on the left, as if it scented a rabbit.

I was damned if I'd play slop boy to pampered Master Wooden Legs.

"My name is Thomas Rose, and I'm come here looking for a Mr. Stubbs or a Mistress Ling. Or a fine horse called Belladonna." I didn't know if he was old enough or sharp enough to understand me.

"How are you on my property? How do you know these things?"

The boy had flushed red when I spoke the names, and pettish to his last button, now he loosed his dog. It bent down to sniff my boots, as if it thought it should do that much work for its master, but then folded itself to lie between us, laid its long head on its front paws, and sighed.

"Good boy, Cromwell," I said, and hunkered down to scratch the dog's ears. That made me more or less the boy's height and no threat to him. Possibly he had thought me a robber, or worse.

"Mr. Stubbs is away today," he said, sulky. "But my mother got me up like this nonetheless." He made a face and stamped so his buckles rang. "You in your boots would not understand how these buckle shoes pinch my toes. But Mama says I must wear them till I break them in, and so I cannot ride until later. I don't want a picture dressed like this! I want to be painted on my new white mare! How did you know she is called Belladonna?"

Belladonna! This was the nearest I had come yet. But I kept my face tight and just nodded to him, as if to say, *Why would I not know that when I know everything?*

Then he grew bright. "Do you know Hélène, then, my new riding teacher? She promises that I will try the highest bar today."

If Cromwell the hound heard my heart go thud,

he didn't show it. But to hear her name like that—and spoken just as she said it!

The boy waved a hand at the paddock, and I could see that some trestles were set up in there. "Look, that one, there. But did you not say a Mistress Ling?" he asked.

I straightened myself. A man and a woman were running toward us, down the path from the walled kitchen yard, the woman gathering her skirts up in a bundle.

"I think you're being called away now," I said to him quickly. "Look, I mean no one any harm. I would like to talk to Ling—to Hélène. I know Mr. Stubbs too, because I work for him in Horkstow. Thomas Rose is my name. He tells me I may come here soon to work at the picture framing with him."

The boy looked confused. But the two from the kitchen were on us before he could speak. The woman put her hands on the boy's shoulders, turned him round, dusted down his fine clothes, and glared at me. The man stood by, silent. He had huge hands, although he was not nearly my height. Both of them wore long aprons, his streaked with boot blacking and oils, hers with flour.

"Master John, who is this pawky trespasser?" she said, puffing. "Could easy be he's a deserter; there's all kinds abroad these bad days. You mustn't take it on yourself to deal with such a thing; you must call out for us. That fool dog isn't worth a bald penny, Jem. Where's the stable lads? Nor any use in them, neither, for when the carriage isn't wanted, they're not astir but in their beds."

I cleared my throat. "I'm no such bad thing, mistress. I work for Mr. Stubbs in Horkstow. I only looked to speak with Mistress Hélène, no more than that."

For a moment those names seemed to work the same magic on the two servants as they had on the boy, and I felt a littler surer of my ground. But before I could mention the matter of the frames again, a light *pick-it pick-it-up, pick-it pick-it-up* of hooves trotting over cobbles sounded from inside the stable yard.

"It's Belladonna!"

The boy's face was no longer pinched and sulky. He shrugged himself loose from the woman and ran toward the tall brick archway. But no farther. For the little white horse stepped through before he reached the opening, lifting her hooves as tidy as a deer, her clever head held high, her golden tail falling clean behind her.

Capriole

IT WAS TRUE, THEN.

Belladonna was a wonder. Even the king must have thought that at Newmarket if he had any gleam of horse fancy in his head. If he'd looked properly at this little mare, *he* should have bought her on the spot, for she was as royal as anything on earth would ever be.

I could take all that in, even though my eyes were fixed on the rider. But, then, I already knew everything about this animal. I could tick the list of all that I knew about her. Tick for beauty and shape. Tick for neatness. Tick for the ears that she wore back, not in a passion but to hear the world better. Tick for a tail the color of ripe barley.

What I had not reckoned was to see Ling herself up, so soon. She sat there so high and mighty in her bearing it was easy to think that *she* was the mistress of the horse, the stable yard, the whole place. Except that no proper mistress would be dressed in the outfit she had on. It was surely the boy's.

The same white knee breeches he wore, but with boots under hers, not stockings and shoes. The long blue velvet jacket like his, though bits of this one were eaten away in parts. But while the boy wore his curls free, she'd set a blue tricorn hat on hers, and the dark length of her hair fell down her back. She looked nothing like a boy, though. If anything, she was like the horse, for her neat size, the hugeness of her eyes, and the tail of hair.

She laughed. "Thomas! I was so hoping you would come here. I rang a bell for you, like a lady in a *salon.*" Her mouth twitched, just a little. So Jack Proctor's stupid story about the church bell ringing out was proved! "Is she not even more beautiful than I told it to you?"

I said "Aye" to her, for a jest, as if I were Ezra Quickfall's man from the north country. What I wanted to tell her was that she was the beauty in question. The strange thing was, the boy's clothes she wore took nothing away from her look, but added to it.

She turned Belladonna so that the mare folded her

head shyly against her neck. Almost like a swan, I thought, just as smart as one of my swan friends from Brigg. She didn't flinch or jump when I stroked her neck and then scratched between her eyes. She felt fine and silky.

Ling's eyes laughed to see me making up to Belladonna, knowing well the mare was playing proxy for herself. Then she tightened the reins and sat up even straighter. "Watch me now, Monsieur John," she ordered the boy.

Well, she was the proper bossy boots wherever she went!

"I will show you what I told you about, it was yesterday. The *levade*. One of the great airs above the ground. Watch!"

There was no need to say such a thing to Master John. He stood there, foolish as a washed pig in all his lace and curls, but his eyes never left Ling and Belladonna.

Well, I could not say exactly how it happened, but suddenly that little mare was standing crossways, on her hind legs. But this was nothing like a rear-up, or the sulky fits you might see sometimes in my father's yard. The mare's forelegs were raised high and bent neatly at the knees, and there was Ling sitting easy as a jockey over the jumps. She carried her hat in one hand, and her head was bowed. How well she knew the picture they made!

"That was the *levade*, Lady and Gentlemen!"

Who was the lady? I looked around but there were only the two servants from the kitchen, scowling away, the boy with his washed face and feathers, and me. Ling was being kind. But she hadn't finished.

"And now," she called. "Watch me again. . . . This is the most magical of all the steps. I promise you. "

Belladonna dropped down again, lightly, and tossed her head. Ling looked at me. "If only you had a drum, *mon ami*. She loves to hear the drumroll when she does this."

She pressed with her knees and, leaning well over, murmured something into the mare's ears. Again, Belladonna reared up, but not so high this time, and while she hung there, she appeared to have a second thought. She thrust herself forward and jumped, so that her hind legs lifted off the ground too. She kicked them behind her, straight as they could stretch.

With all her legs off the ground, Belladonna flew.

For how long? I would never be able to reckon that much, but I saw it happen. All of us there did.

"*Madame et messieurs,* you have witnessed the *capriole!*"

Lord knows, she was proud as puppet Punch after he killed his puppet wife stone dead at the fair in Brigg. She put her tricorn back on her head, rose up in the stirrups, and bowed. Beside me, the boy clapped as if his silly noise could make it all happen again. "You see that?" he said to me. "Next week I'll be doing that too."

"Next week you'll be taken off with the thieving Roms if you're not careful, Master John," the kitchen woman said. Her face was tight and well turned away from Ling and the horse. She sniffed as if she had a high winter's cold. "Come away inside now and have your eggs before you get mucked up out here in all your finery."

The woman beckoned me forward. I took two steps, no more. She looked me up and down as hard as any schoolmaster ever did, and her eyes were as mean.

"I know nothing of what you can do, lad," she said at last, "but this I'll tell you. It's my lady who gives out the work here, not Mr. Stubbs, and we have as many bodies here as we need, and more, and no settlement for any others, on horse or foot. They're looking for rope makers down the wharf, though, and the wherries from Norfolk are always good for new hands too, they say."

Whewwies, she said. *Wharw.*

She looked at her companion, the man in the dirty apron, and something seemed to pass between them. Then she sniffed again. "So, young man, you can come to the kitchen door for a cup of milk and bread, if you want, before you show us your heels."

"But he says he can make picture frames, Julia . . ." the boy began. "And he says he knows Mr. Stubbs well."

"And so can my husband do that," the woman said,

sharp. "It's his job. And he knows Mr. Stubbs too, and there's an end to it, Master John. The lad's been told."

She turned her back on me, and the little party moved off toward the kitchens. The boy turned his head more than once to look back at us. I felt sorry for him.

"No settlement for any others, on horse or foot! The wharw and the whewwies and the whewwies and the wharw, and there's an end to it!"

That was Ling, still sitting up smart, but spilling out every one of the housekeeper's lisps and spits. Then she moved closer to me and started over again, and I had to get out of her reach.

"You're drenching me!"

But she followed me. She leaned forward, and speaking her French, she coaxed Belladonna to suck the back of my neck, my hair too, until I had to hold myself across the belly, helpless for laughing. I had to beg for mercy from the pair of them.

There was a change in the climate then.

From the stable yard, three men led out four chestnut horses, already harnessed, save for the collars. They walked them past the paddock with the trestles, toward the front of the house. They spoke nothing to Ling as they passed, but one man said something to the others and they made a guffaw, all of them, whether about her or me or both of us wasn't clear. She kept her face steady, looking at me, but her laugh had gone. She swung her left leg over and jumped from the saddle.

"I was going to say, you seem right glad to be here," I said. "But I don't like it that you have those under-strappers tormenting you. I'll go after them. I'm well used to putting manners on the likes of them." Why, even my mother, the kindest of all women, would call those men ignorant pillocks.

Ling scowled after the men's backs. "No, Thomas, you will not," she said. "That, it is nothing. They're only *martin-bâtons*, only donkey men themselves, but they think I'm a Rom, a gypsy girl. *Tant mieux*. Better let them have that idea sitting in their big pumpkin heads for now. They probably hate the Roms more than they hate the French, anyway, and perhaps that is why they have not come after me yet, for a girl. But I always have this, Thomas, never fear."

She lifted the coat and showed me the blade, tucked inside the waist of the breeches.

"You see? I am safe. I told you how sharp my blade was. You should carry one of these too, Thomas. Or something." She passed the back of her hand across her forehead. "You want to know where I sleep these two nights past? In the stall with Belladonna and a little black cat. They tell me I can sleep in the house under the kitchen stairs as long as I am to teach the boy, but you know, after all this time I need to see my horse. Though I know she is safe — yes, I know they will not harm her, for they think she is the perfect horse for the young master. Hah!"

"And this Master John?"

I was trying to think what the foxy-haired boy had said. It was more than the story of the wooden legs; it was some matter about the way he treated people. Or might do, if he got a chance.

"Oh, he's not so bad, that one. He loves me a little already, and I teach him how to be kind with a horse, the way he should be, not like you English, who kill them with work too much and whippings."

She stroked the pure-white muzzle of the mare and then pressed her fingers against the long, curled eyelashes. Belladonna closed her eyes like a baby in milk bliss and wobbled a little on her pins. "See, they feed her well here, *la petite princesse*. She grows nice and round already."

"But your mother, Ling? Zéphyrine? She'll have no word of you yet, will she?"

For answer, Ling simply stared at me, but I could see nothing in her eyes, not a spark. It was a strange look, as if her soul had drained away in a moment. It made me uneasy, so I patted my satchel.

"Look, I have some apple cake here in my bag, or what's left of it. Let's take Belladonna back to her stall, and you can tell me what you're going to do now you have found her safe."

What Lies Beneath

LING'S SHABBY OLD GOWN hung from a rope that ran across the stall. Of course it wasn't wide enough, but it made a door of sorts, she said, and that was all she needed. The straw bed bunched up against the wall inside the stall was clean, and there was no dirt or dung on the floor.

We sat down on the bed to eat, I like a dog with my hunger, Ling dainty as a bird. She didn't finish her piece of pie but pinched some of the apple out of it and fed it to Belladonna, who sucked the soft fruit up as if it were water.

"Whoa, then, Ling, I'll eat your crust if you're thinking to give it all away."

She swished me with a straw but let me take it.

For a stable yard in a great house, it was strangely still. My father's yard was a busier place for sure. The only sound came from a stall across the yard, a lazy iron pinging against an anvil, and it was no Jack Proctor working it. There were martins here too, though, with their shuttlecock tails, flitting through the open doors, and for all the size and space of the place, the birds didn't look any different from those that built nests in my own yard.

"Are those the boy's clothes?" I asked.

She nodded. "He has so many new ones, him. His mother, the milady Nelthorpe, she does not care what I wear, only that I teach him how to make the hunt. I tell her all my good clothes were robbed on a stage coming from York. Monsieur Stubbs tells her I am from a good French *haute école* family. He does not tell her the truth, that Belladonna is mine, so I say nothing about that either."

I would act the sage without frightening her, I thought. "Better not," I said.

She looked hard at me, as if, just once, I might know something she did not. I shrugged. "The less they know the better for you."

Her face cleared. "But you, Thomas? How did you do with Monsieur Stubbs and his *grand travail*?"

I told her everything. About the crane for lifting the poor dead beast, the knives, the veins like rivers, the scalpeled curls of skin, the monkeys he'd known that had fingernails like our own, the yellow soap and vinegar against contagion. The smell.

She said nothing, but her face came over stern, halfway to bulldog. I had an urge to kiss it and see what it would turn into then.

"It was a giraffe you said I was like, wasn't it?" I said. "Stubbs has seen them in the parks of London."

She smiled suddenly. "Tall as a tree with big soft eyes. Just like you, Thomas. I saw a giraffe once in a park, but she was shy. Now, is that not something else you have in common?"

I reached to hold her wrists, to pretend to be fierce, a lion or some such, not shy Mistress Giraffe. So small those hands felt! I tried to cup her face, but she wriggled away. She stood up and put her tricorn on my head where I sat, but it tipped down over my right eye.

"This one is not as good as my invisible hat, and it's too small by half, *mademoiselle*."

That was the first word of French I had tried on her, and she clapped me for it, making a mock, but her smile took the harm away. It took me away too. Then her face turned stony again.

"Monsieur Stubbs. Yes. I think I change my mind about him again, you know."

"He thought well of you. He thought you were half horse and half human."

I got not even the ghost of a smile for my wit. She lifted her hands up. There they were, so slender that the cuffs of the jacket slipped back down to her elbows.

"You see this? My clever hand? It can play a flute, though you do not know *that* yet, Thomas, and must take my word for it. My hand can give a handful of feed to a horse and slip a bit into her mouth before she knows it. It can find an egg under a duck, yes?" She touched my ear and I flared. "But Monsieur Stubbs and his knife, he wants to pick out all the strings under the skin of my hand and say, '*Celui-ci, il fait ça*. This string does *that;* that one does *this*.' We should not make these questions, Thomas. That is how we lose our powers."

I thought of all I had written and drawn into my own book, and for the first time I did not agree with her judgment. I took one of her hands and spread her fingers across the back of my own palm. Hers were half the size of mine, but I thought that together they made a fine pair.

"Yes, but he doesn't cut up *people*, Ling. Your hand is safe." Did I know that for sure? If people were dead, was such a thing allowed?

But she rushed back at me. "He thinks he can discover what a horse is made of, Thomas, as if a horse is just a *marionnette*, or a *poupée*, a doll stuffed with sawdust. But I say he will never find his answer."

Pegasus

THESE DAYS I WAS learning more than my prayers, as my mother would say. I heard who Pegasus was. Or *what* he was, more like.

"On my second day the Dane called me and Augustin together. I thought, *bien,* now we will start, but no, first he had a story for me, he said." She tapped my arm. "What do you say when you begin a story in England?"

I thought for a moment. "When Nan begins one of her stories it's always, 'Once upon a time.'"

"*C'est la même chose!* We say, '*Il était une fois,*' Thomas, but it is the same. Now I will tell you this once upon a time story, and then you will understand Belladonna better than Monsieur Stubbs ever will."

She told me that long ago, before there were any countries with the names of France or England or Persia, white horses could take to the air. They flew as gracefully as a long-legged crane, and as far.

"Pegasus was the first of these horses who could fly. But his parents were not a sire and a dam like other horses. He was born from a battle and made from drops of blood and salt water."

I must have smirked, or worse, because she thumped me.

"Have faith, Thomas! This is a noble story about a noble horse."

"Who was made from blood and salt water. I understand."

She glared at me. "You do not understand at all. The blood was from the Gorgon lady's head. The water was taken from the dark seas of Greece."

"I thought you said there were no countries then."

"There was Greece! *Tais-toi*, Thomas. Keep quiet." She pressed my lips closed so tight together, they turned up. I must have looked like a duck.

"Pegasus took heroes on his back, and they had many adventures. But when he flew over the mountain where the gods lived, his long white feathers made the sun dark, and the gods were furious. They sent a hornet after him to poison him and bring him down to earth."

"I bet it was a cleg, a horsefly. They bite like hell."

That put her off for a moment. Then she shook her head. "I am sure it was nothing that lives in England, but it is no matter. Ever since that happened, no horse has wings. Maybe there are some now in Greece. I do not know this, but everybody knows that it is the white horses, more than any others, who still try to fly. That is why we teach the lessons of the *haute école* to white horses. The Dane said so. *Ainsi soit-il.*"

"Amen," I said.

She pointed to Belladonna. "The Dane said she was the best-schooled horse he had ever had and that I must learn the same lessons quickly or he would send me away. He told Augustin to ride out his new horse Tournesol and to put me on Belladonna. He was to bring me to the park and teach me the *levade.*"

"I thought Augustin hated you," I said.

"He did, but he did not dare disobey the Dane. None of us did. So he took me to the park."

"Were there statues there?"

She considered. "No, Thomas, this was a different park. The young men came to this park in their carriages to show off and crack their whips. The carriage wheels went so fast, you could not see them turning. I thought they would catch up with the poor horses and roll over them."

I thought of Pell's poor old horse and the broken wheels of the wain. "Then they would need my father," I said.

But Ling shook her head. "I hope he would not go to help them. They were fools, those drivers."

"Perhaps they were trying to fly too," I said, though I had no interest in the carriage drivers. "How did Augustin teach you?"

She brushed crumbs from her breeches, chasing them all the way to her boots.

"He said we must leave the *allée* where the carriages were making races and go to an open space for our lesson. I was going up-down up-down, just right, and Belladonna was pleased with me—I knew that. But Augustin, he was not paying attention, and he had a new horse. That is dangerous."

I nodded. As if I knew what it was like to have a new horse! Our poor Ox would stay steady on his pins if a roof flew off a house right in front of him.

"*Alors,* there was a little piece of lace, some fine lady left it on a bush in front of us, and the wind lifted it in the air. Tournesol, he thinks the lace is a bird or something strange. *Donc,* he jumps up high on his back legs, and Augustin falls to the ground."

She thumped the straw.

"He makes no move, and I think, Augustin, he is making a trick, to spite me, so that I will not learn anything. Tournesol, he has stopped running. He is eating the grass like a good horse. But then I see that Augustin is as white as the lace, so I say to him, 'Are you really hurt?'"

Belladonna stopped neatly beside the boy, who was curled up on the ground. He had difficulty speaking because his tongue seemed swollen and his teeth chattered, but at last Ling made out what he said. "S-s-snake," Augustin gasped. "B-b-bit me. A viper."

"He showed me the holes in his arm where the snake's teeth went through his skin. There were red rings too, but his skin was cold like ice. I told him I knew what to do."

And she did, for one time a snake had performed onstage just after Zéphyrine and Hélène had danced, and that snake too had raised its black head in a temper at one of the stage boys. They had watched what the snake's owner did to the bitten boy.

"What did you do?" I asked. I hadn't seen a snake in years and had never been bitten. In our village only Jack Proctor had salves for snakebite. That man had salves and simples for every mishap under the sun.

"First I sucked the poison out. It was so *dégoûtant*, so foul, I knew it was poison that could kill. Then I took my coral knife and cut deep around the bites so the badness was all gone. He screamed, but I tell him he must not be poisoned in his skin like poor Pegasus."

"Poor Augustin," I said. I knew how sharp her knife was. "Did he teach you well after that? Did he hate you still?"

Ling laughed. "What do you think?" she said. "*Mais oui,* Augustin was a very good teacher. Because it was not so long since he had learned the steps himself; he knew the *un-deux-trois* that you need to know when you begin something new. And then Belladonna was my best teacher. Over the months she taught me too, with every little part of her back and neck."

She paused and looked at me full in the face. "It was strange, you know. Augustin and I became the best of friends after that. I wonder how he is now."

Her face emptied again in that way I was beginning to recognize. I had no words for her when she was like this, but I was made curious.

"When did you last see him?" I asked. "Augustin?"

She didn't answer my question, but she took the coral knife out from her waist and held it up. Close up, I could see how fine it was.

"That is the proper way to use a knife on a person or an animal, Thomas. To take away the bad thing. Not to kill, not just to cut open and see what is inside."

Duck Country

WE HAD a proper argument now. What Ling said was true. But I knew that Stubbs was right about the frog skeleton. When I had drawn that little creature made of bones into my book, I knew it better than any living frog I had ever held prisoner on my palm.

She was able to see my doubts on my giraffe face, for she kept going. "And remember this, Thomas: Monsieur Stubbs told me himself that if he found Pegasus, he would cut his wings away to see how they worked. That is just what *Barbe bleue* would do! He cannot be trusted, this man. I asked him, you know, when we came here the first day, why he did not paint my Belladonna, and do you know what he said?"

The bulldog face was back so stoutly that I had to fight to keep my own straight. "He said that she was made in a way that he did not yet understand! That she was not like other horses, for her back parts were so prom-in-ent, he said."

Immediately, as if she had perfectly understood the insult, Belladonna shifted those very parts of herself and blew wind out of them. A volley, like shots. I had to cover my mouth and nose to keep back the laughter, but Ling took no notice. She still raged.

"Prom-in-ent. My beautiful Belladonna. He made her sound like a fat washerwoman from the sluices of Paris! Like Madame *La Vache* Lorraine, the *salope* who rented us that dirty room in the rue du Bac and yet made me haul water and stink for her."

Now I knew the reason Ling had made such a rumpus when I'd said she might do some house task for my mother.

She stood up and stroked Belladonna's white rump, ran her hand across the curve of the barley-colored tail. "*Ma belle,* maybe she keeps her wings right here under her skin! And Monsieur Stubbs, whatever he says, he will never find them, because he looks only for strings and bones."

She sniffed. "It is true that he has observed well this one thing, her fundament. Look, that is how she is strong enough to stand up and perform the *levade* and the *capriole*. The *capriole* is like flying, Thomas, truly it is. I will hold Belladonna's head for you and let you try it before too long. Though she is much too small for you, she will allow you sit, for she is a good teacher."

She stopped. "Come, I have something to show you." She pulled me from the straw pile to my feet. Then her arm was through mine, the lightest touch, steering me across the stable yard toward the back, away from the archway entrance. If the kitchen woman appeared again to shake her apron at me, I wouldn't care. The lumpy stable boys could stand well back too.

She ran her fingers along the doors of the stalls as we passed along. Then she laughed and flung her hat up in the air. She tipped forward, just a whit, just enough that the hat fell back again neatly onto her head. She looked perfect.

"Now you will see what I found," she said. "Close your eyes."

When I opened my eyes, she was gone, hat, boots, and all. But, no, there was her arm, all on its own in the air, beckoning me. Impatiently.

Clever girl. Between the end wall of the stable block and the high boundary wall, she had come upon this narrow passageway that she called her road to liberty.

Libertay, she said. She lifted my arms and stretched them out to show me how a small horse could make its way through if it took care, or if it was led. We picked our way over fallen bricks, where the weeds burst through, and then through grass so long it had fallen over on top of itself.

When we came out, we were on a rough path that ran behind the outhouses. I could easily recognize the chicken roosts and the pigpen from the smells, but there was a strong smell of ferment too. Perhaps there was a cider house here. We could not see the big house at all now, though it must lie somewhere to our right. On the left were bramble bushes with fat blackberries dangling like jewels, red, black, green, and purple. The sun was settled high into the south, so it was well past noon.

"Where are you taking me, Ling? I must head for home soon."

She pinched my arm. "Perhaps clever Ling finds you a quick way home, *hein*? You see how we are invisible here? So now I bring you to where it is possible to come and go just as a *fantôme* moves through a wall."

I felt something like a shiver, despite the heat. She had said that word so clearly that I knew it must mean a phantom. A barrow spirit walking out of the earth.

We walked and then stopped. Ling put her arm out across my stomach to stay me, and if we hadn't stopped, we would for certain have broken our legs in a nasty fall.

As it was, our toes hung over the half-cut block stones of a ditch wall that dropped away, sheer, to rough stony ground. From that place below the rising, ground began and led up and away, steadily climbing. Clumps of furze appeared until on the height there was just a giant spread of thorns.

Pyewipe country. That was what my father would call this sweep of land, fit only for rabbits and birds and the hawks that sought them out. I could hear larks, far up in the blue, invisible. They were the ones who would be able to see the best paths through the furze, although they had no need of them.

But Ling was right. Once down from this wall, I could climb through the scrub and reach the wold and have no need to go back through the wretched town. If I didn't at once find the road that led down into Horkstow, I could simply take the fields until I did, keeping south-west all the way.

"I must take her away soon, Thomas," Ling said slowly. I knew this was her warning to me. "I know the boy will leave here soon, to go to his school. Do not judge me, please. Belladonna is mine and she is all that I have left in the world."

"But what about your mother? Does she know where you are?"

For answer, Ling placed her little finger over my mouth. There was a piece of the apple pie left on it, and after the smallest gap of time passed, I sucked it clean. She did not stir then, unless to move closer is to stir. I pressed her tight to me and so could barely hear the words she whispered.

"Come again, Thomas. Soon. Before I must leave, *avant que je ne parte.*"

I wanted to tell her that was much too soon a plan, and far too much French for me, but she pulled my face down and kissed me on the mouth and inside, and I had no thoughts left at all.

For it was she who first kissed me, her giraffe, not I her, and I knew then that my play the night we were in the meadow was just that, a childish game. I was a man before her now — she knew that — and I was good enough for her.

New Territory

"NOW, INSTANCE YOUR FRIEND, Hélène," Stubbs said. The stinking air seemed to part for those words.

He folded a skein of skin back over his wrist so that it hung down like a curl of hair. I could see the scarlet parts where the horse's long nose had been uncovered down to its muzzle. *What about Ling?* I wanted to shout back, to hurry him.

"When she decided I was not an ogre after all"— here I got a quick sideways look—"she told me a sad story about a baby brother and a visit to the anatomy theater in Paris. I told her she was correct in what she did, taking her mother away from the place. There was nothing that doctor and his knife could have done for them, for it was probably an eight-month child, poor thing, and so its little lungs could not open and close as they should. I have seen such things for myself before now. Now, best look away here, Thomas."

Stubbs dealt swiftly with the eyes, and I didn't turn around until I knew they were in the bucket. The wretched man did not drop his lesson as easily as he did the poor cut-away parts, however.

"The eye of a horse," he said, "it looks so beautiful to us because it's dark and has great depths, and we think we see a soul. But a horse is a prey animal, not a hunter, so it needs big eyes that can see in all directions. Did you know, Thomas, that without even twizzling his head, the horse can see us seated on his back? In all our inelegance, they see us — how can they forgive us that!"

Belladonna has nothing to forgive, I thought. But Stubbs was there before me.

"I take that back, of course, in the case of your young friend, who could have taught Xenophon the Greek a thing or two. It was he who said horsemen should work their animals with joy, not fear."

Well, I could pass on to this Greek fellow something he didn't know. I told Stubbs how Ling had first met Belladonna on the fairground outside the city of Paris and how she won the mare's heart by giving her a crust of the nobleman's soft bread. "She had never been on a horse's back until that day," I said. "She let Belladonna teach her what to do, so they made a perfect pair."

Stubbs smiled. "Little wonder," he said. "She brought the instinct into the world with her, that one. What a stir such a girl might make at Newmarket if they were ever to let the ladies enter the field!"

I thought then of the king and the huff he had taken against Ling and her company. Perhaps that was it! She had mounted a horse in front of the king and raced, though likely not on Belladonna, for the mare was surely too small to race. I was sure of it.

We worked in silence until Stubbs said it was time for him to make his first drawings of what was now laid bare. I had been pressing myself to look more boldly at what we did. At first look, the head and face of the horse, stripped as they were, looked like raw meat. There was the white fat, there the red flesh, there the trapped dark clots of blood. But I knew I was seeing more than meat.

The open cheeks of the horse were rolling country-side, through which the veins of the rivers flowed. Then there were the muscles. Now that I knew what those tight bands were, I saw that they were the fields, harrowed by every movement the poor horse had made in its life. I must have muttered some such thing, for Stubbs looked up from his quick sketches, surprised.

"It's like a new territory," I said. "Like a map of the head."

"Well put, my boy," he said. "And almost as new for me as for you. They don't teach us these things at school, as you well know, Thomas. Look here—have you noticed this?"

He pointed with his pencil. "Because he does not have to smile or scowl or tell lies, the horse does not have the web of muscles we have in our faces. Monsieur Horse uses his ears and eyes to talk, and so he keeps himself honest. His power is in his jaw, the muscles here, and here, and the great mandibles, where the teeth grow, all for the munching of grass. Look, Thomas, take this piece of paper and copy the words I have already written."

"But . . ." I was flustered because I had warned him already of my lack in that region.

He stopped me. "My hand is a clear one. Make as if you were tracing a path with a stick, like a child going from one stook of hay in a field to another. You shall see the point of it in a while."

I confess that I forgot the smells of death and decay when I took the pages to the table and began to copy the marks the man had written down. It was weeks since I'd been forced to hold a pen, and my right hand trembled when I took this one up and dipped it in the ink bottle. The miracle was that if I pictured following a path rather than writing a word, I could make a fair enough copy of what he'd dashed off in rough. Really, it was no different from working in my own notebook. Nobody was there to harry me, or worse.

Some words were long, and I couldn't reckon any sense of those. But some of the shorter words seemed to form shapes, and while I couldn't read them, I felt I might know them again. If Stubbs would speak the words out for me, it would help. At least the letters held steady in front of me and did not do that terrible dance.

"Do you know your numbers, Thomas?" Stubbs asked, without lifting his head. "If you do, I would like you to label the notes you copy, as to one, two, three, and so on."

To make a digit was no hardship. When I started at school in Brigg, I was able to compute sums entire in my head, but because I wrote down my answers with no workings attached, the master was driven to a fury. That was when I learned to pretend I had no numbers, any more than I had letters. Nan knew the truth of it, however. Her *"Help me do my sums, Tom"* was the only credit I held when our skills were reckoned together.

For a while we were all scrape and scratch, knife and pen.

"The walls are so thick in here," I said. "I thought we might hear the church bells, or the sounds from the fields. We hear them in my father's shop."

"You're hungry," Stubbs said, turning around. He was amused. "Pen work is as tiring as any other labor, I know that well. Have patience a while yet. But, yes, you're right about the walls. There isn't a malt house near that's built sturdier than this place, and that suits me well enough, for what must be done here."

He looked up from his head and toward the window, and his face lightened. "You're in luck, Thomas. My Mary comes with our food, and whatever it is, I daresay you'll welcome it."

Mary Spencer came through the door in a bustle of baskets and cloths, but she would not dole anything out until we had both scrubbed outside at the rain barrel, first with water, and after with vinegar. Then we sat down in the other room with the cheese, cold potatoes, and oat bread she'd brought.

"You didn't bring the pup today," I said to her.

"You won't believe my story," she said. But she was smiling, so I knew I'd hear nothing bad. "Last night George and I met your father's man, Henry Harkin, down by the shore. I knew him to see, but we'd never spoken, he being so shy and stiff in himself. Then Zachary bounded up to him at his traps, and do you know this, Thomas, it was like watching snow melt to see that man come alive with the puppy's playacting."

Henry Harkin. I could not think when I had last heard the Clock's full name spoken.

"He told us that he'd had a small brown dog when he was a boy. I thought then it was fitter and kinder for him to take Zachary, for they had a bond on the instant, and I'd him only a day or so, with nothing so special showing between us."

Mary rubbed her hands together. "I tell you, the years fell from that man's face. He picked up a natural way of talking the more he carried on. I told him he could leave the pup behind with me when he went working, but he said your sister would surely take a turn there."

Of course Nan would love her turn with the puppy. But imagine that it was the Clock that said so!

Stubbs had not taken any part in the talk. Now he spoke.

"I was sorry to lose the dog, for it had an extra claw on its hind legs, like a chicken has, and that to me is an interesting thing. But also because the beast would be company for Mary when I go to Barton."

Mary shook her head. "It was the right thing, George. Ottleys have a litter of sheep pups growing, and I can take one there if I need company. Zachary belonged with that man."

An Evening Walk

STUBBS SENT ME home early, barely after mid-afternoon, when the sun was still high and bright.

"We rub together well enough, you and I, Thomas Rose," he said. "I like the matters you raise."

He went to the drawer where he kept his fresh paper and handed me a long sheet and a pencil. "Take this away for your own work. You can show me what you do tomorrow, if you wish, and it's no matter if you prefer not to. I know what it is to put oneself forward for the opinions of others."

I was well pleased, for a number of reasons. I had time enough now to go the scrub way to Baysgarth and be back by dusk if I stepped out handy. Nobody at home would expect me so early. Or want me either, for I was still living down my thievery.

Hugh had laughed when he saw his broken birthday pie, he told me, but Nan wept, the silly, and my mother had been quiet all evening, a bad sign. When I turned up at the end of my day at Baysgarth, my father slapped my face and called me a wastehands and a go-the-road who'd be pressed for the war one of the days. Then Mother had cried for us all to keep the peace on Hugh's birthday. The worst was seeing her eyes, dark as bruises.

I reached the village road, quick as a frog to water, and cut straight up to Middle Gate Lane, the old road, rather than take the turn at the church, where anyone standing around at this hour would see me. I joined the wold road well above the church and began the trudge uphill.

My grief began when I'd gone only a few paces. There was no hiding from the voice calling me from behind, so I turned and waited for the short figure in the tight green jacket to catch up.

Jack Proctor in his Sunday best, though it was not Sunday.

"Well, young Tom, you're at your liberty good and early in the day. Taking a walk up the wold, then?"

I heaved a great breath before I answered him. "I needed the air, Jack," I said. "The smells are that rotten. I couldn't stomach going inside four walls again right off."

"Well, if you're going toward Barton, you may have my company for most of the way, whoever else's you'll have at the end of it."

At least Jack shut himself up sharpish on *that*. All his curiosity was for Stubbs. How the man set about his business with the misfortunate horses, what instruments he used for the butchery, what his true purpose might be, working such a trade. He nodded when I named some of the knives we used.

"He's not just a fumbler, then," he said, pleased to show what he knew. "Not like Bart Ottley, who left your father's shop today on account of that wheelwork did not suit him."

That news shook me a little. My father's hold on me would be stronger than anything Stubbs might muster, if it came to a push for hands on the job. Jack seemed to put little store by it, however, and stopped me only to point.

"Aye, but look at that spectacle, Thomas! The fighting ships out there!"

Again, I stood on the crest of the wold and felt the tingle along my skin when I looked down at the moving waters of the estuary. I saw nothing I could call a ship, only the lines of the land stretching along either side, until they became faint blue traces, like pencil marks on paper.

I looked to my right, where the scrubland began to slope away down, toward Baysgarth and its stonework ditch.

"Jack, I'm going to tramp over that way. I might take a rabbit or two home with me for the pot."

We eyed each other.

"Plenty of bunnies grubbing their way in the after-grass around Horkstow, Tom," Jack said, his voice level. "You don't need to traipse all this way to find them on pyewipe land like that. Watch out for yourself, lad. And stay out of the town. Those are two big ships out there. Your father has a bee in his bonnet about the press-gangers, that's true, but that's not to say there's not a crowd of the king's poison wasps swarming from time to time, looking for any folk they can sting."

"Best not tell Father you found me here, then," I said to Jack. "Or the air at home will poison all of us."

I stared him down, but he only gave me a quick pat on the arm before taking himself off down the smooth-cut road that ran from Barton all the way southwest to Brigg.

I watched until Jack was only a speck and then clambered over the ditch and made my own path downhill, past thousands of cruel furze fingers that tore any bare skin they could find. When I got past the ditch wall and onto Baysgarth land, I began to see bits and pieces of the place I'd not laid eyes on before. I could blame Ling for my blindness of yesterday, of course. The thought gave me a warm feeling.

A smith must once have worked out of one of the stone sheds here, for there were shoes scattered everywhere outside, along with the chewed leather scraps of a bellows. Farther on, white birds, like pigeons but prettier, flocked to an old cote standing on a pole. They sounded like girls giggling together. I could still hear them as I came along Ling's secret way, between the stable block and the wall.

There was no sign of her or Belladonna inside the stall. But stretched out on the straw bed, welcome as nettles, was Ezra Quickfall. He was running Ling's red kerchief back and forth across his mouth as if his breath depended on it. I grabbed it from him and didn't mind that I cuffed him doing so, though he raised no hand against me and took a fit of coughing instead. I hung the silk piece up with her dress.

"Did your gram die already, then?" I said to him. "Is that what brought you here?"

The boy turned dark as the silk. He sat up straight and glared back at me. "What's it to you?"

"Would you not wait till she's in the ground to come around here fingering items that belong to others?"

Now the lad looked half his right size, which wasn't much to begin with, and pasty as meal, and I felt a pang. There was no gram in his life, I was sure, alive or dead, but that was for the boy himself to fiddle around with.

"You've brought no honey with you today, I suppose?" I softened my speech to meet the miserable look of him. "Have you met Ling—Hélène? Is she here?"

At Ling's name, his face lit up. "She's coming back straight. She went with the boy to show his ma all he can do now, a jump or two he wasn't up for before. They're across by the front of the house. Did you ever see such an animal as the one she has? I had to rub my eyes over twice. She says there are horses that fly where she comes from."

I grunted to let him know I heard his simple talk. The black cat padded in from the yard and rubbed herself against my legs, purring loudly, while I stewed in silence. It was *that* unfair. The cat and the boy might see Ling when they wished, but there'd be no time now for me before I had to turn around and take myself home. Why was the idiot boy here, anyway? He hadn't the right of kissing her that I had, and surely she'd not waste her time telling such a poor nobody all the story of her life.

We heard her then, both of us in the same instant, because our eyes locked. A smart trot turning under the archway, across the cobbles, and then the light spring down and the soft shadows across the doorway.

Today she wore only a shirt with the breeches, but the Nelthorpe boy's lacy bib was not at all foolish on her. It made a summer cloud under her face.

"Thomas! How nice! Look, it is I who brings the gammon now."

She held out a platter, a mound of fatty meat and a mash under it, enough for a family to eat. "That Julia, she says, 'Where do you put it all, for you're only a button size bigger than a *dwarw*?'" She sniggered. "But she is so happy I do not want to eat in the kitchen with them, she gives me more, and so I have plenty here for Ezra and now maybe even for poor hungry Thomas, too."

She turned to Ezra. "I tell my friend Thomas he is a giraffe, for he is so tall."

Ezra was staring up at her face as if she were an angel. As if the likes of him might ever know what a giraffe was.

I waved the platter away. "I'll eat at home. Let him have it. He needs feeding, with that cough he has."

Then, desperate to speak with her, as I needed to, I blurted out my fill without any shame. "Ling, will you walk with me a little way when you've had your supper? Just you?"

A Marriage

IN THE END it wasn't so awkward to arrange. Ling gave Ezra all the different combs he must use to make Belladonna beautiful for the night and came with me, this time as far as the furze. I made a little noise at that.

"It's not safe to walk back through the scrub on your own. Suppose you fell? The place is pocked with rabbit holes, and you'd be left lying there."

"Me fall, Thomas? *Moi?* I am a dancer, you know, and so my feet never fail me."

She tapped my nose, pretending to be cross. "Anyway, Ezra would come for me. Poor one, he does not know what to do on his own, and he is afraid for his poor horse. He takes it around to crop the grass under apple trees in the town, but the winter will come soon. Maybe he can get work in the stables here."

I thought of the pair who were in charge in the kitchen and saw no hope there for the scrawny boy, but I had more on my mind. "That fellow stays in the stall tonight? With you?"

"Thomas, do not be so silly. I am sorry for him. I know what it is like to be him. You do not." She put a finger through one of my buttonholes and poked my chest when she said "you." I shivered to be touched like that, but it was pure pleasure. "Remember, you had a fear about the donkey men? Well, now Ezra can stay to protect me, so you must think that is a good thing, *n'est-ce pas?*"

"Him? He couldn't swat one of his darling bees."

"Ah, Thomas." She shook her head, making to be sorrowful, as if I were a bad child. "All is not quite as it seems. It never is."

"What do you mean?"

She took my hand and pressed it against my chest, though I confess it had a hankering to go toward her own. Well, my heart would make a fine school lesson for her, for sure. She might feel how it pounded underneath my ribs. Let that tell her what it would.

But she only looked concerned. "You are kind, here in your heart, Thomas," she said, "but not always, I think," she said. "Like me. I was not kind to my poor husband."

"*What?*"

She pointed at a patch where the furze did not grow, where the rabbits had left some grass. We sat down, as close together as the space forced us, though I could have sat on thorns without noticing them if they'd bring me nearer her.

"Thomas, you saw the *colombes* we passed, and their little *maison*? You call those birds doves, yes? They are for marriage in France. Well, I was married once —"

"*What?*"

She made two little horns on her head, crooking her first fingers. "*Quoi! Quoi! Monsieur What!* Oh, Thomas, do you not know it is very easy to deceive when it must be done?"

There was a quick nod to me then, from the same family of nods my mother used when she was talking to my grandfather. The winner's nod, my father called it.

"It was simple. We must leave France because we had no money left and the *marchands* were after us, each one waving his long bills under the Dane's nose. But when he told us his plan, it was like we were hit by *la foudre*." She made a zigzag above her head. "This."

"Lightning," I said. "Or a thunderbolt."

She nodded. "The Dane, you know, that man was as clever as the *Chat Botté*, Monsieur Puss in Boots. He said there was a *vicomte* who wanted to marry Sylvie, who was sick with his love like a little dog. We knew this man because he sat in the front row at all our performances with his mouth open. The Dane said he would make the *vicomte* give us money for Sylvie and then we could escape to England. The *vicomte* lived outside Amiens, you see, and that is not so far from the sea."

"But I thought you said *you* were married?"

"*Oui*, Thomas, but you must have the patience." She wagged her finger at me. "Poor Sylvie was very beautiful, but she was afraid to talk to people. He said I must take her place and marry the *vicomte* because I was so bold I would know what to do. I must wear a dark veil and the shoes with *talons* to make me tall like Sylvie. Maman made the dress." She bit her lip.

On the wedding day, Ling had fumed while her mother stitched her into the bridal gown and arranged the veil in layers around her head.

"I look like the farmer's wife who steals from the bees! But I could see the *vicomte* and all his chins like jellies, though he could not see me. I could see the cathedral roof above us, which was nearly as high as the sun. It had a canopy of silk, like the silk in my dress, only this silk was made of stone. The windows had pictures made of jewels."

Back at the *vicomte*'s castle, there were real jewels, plenty of them, and gold too, handed over to the Dane.

"But, you . . . ?" I hardly knew what to ask next.

"Thomas, what do *you* think? Do you think I went off with that man to his bedchamber?"

She put her finger into her mouth and pretended to make herself sick.

"*Alors*, yes, it is true I did go to his *chambre*, but not for long. No, I told you how our clever *Chat Botté* was the master in charge of everything. He had a sleeping potion ready for each glass the *vicomte* drank." She laughed. "He drank so many! I was beside him, his wife, poor Sylvie so shy she would not take her veil off until she would be alone with her husband. But if the *vicomte* did not snore when we came to the *chambre*, then I would be Hélène, who had her knife always ready."

But he did snore and she was Hélène after all, and her little white mare was waiting down the road, tied to Tournesol's saddle. Augustin and she made speed after the others, and the ship for England was still singing in its chains when they arrived at the port.

I had almost forgotten the reason I'd been told this story, because I was so caught up in it, a trout gasping in a net. In a veil. But Ling tapped my knee.

"So, Thomas. All is not as it seems, sometimes. You think I am a simple French girl, but you see, you are in the company of a *vraie vicomtesse*. I do not have my silk dress now, but still this Thomas Rose must bow before he ever takes my hand."

I was no drunk bridegroom, but I went home happy that night. Yet later, when I tossed in my bed, my state was as bad as before, because I could think only of that dash to the port and Augustin, the hero, galloping alongside Ling, into the night.

The Linnet

THAT NIGHT FATHER said nothing about Bart Ottley taking himself off, so nor did I. I presented myself to Stubbs the next day and showed him a short passage I had copied from Mr. Defoe's book. Nan had found it for me. He made a sally on it before we started our work.

> *"When they flg abroad, ar, as might be said, are sent abroad, they ga none knaws where; but 'tis believed by same they flg quite over the ses into Hollond and Germony."*

He asked me if it was my father's book I used and then surprised me by saying that his own father had had neither reading nor writing and made only a mark for his name.

"He had no learning, but with you, Thomas, I believe there is some mismatch at work. You've switched your letters around and made this sound like a Scotsman, or a Dutchman! I'll set myself to treat that while you stay with me."

I was warmed to hear that, but if I was, my poor inky hands spent most of their day filling buckets in the kitchen and emptying them outside into the slops pit. Other times, I held what was left of the mare's head at whatever angle Stubbs required. To start with, the mass would slip and slide under my fingers, but then I learned to seize fast on the long bones underneath. I needed less wax for my nose than before, though the smell was growing worse.

Stubbs had been to France and to other countries too. He looked curiously at me when I asked what a French wedding was like.

"What a strange question. Perhaps our *mademoiselle* has been spinning tales for you, *n'est-ce pas*? She's well capable of that, Thomas. It's in her nature, and in her background too."

I flashed fire at that but kept it to myself. It wasn't just that the French words were not so pretty out of his throat, but I'd made sure not to mention Ling, and here the man was, running her down. I steered him toward fresh pasture. "How does the boy stand for his picture?"

He grunted. "Well enough, considering what he wears. You know, Thomas, it's as tricky to paint a silk as it is the gleam of a horse's coat, but I like it less. Anyway, I'll not need you here Monday, Thomas, for I'll be at Baysgarth, painting the last of him. There's hardly any time left till he goes to his school down London way."

Well, that made good news and bad news, both together. Good, because I might steal away to Barton just as before, with nobody at home any wiser. Bad, because Ling's days with Belladonna were surely up now. If she didn't know this already, I'd have to tell her. She would have to make a plan.

The heads Stubbs drew now appeared more finished than those I had already seen, and I knew now it was because of all the deep cutting and layering we did. The poor roan lived on in these pages, with a noble face, her eyes sensible, all her vessels and muscles stretched and full, as if they might flow and move. As if losing her skin had been no matter at all.

I took away the sheets as Stubbs called me to, in case they fell onto the floor, and brought them to safety in the room that Mary Spencer called the parlor. It was her jest. In addition to my little bit of scribing work the night before, I had knocked together a box made of offcuts from Father's shop. I made it to measure from the page Stubbs had given me for my own scribbling. It was a rough thing, but the man had seemed touched.

"You made this box for me, Thomas? I shall treasure it and my work will be the safer."

Mary came at the usual time, but this day she brought some surprises along with her basket of food. We heard her first in the other room putting things here and about. When I peeked in on my way to the water barrel, I saw that she'd spread loose bunches of sweet herbs and meadow grasses on the floor.

"There's rosemary here," she said, "and queen of the meadow and honeysuckle. They're the best killers of foul smells in a house. *He* doesn't mind the dreadful-ness of it all."

She wagged a finger at Stubbs, who stood now beside me. "But you and I are finer people, Thomas Rose."

Stubbs shook his head at the insult, but he was amused. "Bring out your other treasure for the boy," he said. "It will lift us to a place other than here."

She took away the cloth from the basket, and then I saw the domed birdcage beside it on the floor. A full-grown linnet sat on a bar inside the cage, picking at its red breast feathers. It opened its bill then and sang for a heartbeat or so. If we closed our eyes and our noses we might all have been outside, walking by the hedges of late summer.

"My uncle showed me how to catch a bird with lime and twigs," Mary said. "He brought them to sea with him to remind him of home. Don't think me cruel. I let my birds go free in the evening, but meanwhile you'll have their music."

The linnet put its head back and obliged us again. Its song was fast and full of notes, but it would break off after only a few bars, as if it suddenly remembered it was a prisoner. I wondered if the bird felt as helpless as I had when I was shut up in the classroom at Brigg. I whistled and the bird answered me.

"He thinks you're the hen!" Mary beamed at me. "You're some hen, Thomas Rose, the size you stand in your boots."

It seemed nobody in this world would ever liken me to a lion, which was how I preferred to see myself, but I could put up with that. I knew now giraffes had their uses too.

At the end of the day, Mary was true to her word. Before I left, she took the cage to the front of the house and opened its small door. We all watched while the bird stayed on its perch, moving its head from one side to another, until it seemed to understand that no gate stood between it and the sky. It hopped to the wire door-sill, where it waited. Then it lifted its wings and took off, leaving a solitary red breast feather behind on the floor of the cage.

I reached inside for it. "For my sister," I said. Then I bade them good night.

Past the granary, the Clock was stepping out again for home, but not with his usual head-down stride. Instead he was pausing, looking around and behind him, distracted.

"There you are, Zachary," I called out to the pup. It raced from the ditch and tried to jump as high as my waist to greet me. "God speed you . . . em . . . Mr. Harkin," I said. I hardly knew how to greet him now. He mumbled a word or two—that was all—but his bony face was lifted up and open to the sky. Then he clicked his fingers, and the pup ran after him, gathering its legs, its string of a tail stretched behind it.

The Letter

NAN WAS HANGING over the gate, looking out for me. She ran into the road, waving, as if I were a ship in danger of sailing past her.

"Did you see Zachary?" she called. "Our new pup?"

"The Clock's pup," I corrected her. "Henry Harkin's pup."

"Yes, that's what I meant," Nan said. "Silly billy *you*. But he's half mine too, for every day except Sunday. And do you know there is a letter for you, Tom? What will you do with it?"

I had my hand on the gate, but this news stayed me. "What type of letter is it?" I asked. As if I or Nan knew what manner of letters made their way around the world!

"It's wrapped in a cloth and tied tight with a bootlace. The cloth has your name written on it. Not in a proper pen, only in charcoal, but very black. A man left it here at noon."

"What man?"

"Just a man, Tom. I didn't know him and I asked who he might be, but he said nothing, only would I see you got the letter. I watched him go, and he went down the track to the river. He had lines in his pocket, I think, but it was too early for fishing."

"Did Hugh say that?"

"I didn't tell Hugh! I didn't say anything about the letter to anyone. It's *your* letter, Tom. Look, you can read your name here."

Nan took a grimy piece of cloth from the pocket of her pinny and showed me where my name was written, in thick dark letters. Then she put it back.

"You mean, nobody else knows about this, Nan?"

She shook her head and set her chin in a point, as if to dare me cross her for what she had done, but I could barely believe my sister had such sly craft in her. I wanted to lift her in the air and dance her down the road.

"Come down the way a bit with me, Nan," I said.

A glance across the yard and I could see that Father was still in the shop. The doors of the shop were open, and we could hear the special clatters and bangs that belonged to the end of the workday.

"We'll have supper soon," Nan said slowly.

"But just to take a look. Perhaps I'll need your help. You know why I might. Silly Tom and his wooden head."

The soft thing smiled at that and took my hand. We went up the small incline of the road and past the grange, the long low farmhouse set back from the main thoroughfare. I stopped there, and Nan handed me my letter.

My hands were so eager to work the knot that it tangled itself into a worse mischief. Nan giggled while I struggled with it and again when a piece of rough paper fell onto the grass between us.

I picked it up and looked at what was written. "It's no use, Nan," I said at last. "You must help me again. The hand is odd."

Of course I'd expected Ling to have a penmanship all her own, but this one was a fright, just as my own was. The letters had large loops and fell away from the straight, so that the words tramped across the page like loose cattle. Yet the message itself was short, I could see that. There *was* an *X* but it sat in the middle of the page, like an impostor. Perhaps someone else had written it for her.

Nan put on her reading face.

> *"My deer Thomas*
> *Will you meet me at the market X in*
> *Barton on the moro erly? Im in a pickle like*
> *a poor sprat and need yr help. Toward 7*
> *ours if you ken be there.*
> *Yr own E."*

She looked puzzled and read all of it aloud again. "Why is it signed *E*?" she asked. "I can write words better than this. I thought this letter would be from Ling. But Ling is very smart."

"She is," I said. "Of course she's smart, Nan. And this *is* from her. But she's French, so she probably doesn't know to write our words so well. Can *you* write French words? And her real name is Hélène. Perhaps that starts with an *E*."

I was unsure. Even if I was right about that, all the other sounds in the letter were wrong, because Ling did not talk that way. She talked so that I wanted to listen forever, and surely she would write that way too, with her words put together to please, just as Mr. Defoe's did when he wrote about our wildfowl and their ways.

I slapped my knee. Of course! That Ezra had written it for her. It was a wonder the pest could write at all, but that was no matter. And whoever had delivered the letter was just someone the boy had found, someone who was coming to Horkstow.

"I didn't know she was *French*!"

Nan's voice was climbing high. My sister heard only bad things about the French, that was for sure, all those bloodthirsty mutterings about the war. I'd known little more myself, until this last while. Now I saw parks with statues, palaces with gardens, hospitals with domes, cathedrals with ceilings of silken stone. That was France. And French children no older than Nan danced for the pleasure of lords and ladies and taught them their fables. Was there anything as rare and precious as that anywhere in England?

"Will you go, Thomas? In the morning? A Sunday morning, too?"

Her face was upturned and to one side, like a bird's. She looked distressed.

"With your help, I'll pick Ling out of her pickle jar," I said, trying to make her smile.

"Look, I brought you this." I tickled her nose with the red feather. But she just stared at me all the while I was thinking of a way. "Will you tell Mother I had to go to Appleby tomorrow on an errand for Mr. Stubbs? I'll leave before anyone is up. I'll sort out the pickle and tell you about it after."

"Mother does not like the man who chops up horses in his kitchen. And I don't either."

Her voice was just a whisper.

"Oh, Nan, I know. It's hard to explain what he does so you might understand that it's not for bad reasons. You saw his big horse, Walnuts. He cares about *him* and keeps him well away from the butcher's work so he won't be frightened. And he's a good man. I've told him about you." That was true. I had told Stubbs and Mary Spencer many things about my family.

Nan let out a breath, very slowly. "All right, Thomas. I'll do it. But afterward you must tell me every single thing you do tomorrow. And you have to tell me much more about Belladonna. Is she French too? Are there horses in France? Is she really beautiful?"

I laughed and hunkered down to reach out for her. "Quick, hop up on my shoulders for the way back. While we can still do this. Before you grow into a giant like me."

From her perch, Nan thumped my head.

"Next time you see her," I told her, "Ling will tell you about the horses in Paris, how they dance and how they fly."

A Sprat in a Pickle

AFTER WEEKS of dry earth and heaven, it was raining just after dawn, a light rain of dribs and mist rather than a full drench. The sky to the east was the color of pigeon wings.

On the road, the cart ruts were soft and pooling with water, and I had to pick my way with care. Before long the thick broadcloth jacket I was wearing, Father's second-best, was wet through, the shirt stuck to my skin, and water puddled in the heels of my boots. I thought of the open marketplace and hoped Ling would find some shelter there.

On the height, it seemed I was walking in a cloud that had sunk to earth with its bellyweight of drops. If the river was down there, today it was just a gray sulk, like everything else. I could see nothing sharp ahead until I came to the outskirts of Barton, and even then people gave no warning of themselves until they were right upon me. All sounds were muffled, even footsteps. Of the few people that passed, not one returned my civil Sunday greeting.

Even bad old Brigg was not so sour a place.

The marketplace was ghostly and shapeless. I walked the four sides of it to get my bearings and saw only a couple of men taking shelter under a gable end. I must be too early for Ling, but that was all right. She'd see me first, anyway, with those quick eyes.

I set myself up outside a joiner's shop on the Baysgarth end of the marketplace. Even though the shop was well shuttered, I could smell sawdust and fresh oak. If I closed my eyes, I might believe myself in Father's shop, with the door open to the east.

But when I opened the same eyes, it wasn't Ling who approached. All the gray morning could not darken the blaze of Ezra Quickfall's hair, sleeked down and wet though it was. Worse, he looked as eager as ever. He smartened his step as he drew near and kicked out his skinny legs like a soldier. A very poor soldier. He'd be saluting me next, but for the piece of horse blanket drawn tight across his shoulders.

Cuckoo boy.

"Thomas Rose! There you are!"

"Where's Ling, then?" I said roughly, for it hurt me to see him. "Can she not come after all and sent you instead? That's a poor swap."

He stopped, with a puzzle spreading over his face. "But *you* said *I* was to come here . . . that your father . . ."

"That's the pair of 'em now! Don't let 'em lunge at ye!"

Hands like pincers grabbed my wrists from behind and had a rope around them before I could twist them away and land a punch on my attackers. Two brawny men, short but strong, one breathing like a bellows, had me. I dipped my head down then to go at them like a billy goat, but that only helped them, for one of them dropped a foul-smelling bag over my head. For a moment I thought I might choke, for something fishy had only just been dumped out of the thing.

"Thomas Rose! Please mind me!" That was Ezra, but of course I couldn't see anything of him. He kept calling my name, then I heard him coughing and gulping air down, but that all grew fainter, until he was pitiful as a lost lamb in the darkness. However, just before I was blinkered, I'd seen the man who'd shouted the order, the one that grabbed Ezra, even as the other two had found me.

The shouter was the kitchen man from Baysgarth. Jem.

"Aye, good work, that'll make them civil," one of my captors said. "You'll get your shillings for this, Hasp, or else you'll get your comeuppence. All hangs on what use they are. And if what you said is so."

They pulled me along, for all I dug my feet down onto the wet clay of the path and tried to stall them with my weight. They simply lifted me by the arms then and dragged me deadweight, so that it was easier to give in and let my feet walk for me rather than have my boot soles scraped raw.

I heard no more calls from poor Ezra, but shouted out myself. "Help us! Someone, help us, please!"

But of course the men had planned their time to suit their deed. *On the moro erly.*

I reasoned my two had to be gangers, impress men. If they weren't the men who'd been watching me the other day at the market, they were hatched from the same rotten egg. What were they after? Money or badness?

Nan had been right, bless her, and I was well paid back now for believing that Ling would write such an ugly letter. For sure, some other note must have led Ezra to the same place at the same time. What had he said, something about . . . "your father"?

I tried to think of what I knew of the impress men. Father talked enough about them, goodness knows, though he always called them crimpermen and spat out afterward to cleanse his mouth. The war with France was on, and the navy took the men that came to sign up. And if enough didn't choose to come, the king's men went looking for more and took what they could find. But not everyone. They'd turned away Tom Pell last year, for he was not old enough at fifteen, they said, though he was as hot as mustard to serve England.

So they did not take boys. And Ezra was only the slightest of boys, hardly more than a child, surely, for all that I'd built him up as my rival with Ling. I felt chill at that. I'd be safe enough, I was sure. All it would take was mention of Father's name in one ear and Stubbs's in the other. But who'd speak for Ezra?

Who'd speak to Ling? I had to let her know about the boy going off so soon to school.

We were taking a turn now, probably heading down for the wharves. *The wherries and the wharves.* It was no joke now and there came a real burst of fear, a knife turning itself over and over in my belly. Only yesterday Jack Proctor had seen ships in mid-channel, navy ships.

Out there so far from land, who'd ever know what might happen to two fool boys? Who would care?

I lowered my head and shook it like a mad thing, like an ox with biting ticks in its ears. The bag came off and fell under my feet, and under the nappers' feet too, and was trampled into the damp ground. I got a thump on the back for my trick, but the men didn't stop. Probably the blindfold didn't matter now that we were far enough away from anyone who might lift an arm for our sakes.

The Rose

I STARED WILDLY AROUND.

We were almost at the waterfront. Where the men stopped was just as mean a place as the streets that led to it, just a straggle of sheds that followed the water. The sheds were made of rotted wood for the most part, with gaps between them, like a mouth of bad teeth.

That dirty crab Hasp scuttled along behind, with Ezra trussed tight in his claws.

Here by the water, it was as gray and moody as it had seemed from on top of the wold earlier. Nothing could be known unless it was close by. There might be a ship sitting there or there might not. My two men called out and got an answer that seemed to come across the water like the skims of a stone. Then we were all on the move again, toward a shaky platform that marched out over the tide, on stilts like those fowlers used, to stride high and dry across the fens.

At the end of this walkway, a boat was moored. But if this was the king's ship, it was a poor thing that his majesty had set aside for himself, here on the Humber. It was low in the water, and its cabin was hardly higher than the rail that ringed it. Only one mast rose from its belly. It had a name, however, painted high on the bows in measled black letters. A name that gave me no bother at all. The *Rose*. I would laugh if I didn't want to cry.

"Come on, then, Hasp." Bellows-Breath was gruff. He meant business. "I need to make the rendezvous fast, so tell me what we have here. Facts, Hasp. A short lad and a long one is all I see here. I need names, ages, and residences. Take the bag off the shorty lad and let's see to him. If we can add two to what we've packed down below already, well, six ain't bad pickings."

"No!" I shouted. My poor call made twins of itself, and then more, so that there seemed to be a navy of *Rose*s out there in all the fog and water, every one as use-less as the one on land.

"NO-OO-OO!" they mocked.

I had to shake myself out of it. I turned to Bellows-Breath, who seemed to have more heft than the others. "Whatever that man there told you is a lie. I'm only fourteen years old, and I'm bound over to two masters. To my father, John Rose of Horkstow, wheelwright, and also to Mr. George Stubbs, who works in this town as a painter, and in Horkstow too, making an anatomy."

The man looked back to Hasp, puckering up what bit of a forehead he had. Hasp spat from the corner of his mouth and shook his head.

"He's a liar and a vagrant, like the other one," he said. "They moved themselves with no settlement onto my mistress's lands and offices, just because she was bad guided enough to take the gypsy girl in —"

I yelled him down. "I don't need a settlement. I have one, a better one than you have, for it's with my own kin. And you know it full well, for that's where you brought your letter."

I went back to Bellows-Breath. "Send for John Rose to Horkstow, sir. My father will vouch for me. And he'll tell you too that boy is only eleven. Get the bag off him, look at him close, and you'll see that."

I had no idea what age Ezra was. Eleven sounded safe from the sea, but was it? Perhaps I should have said ten. Let the devil take it — they could have the works from me now.

"He has a grandmother that needs what he brings

in, and a horse that he jobs with. He visited the lady's stable only to learn what a horse can do if you teach it right. He'll not do it again."

I was wild now, spinning my story like wool. But Bellows was growing doubtful—that was clear.

Jem Hasp bared his teeth when he grew desperate, like a dog. "Fourteen, the great lummox says," he snarled, "and a fine name that he picks off the bows of that boat of yours for himself, like an apple off a market stall. I ask you, sirs, was a creature that lanky ever *fourteen?* And you saw him for yourself the other day, idle in the marketplace . . ."

Bellows was shaking his head. "If you've messed with our day of rest, Hasp . . ."

He and the other one had the bag off Ezra now, and I sickened at what I saw. The boy seemed choked or half dead, for his head lolled to the front like an old turnip skull on a scarecrow, and his eyes were closed.

"Did you squeeze the last breath out of the lad, fool?" said Bellows to Hasp.

Then he was up the plank to the boat with the speed of a lighter man, and back down again with a bucket. He threw what was in it into Ezra's face, and as the boy gasped and spluttered, he grunted.

"He's right. That's no more than a sprat. That's no bloody use to us, Hasp, and trouble if we tried it. The long one's no vagrant either, I'll wager, let him be Rose or Thorn or whatever he wants. That coat he wears and the way he talks! I'll not risk that much trouble and then the bringing back and the ballocking I'd get for it. Get the ropes off them both, and then get back to your stink hole, you damned fool."

We were loosed, though it took both of us a long minute to feel free, so long I got a shove to move me along. Likely I needed it. My head was reeling as if it had got a worse clout, all for what I had seen.

It had been there for only an eyeblink, but the mercy was that nobody bar myself seemed to have noticed. When the water hit Ezra, it soaked his horse blanket so that it clung to his skin. He'd had no hands free, and a cough starting up, but quickly he'd pushed his shoulders forward, as if to steady himself.

Too late.

What had Ling said the other night? *All is not quite as it seems.*

Ezra's game was up.

Dido

WE MADE OUR WAY back through the miserable alleyways. I thought we'd surely take the main street to reach Baysgarth, but Ezra took hold of my arm and pulled me down another way instead. There was no word out of him, just the little gasp and wheeze of fear he hadn't yet thrown off, even though we were safe now and a good stretch grew between us and the wharf.

Him, indeed.

"So what *is* your name, then?" I asked. "And don't muck me about. I saw you back there, your girl's chest and all, before you got it covered up again."

"Esther. Quickfall, the same."

"Then why Ezra? Why all this fool play?"

Of course, *I* was the fool, and it was that which had me boiling. I could forget the trap letter; that was done with now. But Ling and this creature had me rightly twisted between them.

She stopped so sharp, I almost toppled her over. Where we were was no more than a laneway, with low cottages along one side only, all joined together as if they were only one brick wall, all damp and dripping from the roofs. Not a patch of sweet earth in front of any of them, not as much as a houseleek planted on a window-sill to keep the home safe.

"In here is my place."

Small as she was, she had to duck her head to go through, and I felt I was a bull breaking into a badger's den. Inside it might as well have been a den, because everything was earth, or the color of it, and the smell of it, and empty as a hole in the ground. There was not a stick of furniture, not a chair, only some rags in a corner and the tall pitcher from the marketplace.

She knew well what I was seeing. "It wasn't always like this. The lender man came for all we had when my gram died. She was dead when I met you, but I didn't let on. I don't tell everyone, for they get ideas, and they get worse ideas if you're a girl. So. Anyway, I'm not right used to it yet."

I didn't know whether she meant being a girl again, or being a boy in the first place, or her gram being dead, or all of those things together. She was so pale and out of blood, the freckles stood out like fleabites on her skin. Her breaths were shallow and rough.

"I have some well water outside, so do you want some? And I've that blessed honey—look—but no bread to put it on."

She pointed to the pitcher and laughed. "I whipped that at the market the day I met you, not a bother to it. You throw your shape at something else and talk it up, and they'll never see what you're rightly at. I was minding to bring the honey to Ling today, after we got the other thing out of the way."

"What did your letter say?"

She sang it out as easily as I could have done mine.

"Foxy Boy
      Thomas Rose nown to you says you ken
bring your old horse to his da for best free
grass in Horksto. Meet him at the market X
in Barton on the moro erly. Toward 7 ours if
you ken be there.

"It was Ling read it for me, and she said it looked a pretty poor effort, but she said too you had hardship writing, so that was that."

I flushed to hear that much, but Esther breezed on. "When that Hasp saw me in the stable, he didn't know my name, but you were told it right well by me, so that should've been fair warning. Foxy boy indeed! But I was that keen to have the grass, I never heeded. My old Dido was put off the priest's apple field yesterday, and there's nowhere left in town will have her that she hasn't munched down to bald. They want to take her off me too, so I'd do anything, you see."

She went to the small gap that did for a back window, without an inch's worth of glass or shutter across the space.

"There she is, Thomas Rose. My Dido, same age as myself, thirteen. We were born the same day, back when I had a mother and a father, both."

I peered out at the muck yard.

I'd not say it to her, but the first thing I thought of was the roan, the day Ling and I first saw that poor beast on the road. Dido had the same thinness, and her coat was hardly better than the roan's, though there was nothing wrong with this one's eyes, and her legs seemed trim enough under the splashes of mud. She was small-sized, no higher at the withers than our Ox. Under the rain she was gray as the weather, but no doubt she'd come whiter when the sun shone and she was clean.

"We'll take her with us now and get some oats out of them," Esther said, fierce. "That Hasp won't make peep in the stables above, after all this business, and it'll be quiet up there, anyways, because the lady and boy are going out in the carriage. Ling will think of something— you'll see."

She would have to. So would I.

"Let's be going, then," I said. "I have news for her."

She looked at me, suddenly impish, like Nan when she had some trick or other.

"She'll be right sorry it didn't work out. The grass for Dido, I mean. She said she was faring to think you might have a proper heart in you after all, Thomas Rose."

The Brown Dress and the Barley Tail

BUT LING WAS in no mood to make mock of me, or to sample Esther's honey either, though she took a little time to admire Dido. She ran a hand over the mare's short neck and put her head to the chest and gave out her opinion that, despite all the odds, the mare was sound.

"You look after her like her *maman*, Esther," she said. "If only my Belladonna had time to show your Dido what it is to be a white horse of the *haute école*, then we would see something."

Esther made a little show with her mouth, but you could see she was pleased pink. Far too pleased to take note of the words let loose into the stable, or the stiff voice that had said them. Instead, she started rattling off what had happened down at the marketplace and afterward at the wharf.

"That Thomas, he isn't so bad after all, you know. He helped me, Ling, he did. The way he said things, well, they just had to listen. He said I had a jobbing horse and a grandmother to feed and I was but eleven. Eleven!"

Ling nodded. She reached for my hands and raised them to her lips. But her eyes were full of something dark dragged from the bottom of a well, and so it was I who spoke.

"Esther, you take Ling's combs and see what you can do with your Dido to make her smart."

Esther raised an eyebrow to hear the likes of me giving an order in the stable, but she set to anyway and seemed glad enough to have the fine tools for it. The dust from Dido's mud patches rose and then settled over everything close by. She sneezed and sneezed.

"What did you mean 'if Belladonna had time'?" I asked Ling.

The blades of her cheekbones were sharp as knives; her skin was drawn that tight over them.

"The boy goes to school next week, Thomas, and so

the whole household goes to London. Only Julia from the kitchen and your *meilleur ami,* Monsieur Hasp, will remain here. Milady told me that this morning. She sent for me to the house."

She took a breath in, and I knew then that she'd been crying before we came. I reached my arm around her and she put it back by my side, but gently, as if it were a valuable thing. "*Pas maintenant,* Thomas."

Tohmah.

"She tells me that Belladonna must travel all that way too, so the boy can practice his riding whenever it is possible for him. I am to bring her so far, if that is my wish, to ride on her back all the way, beside the carriage and the carts. This is not for my pleasure, of course, but for Belladonna, in case she will have fear on the long journey. But there will be no place for me in the city, not even in the stable, like here. Belladonna will have her lodgings in a special *pension pour les chevaux,* near to Master John's *pension,* his school."

Her own little nostrils flared, like a horse's. She thumbed me on the chest, as hard as before she'd been soft. "Your *dear* Mr. Stubbs, he tells her all about this horse *pension* and gives her the name of it, says it is dry and well aired and will make a good stables for my Belladonna. Did he tell you that?"

I shook my head. My stomach churned. "He said something about the school, yes, but not that."

She lifted her shoulders. "So you see. *C'est la fin.* I must take her away today, for now they make a visit to some other milord, and nobody is here who has a care. They are all inside because of the rain. The pigman, who might hear me, is drunk, and the donkey men have gone to the town. I will take her through the passage so nobody will see. If you had not come so soon, you would find I was all gone too. Eh *pouf,* like that."

She blew a puff of breath toward me. "I wanted to see you, Thomas. I would have stopped in your village, to tell you this. But not with a bell, *non.* Not this time."

I wanted to believe her.

She was staring hard at the two round rumps of the mares, so close together, one white with a tail of barley, one gray white with a white tail. Only now did I notice that she had all the fine clothes on, the jacket tightly buttoned over the frilly shirt, the breeches tucked neatly into the boots. Her dress no longer hung across the stall. Belladonna was saddled and bridled, and a sack of something hung from the saddle. Likely oats for the road.

"Oh, Ling. They will find you."

I stopped. Ever since I knew — and I had always known — that she would run from this place, I had not been able to rid my head of a story Jack Proctor had told us. Jack had been there, so he'd seen it for himself. A kitchen maid hanged in Doncaster after the last assizes.

And for what? Because she had taken the full arm off her master with a carving knife.

"It didn't matter, not her age, which was seventeen, nor that he was after her like a dog, they hanged her anyway. And they do the same to horse thieves and sheep gangers too, if the judge is minded for it, God blast them."

Mother had put Jack out of her kitchen that day, first for telling the cruel story in front of Nan, and then for his curse.

Ling was shaking her head, warning me off. "Useless to open your mouth, Thomas, for I will not listen. You know that Belladonna is mine. If I do not have her, I do not care for my story anyway."

There was no talking to her. If she was to go, she should go as fast and as soon as possible, and I had to keep my fears bottled up in my own head.

"What way will you go, Ling? Where is your . . . the company gone?"

"I will go to York. I know some Rom people there. They will keep me."

Again, she'd said no word about the company, and so I knew at last the Dane must have thrown her out or given her up when she went to hunt for Belladonna. I tried to think, though my mind was thick as mud.

"Best, then, you go the back way, like you say, and when you're safe out of Baysgarth, climb the scrub up the wold. You saw the way I went, going southwest all the time. When you get near Horkstow, come off the road and take the lane instead, for you don't want to come out near the church. There's always people there, gossiping. Make for the shore then, and follow it, because you must go as far as Winteringham to take a boat across the water."

That was as far distant as I knew. After that she herself knew more. York! Even Father had never been to that city. But she waited for each word as if it were a piece of silver dropping from my mouth. When I stopped, she pulled my head down, just as she'd done before, and kissed me on the mouth, but it felt nothing like the last time. It was a piece of business. No, that was not fair. It was more that the world itself had taken us and thrown a sack over our affections, and from now we had no time for sharing anything but facts.

Ling moved to lead Belladonna from the stall.

"Ling, no!"

She turned.

"Go to the Clock's house instead," I said, nearly out of my skin for thinking of what I might have put her to. "It's Sunday, so there'll be no boats. I forgot that. The Clock won't go out today, and he'll keep you safe if you ask him. Don't mind that he's odd, for you can be sure he'll not utter a word to anybody."

I told her where she would find his house, low and hidden in the long spike grass that grew by the shore just beyond the Ancholme crossing. I'd never been inside the place, nor had anyone in my family, unless Mother at Christmas. Nobody from the village would go near it either. The Clock wasn't feared, but he was looked on as a trial and best avoided. If he was shocked to find her at his door, he'd say nothing to anybody. I hoped she'd be another Zachary pup to him.

"I'll come there later tonight. I'll bring whatever I can find for you. Go!"

She was up on Belladonna then, and they were gone out of the stable in a burst of air and a confusion of birds. But when the noise was done, it was as if they had never been in that place at all.

Esther stirred then. She dropped the horse combs on the floor, one by one, and came to stand by me. "Listen, Thomas," she said. "That Hasp and his woman are in the front room of the house, stuck to the seats, letting on they are fine folk. I saw them when we came, while you led my Dido across the paddock. This is what you'll do."

She told me.

So, while I filled a sack of feed from the grain barrel by the door, Esther fished out Ling's dress from under the bed of straw and pulled it over what she already wore. It hung like a tent on her, for when all was told, she was still only like the thinnest of lads, a right stick of celery.

She took strings of straw then and, quick as a hay-maker, bound them around Dido's tail, so that when she'd finished, the horse appeared to have only a rat's tail hanging from her quarters. But if it was a rat's tail, it was also the color of barley.

She dipped down again by the straw bed and rootled around, coughing as she did. "Here."

She held out the dark-red silk kerchief to me. "She forgot this, and it won't cover all my red, so you take it and mind it for her, Thomas Rose."

Well, this item was turning into a proper holy relic for me. I folded it and slipped it into my pocket. Esther tied her hair back with the piece of blanket from her shoulders so that no bright strands stuck out to give her away, short though they were.

"There! I look like a fish girl, I know it, never like Ling in a hundred years, and there's my poor Dido, who needs all the eye-dazzle she can get too. But I'd say we'll pass for her and Belladonna on a misty day like this. If that dirty maggot gets a view of me from the door of the house, he'll see me and Dido heading east for the village of Barrow, and others will too, for that's the way I'll make sure they'll see me take. And all the while Ling is going your way. Go now!"

I ran through the archway and took the path to the front of the house, the wide face of it, and all the cruel unblinking windows, with the rain driving against them. The brass clapper on the door had an animal's face. I picked it up and smashed it down, then again, and again.

It was worth anything to see Jem Hasp's face. He opened and shut his wet mouth like a fish, and behind him his Julia was dabbing her apron to her face, not a word left in her.

"I came to tell you that my father will be coming after you for what you did this morning," I said. "In case you thought you'd get away with it, for you won't. I have the letter you sent and the one the boy got too."

He said nothing, but I waited and watched until I saw his eyes open wider than my bit of bluster would ever give cause for. So I turned then and followed his gaze. If I squinted, what I saw at the end of the avenue was the quick trot and turn of a white horse with a yellow string of a tail and a girl on top. The girl kicked her animal, just a touch of bare legs showing under a dull dress. The horse bucked at the kick and whisked its tail. They passed through the gates, turned right, and were gone.

Home

HUGH LAID THE FISH on the kitchen table beside the bowl of new-dug potatoes. A brown trout longer than his forearm, with a fat yellow belly and spotted back. I ran a finger against the scales so that they rasped against my skin. I yawned. I was washed and dry now, in fresh clothes, and if I could I would put my head down on the table beside the trout and sleep. But the evening ahead would be as long as the day past.

"So clever you are with your fishing lines, Hugh," Mother said. "But was it proper to be doing that on the

Sabbath?" She shook her head, but not only at Hugh, at me too.

"Mother, I never caught this one!" said Hugh. He laughed and held his hands far apart for her. "A trout so big needs proper feathery flies and all the time in the day to work it. Father and I met old Pell coming our way, and he gave us the fish as goodwill for that big old wain we fixed for him."

He looked sideways to check that Nan had her ears open and gave me a dig. "Old Pell said he didn't know that his horse was become a Christian since it died. But he believes there's a marker stone standing where the poor thing fell last week. He was wondering, Did someone christen the animal without him knowing? Percival Pell?"

Nan darkened and burst out. "That was his *name*. Old Humphrey told me that himself! And why shouldn't a horse have a stone for its life? I showed it to Tom's Mr. Stubbs when I met him this morning, for I wanted to plant it early when the ground was so soft. And he said I had a good heart and made a good effort doing what I did, when I'm only ten!"

"Hush, don't row," Mother said. "What did that man send you across to Appleby for, Tom? When the day was Sunday and raining enough to float Noah off his mountain?"

I still had no proper story in my head that she'd believe. What was the word Esther had used? *Eye-dazzle.* Trick them. I turned to Nan.

"So you met Mr. Stubbs and you liked him? There, Nan, I told you he wasn't half bad a man when you get to know him. He's worth a drenching or two. Tell Mother what he's like."

And she was off. When Mr. Stubbs had seen what she was doing with the stone, he took the little chisel from her hand and graved the prettiest horse's head under the "Percival Pell."

"He had a charcoal stick in his pocket, and he blacked the lines so they show up nice for me. I told him the head was too pretty for such a big horse, but he said he did it that way for me because my cheeks were rosy and jolly. That's what he said."

She blushed, Mother smiled at her, and I marveled at how easy it had been. Clever me and clever Stubbs, together. And clever Nan too, because she had remembered not to betray me.

Duck tales.

Hugh picked the trout up by its tail, pretended to stagger under its weight, and brought it out to the yard to clean it. We heard him call the cat to help him.

"Good old Tassie," I said. "She'll be fat and happy tonight." I wondered if the little black stable cat at

Baysgarth knew already that Belladonna and her mistress had gone for good. My eyes drooped.

When I opened them again, my head was on the table and my neck stiff when I moved. Father was sitting in the plain chair opposite, while I still held his. Everyone had a plate in front of them, with mounds of potatoes and white-fleshed trout and podded peas, all buttered and salted. I struggled up.

Father waved his knife at me. "Stay where you are. I'll send to that Stubbs and tell him you'll not be there tomorrow. Look at the state of you. Every worker needs his day of rest, even the likes of Thomas Rose. What were you doing in Appleby?"

"No, no." I sat upright and rubbed my eyes. "I'm right well, don't send to him. I was sent there for a package that came down from London, inks and chalks. It was no trouble."

Nor any trouble to me to think of that. I ate what was in front of me and then plundered the fish's bones to dig out more of it, it was so good. Poor Ling. She'd have to make do with the Clock's boiled duck this evening. That was supposing she'd landed there safe.

"I have to go down to Mr. Stubbs before dark tonight," I said. "He wasn't there when I left the package, and I don't know whether he stays here tomorrow or goes to the house in Barton. We may practice some letters, too. He teaches me, Father, when he has spare time. So don't wait on me. "

Mother looked so pleased to hear this last that I wished I could unsay it, even though there was a hank of truth there too. But of course Father was not won so easily.

"That's a rum thing that can't wait till morning," he said. "I'll tell you something else. I heard the crimpermen were out in strength in Barton all week, even up to the Sabbath today. Have you heard that, Tom, with all your new connections?"

Did my father know something, then? I answered carefully, picking my words. "I heard Jack say something like that, Father. I don't think I'd know one of them if I saw one, but I doubt they come down as far as the carrs to hunt for their men."

Father stared hard at me. His blue eyes on mine, the thick caterpillar eyebrow likely looking just as cranky on my face as it did yonder over his nose.

"Keep your wits tight about you, Tom, and think of what you're put to. Don't be gandering after anything else. Here. You forgot to take this bitty thing out when you put my poor wringing wet coat back on its nail."

Oh, but my blessed father had wrapped Ling's kerchief safe in a scrap of billing paper, so that it looked innocent as wool, or cheese, or a pair of spectacles!

Quickly, before Nan or Mother could catch a glimpse of the silk, I had it in my pocket and mumbled something back, surely boiling red all the while.

There was still a good ration of daylight when I left the house. Though the rain clouds had passed over at last, they had left the whole country to soak. Every leaf in the ditch carried a water jewel in its heart, and those that dangled over my head held drips on their ends, like an old person's nose. I steered my course in the middle of the road, passing the turn for the Stubbs house, passing Ottleys' place, heading straight for the Ferriby shoreline. I could cut through a meadow and take time off the walk by making a slant toward the crossing over the Ancholme.

There was a hare in the pasture. An evening hare, sitting still on its hunkers, colored like damp straw. When I narrowed my eyes, I could see that its ears twitched — but likely every part of its body was quivering — so that it was ready to run on the instant if it had reason. I'd bet it was a mother hare, and if I could see through her body, I'd find the young hare feeding underneath her. If a dog or a man were to come into the field, the mother would take off, zigzag, leading the enemy to follow her, away from her baby.

A boy was walking from the river. He made his way inside the pasture field, keeping close to the hedgerow.

He wore brown knee breeches and a brown shirt trailing loose, not tucked in. His face looked to be dark-skinned, and his black hair was very short, cut across the forehead into a fringe.

Perhaps the lad had been warned to take it stealthy in the field. But for all that he was brown like the hare, he was not as practiced in those ways as she was. For one thing, he hadn't learned to disguise his gait as he walked along the side of that field. He set his feet down as no village boy in the county of Lincoln ever would.

I looked across to where the hare had been.

She was gone.

Walnuts

As she came near to me, Ling was tugging at her short mop as if she might lengthen it that way, but instead it stood up on her head in points, like a hedgehog's prickles. If anything, she looked a rarer thing cropped, for now her dark eyes seemed to occupy a full quarter of her face.

She made a play of wrinkling up her nose, but she was smiling. "Thomas!"

Tohmah.

"I was coming to look for you. You are too slow, you *grandes girafes*! But what do you think? Am I not made a good and proper boy this Sunday?"

She stamped her left foot in its boot and thrust out that hip so the world could see the coral blade stuck into her belt. As if it were the mightiest sword and she some kind of knight at arms.

I grabbed her arm and pulled her down into the hedgerow, where nobody passing on the road above would see us against the sky. She had done just the same thing to me, oh, how long ago was it? Hardly at all but it seemed an age.

"Ling, you are mad. If they come out this way, looking . . ." I almost preferred not to tell her about Esther's dressing-up trick. If she didn't know that a little time had been robbed for her, she might keep herself sharper. She needed to.

The kitchen maid hanged at Doncaster. They do the same to horse thieves.

I told her all the same, and she clapped at the end, as if she could see for herself the neat turn and twist Esther had coaxed from Dido at the gate of Baysgarth House, all the better to show off the tail of barley straw.

"How clever is my Esther! And now she is a girl again and I am become a boy in her place. You know, Thomas, I think you would make a very beautiful girl. . . ."

She reached to pull my hair down, to wind it on her

fingers as long as it would stretch, but I caught her arm, so she kissed me instead, for my face was over hers and her head was almost against the ground, and then we found we had to lean back or fall, so we pressed as hard and as surely into that wet bed of ditch as if we were one creature.

Time moved strangely down there too. When I opened my eyes, it was almost full dusk.

Well, if the sun had bounced back up again and blazed right in front of us like a torch, I would say there was a better wonder in the world. Hadn't Ling and I found each other? Nothing should have fitted us together, but it had. We were our own place with its own map, in that ditch and everywhere else too. We had no need of sun, moon, or stars to light us.

It was Ling who untangled herself first and sat up. She picked the burrs and prickles off her brown clothes, and now I could see they were just the same clothes she had had on earlier, the Nelthorpe boy's, but baked dark. They were soaked through, and mine felt almost as bad. She stretched her legs out, patting smooth the seams of the breeches. Then she reached for my hair, the cause of all the trouble, and smoothed it back behind my ears. I had never seen her smiling so freely. Only she and God could see what my own face was at.

"We did an experiment, Monsieur Harkin and I,"

she said at last. "I did not want to dishonor this shirt of Master John, for it was a creamy white, like good Paris bread, except that Monsieur Harkin wanted to show me how he could turn it into this dark shade. The *pantalon* too. And his potion, it worked in an instant. And, look, my skin too. I am made into a proper Rom boy!"

She stroked my cheek.

"And so now that good man is believing that we can do the same for Belladonna. We can turn her into a dun horse! But he needs more potion. Thomas, will you help me find walnuts tonight? That is one reason why I was coming for you. To ask that of you."

Walnuts? Surely she did not mean to steal Stubbs's animal too? She slapped my hand as if I were a bad child.

"They are *nuts,* Thomas, nuts that live inside big green globes like the world. Monsieur Harkin told me where I would find trees, but I saw them long ago, even before I met you, *des noyers,* a field of them, growing in the garden of that big house past yours. I left two sacks by the river, one for you to carry and one for me. When it gets dark, we will go there and make the pick, yes?"

She meant the grange and the three great walnut trees that half hid it from the road.

I shook my head. "I'll fill them. You stay here, Ling, or much better, go back now and wait with the Clock.

It's too dangerous for you to be about. If I get caught, it means only a beating, but you, they will know at once just who you are."

She thought for a moment and then nodded. "You are right, Thomas. I agree. Thank you."

Away to the west, where the Winteringham ferry lay, well out of our view, the watery yellow light slipped away as if it were sorry for the rainy day just done. Soon it would be dark enough to set out for the grange. I had little fear of being seen. Only a bailiff lived there now, behind the main house, and the trees would hide me from the road. Even if I had to climb them to gather the nuts, it would not be difficult. I would be a giraffe, the animal so tall it grazes from the trees.

"So you won't leave tomorrow, then," I said. "But the next day?"

She nodded. "I think this is best, Thomas. It is a day later, which is not so good, but by then there will be no white horse to see, and I am already made a boy, so we will be safer. Monsieur Harkin, he is so kind. And so *intéressant* a gentleman, Thomas. You never told me this! But I did not see it, who sees everything. Remember, when I was at your table?"

I could hear her again, the bright bird singing to Mother and Nan and Hugh, my father and I apart, watching the performance. What had the Clock been doing while she sang? I couldn't remember.

"Ling, you must go back to the Clock's house now. Please. I don't know for sure that you can pass for a boy. Even with your hair cut so and the dark skin, you're too"—I searched for a word—"dainty. And you'll catch your death with those wet clothes."

She made a face. "Surely I am as good a boy as Esther, Thomas? She fooled you very well, remember, you and Jem Hasp! And I have been one before, you know. And remember you see me now, the way we are when we kiss, so of course you cannot think I am a boy. You do not see how I will be with others, when I act the part."

She put up her fists as if she would box with me. Then she laughed. "I can even make water like a boy, Thomas, when I have to. *Pisser comme les garçons.* Do you believe that?"

I blushed. What on earth could I say to that?

"If you walk with me down to the river crossing, Thomas, I will show you the clever path that Monsieur Harkin takes from there to his house. We will see you then later with the sacks of walnuts, coming to us like so— *un, deux, trois, loup!*"

Her hands swooped suddenly and clasped mine, tight, just as the crimpermen had done yesterday in the market-place. But no two actions could have been more different. I felt the warmth still spreading from my wrists as we walked, Ling making a great play to match my stride.

"I am like a cat who has many lives, Thomas. *Ne t'inquiète pas.* I have had more than one escape in my life, you know. In England too, not only in France."

For once she would not tell me much, only that the winter it happened had been very hard and that she'd been locked up in one of the rubbing-down houses on the course at Newmarket for stealing a duck.

"I had a piece of pipe to make my water like a boy, and a good thief beside me, just as *Notre Seigneur* had, on his cross. He helped me out. Now, Thomas, look, here we are."

She showed me where she'd stowed the sacks for the walnuts, kissed me quickly on the lips, and left. I stayed by the river, watching the small dark head moving through the long meadow grass until it became a speck.

Something made me turn then, suddenly. A crawling under the skin as if someone were watching me, someone too cowardly to show himself. I saw nothing, though I scanned all the world I could see, as far back as the road above the village. The only eyes I could see belonged to a pair of dead crows tied to a cross brace. Though there was hardly a breeze, they swung a little, rotting their warning to all their brother and sister crows left in the world.

The House of the Hare

IF I LIVED TO BE as old as Jane Brice—no, if I lived to be a hundred—I would never forget what I found that night when I came to the Clock's house with the two sacks crammed with hard green walnuts.

If a hare could build a house, it would look just so. It was low to the ground and faced with thick hardwood planks, not with bricks. The winds had seasoned them so that the timber was turned a silky gray, almost the same shade as the sand. A plume of smoke curled up from the small chimney at the gable end.

I knocked softly on the door, three times. "Mr. Harkin," I called. "It's Thomas."

"*Entrez,* Monsieur Thomas!"

Well, that was a voice I knew. I lifted the latch and pushed open the heavy door. And there I would have stayed, my big feet stuck to the doorsill and mouth open for flies, for Lord knows how long, if Ling hadn't run to seize my hand and pull me properly inside the house. She closed the door firmly.

"Well, Thomas, what do you think?" she asked.

Think? How could I think? All I knew was that this room would be in my head for always, like my four stone men on the church pillars, like Ling that first day, climbing out of the ditch and making the shape she did. Or like some of the sights in Stubbs's kitchen. They too would never leave me.

Though the sky outside was black as a cloak, there was no candle lit anywhere in the long single room that made up the house. Only a great blaze of driftwood and old timbers in the hearth sent the gloom packing at all, into the corners. But the fire did more than light the room.

Consider what it did to the fiddles!

There were so many of them hanging on the far wall, and the flame light rippled across them like water dappling in sunlight. The fiddles were all shaped the same, each with a waist and curves and two holes the shape of a dried leaf cut into them, but they came in different sizes. The smallest was no bigger than Mother's Bible book, but the largest one was such a giant that it didn't hang but stood on its side on the floor, big as a barley sack. That one was not yet stained or polished, but had the same raw color as a newly shaven spoke.

The side I had come in had a different look. The Clock must have made the thick shelves that stretched most of the way along the wall between the door and the hearth. But he hadn't stocked them with books or crockery or anything homely. I moved closer to see what was laid out on them.

Everything here was broken, as if it came from a needy shop. Bits of pottery, old hooks, some crusted coins, a couple of ancient knives like bayonets. Perhaps they were bayonets. A quernstone in two halves. A fishing reel so eaten up with rust that Hugh would throw it back into the water. I could see only one thing that seemed whole. It was a brooch, or perhaps a fastening, carved to look like a hare seen from the side. Long ears folded over its back, and its long legs were bent for leaping. *The house of the hare,* I thought.

At the other gable end, facing the fire, was the Clock's bed, a small four-poster that Nan would have cried for. She'd have laughed, too, to see the puppy, Zachary, laid out there like a biscuit on a plate, on a folded plaid blanket.

Tethered to one of the bedposts was Belladonna. She stood easily, one hind hoof raised, as if this warm place were the stall she had been wanting all her life. She had changed into another creature, or almost. One side was still white, but the other had smooth brown patches, like a gypsy horse, and her head was dark as a mole's. Her tail and mane were no longer the color of barley, but had the bronze of beech leaves in winter.

In front of Belladonna, the Clock was bent over a great pot. Now he stood up to greet me, leaving a stained cloth to hang over the edge of the pot. His hands were black as pitch.

"Welcome, Thomas Rose," he said. Still only a whisper of a voice, but there was something new in his face.

"Do you know how we did it, Thomas?" Ling pointed at Belladonna. "It was Monsieur Harkin's secret. He uses the oil for his violins and makes them pretty and strong with the stain. You must soak the green walnuts first and then you boil them. That's how I am become so dark, and now my Belladonna is a half-dark horse, and you have brought the rest to make her whole."

She slid the sacks I'd filled along the floor to the cauldron.

"Now you must go, Thomas. We will be busy here and I am safe. You can see that."

I still stared, for it would hurt not to. I stood there silent for so long that in the end Ling stood on my boots and pulled down my face, in the way she did. She kissed me again, even though the Clock was only feet from us.

"Please come here tomorrow night, Thomas. But now go home."

And so I had, and I stole through Mother's kitchen with my boots in my hands and the hare cottage and its magic within my head.

Who on earth could have imagined any of these things?

The Head

I WAS TO WORK under Mary Spencer's orders all the next day because Stubbs had already left when I arrived at the smokehouse. Mary was standing by the door when I lifted the latch. She pulled me inside, then poured my cup of milk, as was her habit, spilling a little.

"The white mare, Thomas! Oh, there is such a rumpus at Baysgarth. Your little friend Ling is in very great trouble. You must know that, Thomas. You must press her to bring the animal back straight, and then maybe it won't go that badly for her."

I tried to make my face drain away as Ling did hers,

but I wasn't sure I had the secret of it. "What do you mean?" I asked. "I haven't seen her."

She put her head sideways, like a bird, and considered me for a long moment.

"Are you standing there drinking our milk and telling me you do not know what I am talking about? I heard you were in Barton at the house yesterday."

I reddened at that. Was there anywhere I went that I was not spied upon by somebody?

"Yes, I had some bother," I told her, "though it wasn't at the house but in the town. That Jem Hasp, who works in Baysgarth, tried to have me pressed for the navy, and another boy too, a young fellow from the town, called Ezra Quickfall."

Well, that was news to Mary Spencer—that was clear. Her face looked much as mine must have done last night, when I'd stood in the doorway of the Clock's house.

"I don't know which end of the world is up—I can tell you that, Thomas Rose. That very man you talk of was here today at the crack of dawn to waken George and bring him back to Baysgarth. As if he were to blame for what happened there yesterday! But this man Hasp said you were there while the French girl—only he calls her the gypsy—took off on the mare, taking the road to Barrow. They haven't found her yet, though he said any number of people saw her galloping on the way."

It was difficult to show an innocent face to *that*, but I did my best. "She told me she was riding out to check the path of the hunt for Master John, no more than that. I was up at the house to tell Hasp he'd not get away with what he'd done."

I told Mary then exactly what had happened to Ezra and me at the marketplace and down by the wharf. She tut-tutted, *for shame, the bullyboy,* and the like, but then she was back to her own big story again.

"That Hasp says Lady Nelthorpe has all the constables along the Humber vowed to take the girl whenever she may be spotted. He said he had never seen the mistress so full of wrath. For sure, she will belabor my poor George for bringing the girl into her society at all. And he told us the boy wept all evening when they found his little mare gone."

Well, that was a sorry thing, and when I said so, I meant it after a fashion. I had no quarrel with that lonely boy who looked to Ling for his light. I did the same.

"Oh, I don't know, Thomas. He has money enough to sweeten the sour things of life. My care is all for George and his position. How could he know this would happen? And fool that I was, I took the girl in here for a night too. Such deception."

She took the cup from me and picked up a large bunch of grasses and flowers that lay on the table. Stubbs had left careful instructions, she told me. What he required of us both this day was to prepare a clean skull from the roan. In that way he'd be able to make his studies of it at any time, even if he were sitting up in his bed, tired out from painting at Barton.

Mary wrinkled her fine straight nose. "It will not be pleasant work, Thomas. But if you will do the cutting of the head, I can take care of the heating and rendering. We don't boil it, for then the fat would make the bones yellow, so it has to be minded all the time and cold water added. We have our own copper for this, and George carried it up to the house before he left. Wait till you see the size of the thing. Truly you will think a witch had it first!"

But my heart was heavy when we left the smokehouse to go to our work. With constables waiting along the river, all that stood between Ling and the kitchen maid's end was the trick stuff with the walnuts. Who could have faith in that?

"We have no linnet today," I said to Mary when we went inside the house. She began straightaway to spread the fresh grasses over the dried ones of the other day. Still bending, she shook her head.

"I had no chance since, Thomas. You'll have to be my bird today and talk to take my mind away from what we do here and what fares now up in Barton."

Well, I thought, *I can do that only if I stop my own mind turning over all the dangers and traps the world holds for Ling.*

That wasn't going to happen soon, if ever. And there were other notions deeper down that I had no wish to turn over. For the truth was that if Ling came through all, safe and sound, I would never see her afterward.

The smell in the kitchen was an evil blast to the face, and I couldn't reach fast enough above the door to stuff the wax into my nostrils.

"Best turn yourself outside in," Mary said. "Don't think about what you have to do; just do it. I can't open the windows in here, for the flies would make everything worse."

She gave me the great bow saw that hung on the back of the kitchen door. "I'll be in the other room preparing everything else," she said. "If you need me, just call out."

If I think that it is just a tree, I said to myself. If I remember that it had a better death than its life. Out of the strength came forth sweetness. Pegasus was born from a monster's head. *Barbe bleue* was the bluebeard killer, not I.

All this jumble rattled around in my head, and my hands shook and slipped, because in general they were kind enough hands, but I carried off the butchery in the finish. Then, with my nose and mouth closed fast as a trap, I carried the head and neck over to the table.

"I've put the head on the table, Mary," I called out.

"I must go outside for a bit. I'll bring it over to the pot for you then."

Then I ran to the door and made it round to the side of the house before I had to stop. I vomited into a patch of nettles, everything sour and foul I had inside me. When it was all gone from me, I stood there, shivering. The wax had come away from my nostrils, and now I gulped the fresh air of harvest into every part of me.

I washed my hands in the water barrel and picked a long dock leaf to dry them. When I came back to the door, Mary was waiting for me.

"Poor Thomas," she said. "Let us sit down outside for a while and draw a decent breath."

She took my hand and deftly turned it palm upward. She was still staring at it when she spoke. "I'm not fooled, Thomas Rose. I don't know what it is you know, but it's more than you tell. It's true she's a fine-looking girl, and more."

Furious, I tried to take my hand back, but she held onto it.

"I'll tell you this one thing that might soften it for you. The night she stayed here, I took her palm in mine just as I have yours here now. She has the long line in her hand, this one here, the life line. You have it too, Thomas. See, here, where it goes snaking round the mount of your thumb?"

I stared at the net of lines traced on my palm. If my mother knew I was hearing this kind of talk, she'd make me scour pots for a week. Jiggery-pokery never got past Susan Rose's doorstep.

"George has the long life line and I have it too," Mary said. "But not everyone has it. I never knew my father, for he was killed on a ship before I was born, but I was told his line of life ended right here."

She pressed my palm, somewhere in the middle, and she sighed. "Remember that when all seems dark. Life is what counts."

Vitriol

.

IT WAS ALMOST TWILIGHT when Stubbs returned. The rooks from the trees up on the wolds were already wheeling in strings above their nests, calling out before they settled.

I was glad to stay and eat in the smokehouse with them, because when I left I'd be closer to the Clock's house. I didn't intend to return home that night. When Mary and I had finished our butchery work and were walking down the meadow, I'd thought I might see the Clock go by up on the road, but there was no sign of him. Perhaps he'd already passed. Perhaps he'd thought to tell some story to Father. Perhaps he'd say I was to call to him later that night after my work was done.

It was no matter. By the next night, Ling would be gone, and I would take whatever punishment was to come my way. Soon enough too, my father would hear the true story of the crimpermen, just as he'd learn about Ling stealing away with her barley-tailed mare. In Father's eyes there would be so many parts to my guilt that this night's ramble would count for little.

I was weary as I'd never been before.

We'd heated water and scraped, Mary Spencer and I, lifted and emptied, then heated and scraped again, and in the end, we had a passable skull to offer Stubbs. It was much lighter at the finish, because there was only a little stubborn flesh left on the long bones. But it still stank. I would not care to have such a thing on my bed. Yet now that it was bare, it had an odd beauty.

Stubbs lifted the skull easily and admired it. "All the putrefaction gone or nearly!" he said. "I'll take the rest off with a dilute of vitriol. We'll soak it out in the open air overnight. No creature will touch it because of the acid it stands in."

He held up his hand to Mary's questions and said he'd tell his news when he was done with the skull. She had some bacon hanging and made busy with that, grumbling, while I peeled potatoes.

"So, tell us, George, what did the lady say?" she asked when we sat down at last.

He blew out a breath. "They haven't caught the girl yet."

I was ahead of him on that score, of course, but I had to show my hand for what they knew it to be. "That's good news," I said. "She deserves to go free."

"But are you blamed, George?" Mary asked, after a quick eyebrows-up study of me.

Stubbs laughed. "Probably. But she knows it was not in my interest, any of it. And she gets the boy's portrait for nothing. I told her that."

He looked over at me. "A cool customer, your little friend. I pity her, though, when they catch up with her. But my surrender of the portrait fee will cover twice over what the lady paid me for the mare. She likely won't see it that way, of course."

The smallest flame lit inside me. "Does that mean Ling would not be hanged if they caught her?"

They both looked at me and then at each other.

"A relation would have to be made between the two matters," Stubbs said slowly. "And since it is I who am left more truly at the loss now, it is I who would have to provide that knowledge to the judge. But would I do so? That's a question to ponder. It truly is, Thomas."

It was safer to say nothing, absolutely nothing.

"And I hear too that you could perhaps bring a case of your own, if you cared to," he said to me.

Where had Stubbs heard that? Mary had said nothing of it yet, and surely Jem Hasp would be the last to spread the story of the impress men who had spat him out in the end, for all his plotting. It must have been gossip in the stables.

"My father doesn't know about that adventure," I said. "I think it's best he doesn't find out, if possible."

Silence.

Stubbs was looking at me, his forehead all furrowed up, as if he were suddenly seeing something very wrong with me. I held his eyes, but I feared what this man, who could map the inside of a great head, was able to discover in mine.

"Thomas, you cannot go back to your mother looking like that!" he said in the end. His laugh was a great bark of a thing. "She'd be down here tomorrow with a stick to beat me out of the parish for sending her son out into a bloody battle."

I looked down and for the first time saw the filth I was wearing. I was like the worst of men. Stubbs looked over at Mary, who nodded.

"Mary will give you one of my clean shirts," he said, "and I'm sure we have some breeches there to fit also. Now I'll bid you good evening, lad. I want my peace, and to sketch a little, and you've had a hard day. I'll not set you a lesson, but you'll bring me something scribed next time and we'll read it together."

I took the clothes Mary gave me and stepped outside to put them on. The shirt was a little too short for my arms and waist, but the gray breeches were fine, if a little scratchy, being winter weight. Carefully, I took all I had in my own pockets and palmed them into the pockets of the new breeches. When I reached the river, I'd clean the scraping knife I'd thieved. I'd return it when there was no further need for it.

That was Ling's counsel. *You should carry one of these too, Thomas.*

"You won't have to do the like of today's work again," Mary said when I came back to the door to bid them good night. "So I would simply leave those poor carrion clothes in the meadow for the fox."

That was sound advice. But when I thanked her for all she had done, she only raised her brows again.

"I would give more than a silver penny to know what you have in your own skull tonight, Thomas Rose. Go carefully."

Putrefaction

WHEN I HEARD the chink and fall of pebbles, the sound was so close that I looked first to my own feet. But I was walking on clay, the first soft clay of the river path.

I spun around.

Bart Ottley and Jem Hasp must have waited for me to pass them, the fools in their big boots. If they had hung their footwear around their neck and kept their distance, they might have followed me all the way, and I'd have thought any splashings I heard were made by otters or fish. I thanked the Lord for their stupidity. That much, at least.

"Where you going, 'prentice boy?"

Hasp was trying to mimic the ups and downs of my voice, that was clear. But he dropped that play in his next words. "My young friend here has a notion we should take an interest in where you're off to now. He was watching you out strolling abroad yesterday evening when you should have been with the painter man. He thought you might have better company in mind."

My gut twisted. I remembered how I'd watched Ling make her way toward the Clock's house through the sand grass, feeling eyes on me in turn. Perhaps Bart Ottley had been watching her too, reckoning where she went. I looked at him, and he licked his lips nervously and stared into the dark water.

"I don't know what you're talking about," I said to Hasp. "But *you*, Bart?"

It was so very difficult not to reach out and pinch Bart Ottley's pigeon chest.

"My father gave you good work when nobody else did, didn't he?"

"It wasn't a fit for me," Bart whispered. "I'm for better than planing stinkwood with worm in it."

"Pity you didn't settle with Jem Hasp, then, to get you proper work on the wherries in Barton," I said. "But I'd say he's not liked so well down on the wharves any longer."

Hasp's mouth twisted.

"Oh, but the wind might just change, Mr. Hasp," I said. "And leave you there as a gargoyle." For a gaping evil gutter spout was all the man was.

"*What* did you say?"

Gingerly as I could, I felt in my pocket for the scraping knife. I wondered if any shout I might make would be heard by Stubbs or Mary. But the walls of the smokehouse were likely as thick as those of the killing house, and besides it was too far distant.

"It's not for you to ask, but I'm picking up eels for my brother," I said. "Eels don't like too many bodies around them. They knit themselves into knots then and make bad flesh. So leave me be and move on home."

There was a time when Hugh kept eel pots up and down the river. That was no lie, and Bart would know that. But I couldn't reckon with what he might have seen the day before. Had he seen Ling in the brown boy clothes when he saw me? Or was this talk just a hazard? Had he seen the two of us together in the ditch?

That thought gave a right cold kick in my belly.

I turned my step upriver, away from the crossing place. If I had to stay out all night to guard the river and prevent these two from going over it, I would. But supposing Ling came looking for me? She would—oh, she would do *that*.

"Slippery creatures, eels are," said Hasp.

He was following so close behind me that his boot toes kicked against my heels. He grabbed my loose wrist and pulled it, stretching the arm back up, bending it, turning it until one further twist would surely break it.

But it wasn't I who shouted out then, who screamed. "Aagh, my hand! I'll kill you, you dog!"

I held up the bloody knife so that the two could see it clearly. "You'll not," I said.

Hasp clutched his right arm where shiny blood, black in the night, was pooling over his wrist and dripping over his leggings. He was too shocked to move against me again for now, that was clear. Neither of them had a weapon, it seemed. They must have thought little enough of me, the fools, and they were paid for it now.

"Do you see this blade?" I hissed. "Every inch of it is covered in"—I had to grasp for the word but it came—"putrefaction. Filth, to you. You know Mr. Stubbs. But do you know what he does when he's not painting your fine little master? He cuts out scabs and cankers and dirty parts inside bodies, and this is the knife he saves for the very vilest work."

My voice was good and deep now. Perhaps I'd turned the corner at last and become a man in a week.

"It's like the black plague, Hasp," I said, pointing at his arm. "It's in your blood now, and there's only one thing you can do. Go get a salve, and if you don't get it into your flesh soon, you'll likely die before the night is out, not later."

Lord knows, my words might come true. Hasp was become like a ghost; he was white as the rising moon and shaking all over.

"I'll tell you this, though you'd be no loss, either of you: Jack Proctor keeps a salve in his place that he got off the gypsies. If you go and ask him nicely, he might give you some. You too, Bart Ottley, for you'll know where to find him. Run there, fast as you can."

I slapped the flat of the knife across Bart's hand. There was no way of knowing if that blow drew blood, because he screeched like a stuck pig and held his hand up to his chest. I lifted my knife again, and the two backed from me along the water, until they reached the path. Hasp nearly fell there, but he got no help because Bart sped ahead of him.

I waited until I had no sight left of them, though I could still hear Hasp's breathing, a sob in it, as they stumbled up the path toward the village road.

Marron

THE FIRE BLAZED again in the Clock's house. The fiddles hadn't moved either, though the large one now had a coating of the bitter-smelling walnut brew. But something was different in the room, and it wasn't only Belladonna.

"My beautiful princess is now a true *marron, n'est-ce pas?*" Ling said. She had hardly lifted her head to greet me. "She is a chestnut made out of walnuts. But she and I will make *marrons* of everyone else, because *être marron* is to be fooled. See how clever our French words are,

Thomas, while your English is like porridge. That is how we will win the war, with our words."

But there was no winning the war in her voice.

I stroked Belladonna's brown flanks, and the little mare nudged my arm to greet me back, gracious as ever. Nobody would say she was an ordinary one, that was for sure. A person with an eye for horseflesh would see the swagger Belladonna had when she moved. But she was definitely a dark horse now, and dark horses were more common than white ones, especially white ones with golden tails. I sniffed my fingers and there it was, the slightest trace of a bitter scent.

"Will the color last when rain comes?" I asked the Clock. "Supposing it rains tomorrow like it did yesterday?"

The Clock shook his head. "I cannot tell you, Thomas. It takes a long time for the dye to leave my hands clean again—that's all I know. I do not know about hair, or about horse hair. Besides, it will not rain tomorrow. The sky tells us that."

His voice was a wispy thing, like something the fire draft would whip away up the chimney if he went too close. He was sitting on a bench near his big fiddle, Zachary at his feet, and the blaze behind seemed to throw a ring around his spare gray hair. A halo of light, not of cheese, like the one the man at the market wore.

But the Clock's face was bony and open, a proper saint's face. Tonight it was something else too. It was *happy*.

It was the females who had brought about this change to Henry Harkin. First Mary Spencer, then Ling. Even our little Nan had a special eye for the Clock, for she had noticed something only last month.

"Thomas, do you see how dirty the Clock's hands are? Every summer his hands go black, but he is not one bit ashamed of them. He waves them in the air whenever he stops sawing, and I hear him making tunes in his throat out in the paddock."

In all this time, no Rose except Nan had ever heard the Clock sing, or whistle, or make music of any kind. And yet he made fiddles!

As if he knew what I was thinking, the Clock spoke. "I go to Axholme every year," he said. "I bring a sack or two and fill them in the old woods that still stand there. Nobody bothers much with them now."

"He is so clever, Monsieur Harkin," Ling said in a low voice. She went to sit beside the Clock on the bench, laid a hand on his arm, and stroked it. "He finds treasures everywhere. When I am gone, Thomas, he will tell you about them all. He has promised me this."

It hurt me to see what had happened to Ling in just one day. Last night she had danced around the Clock's firelit room, pointing out this thing and that, all the wonders there were inside these four walls. Now she was as dark inside herself as she was in her skin. Cages were made ready in the marshes for creatures so wretched, like the ducks from across the sea. What could the likes of me ever do to prevent a trap springing close on Ling?

I couldn't bear it, nor could I bear another thought that weaseled in: that Ling regretted our encounter yesterday, that she wished me well away from her. I pushed that one back, hard. I would not lose *that* memory. Perhaps all she needed was to have a night's fit sleep, and who could blame her? I was not the one setting out into the world tomorrow with a price on my head.

Quickly, I told them how Jem Hasp had called at the smokehouse that morning, and the news Stubbs had brought from Barton. "So my Monsieur Stubbs has paid for Belladonna in his own way," I said to Ling. "That makes it a little safer for you, I think." I said nothing about Hasp and Bart Ottley down by the river. She nodded, but that was all she gave away.

I went to the door. "I'm going to sleep just outside," I said. "I think all will be well, but just in case someone calls this way tonight, I can shout watch to you. I have a good knife on me, so I'm safe. If you hear anything, Ling, anything at all, you must hide under the bed at once and pull the covers down over you."

It was such a small place to hide.

I pointed at Belladonna, brave new nut-brown Belladonna. "There's no law written down that stops Mr. Harkin from keeping his own brown pony inside his own house."

The pony the world knew he never had. They stared at me and heard out my threadbare thoughts in silence. Then the Clock got up. "I understand you, Thomas," he said. "But before you settle yourself to do that, I'll go and chop some more wood for those of us who'll be staying inside tonight."

Zachary whacked his string of a tail when I joined Ling on the bench. She lifted him up and held him so that he settled across both our laps and closed his eyes, happy to have our warmth.

"I know you are . . ." I began. What word should I say? Fearful? Lonesome? Abandoned? Loath to leave me? Loathful of me?

But what did I know? I knew nothing.

May Day

IT WAS ALMOST MAY DAY when Ling learned that Zéphyrine was going to have another baby. Her mother didn't tell her the news.

"And how could I think it, Thomas? Ever? She was too thin to nourish even the very littlest baby inside her. But Augustin told me there was a baby there. He liked to sleep under the wagons then because he was grown so tall. He heard Maman and the Dane talking about the name for the baby. The Dane wanted his own name for a boy, but Maman wanted a French name. Jean-Louis for a boy, Séraphine for a girl."

I could hear how precious those names were to Ling, even though her voice was dark and flat. She told me that the troupe had come to Lincoln for the feast of May Day. Two bitter winters hadn't killed anybody, the horses were enjoying the spring grass, and the Dane had a clever new production for the children to perform.

"It was a masque. He called it *Proserpina, or the Triumph of the Spring.* I was to play the goddess Proserpina, who comes out of the cold earth and breathes life into the world. My hair was long again, good enough for a goddess. Belladonna had flesh on her bones again. We had some meat on our plates at night. It was all good. Then Augustin tells me this, about the baby."

Ling went to find Zéphyrine. She had already forgiven her, because what else could she do? Her mother had lost so very much in her life, and perhaps this would make up for some of the losses.

"I think she was afraid of what I would say because it was the Dane's baby. I cannot say, Thomas, because I did not ask her why she kept the secret. There was no time."

Zéphyrine was in the wagon, but there was something wrong. She was bent stiff over her middle, like a prawn cooked in its shell, and the floor around her was wet.

"She said, 'Hélène, I think this baby is coming. Too early, again. Oh, *ma petite,* I am so sorry for everything.' I told her not to worry, that I would love the baby as if it were Sebastien."

But Ling knew something was wrong. She could see no sign of the baby, but heat had spread all over Zéphyrine's body, as if she had been dancing herself dizzy under the torches. She was still twisted over and in great pain.

"I went out of the wagon and made the noise of a lion. The Dane came in a rush, and when he saw how she was, he sent me off up the hill on Belladonna for the *sage-femme,* the birth woman."

Ling's eyes were closed. I could feel the terror she had as she searched the streets, calling out for the midwife she did not know. But there was more than one baby on the way that night in Lincoln, and it was a while before she found a woman who would get up behind her on Belladonna's back and come down the hill to the camp.

When they arrived, Augustin and Sylvie were waiting outside the wagon, like the sentries at the tomb of Jesus Christ. One look at their faces told Ling that Zéphyrine was dead. But the Dane had his son, a small perfect child with a frill of silver fair hair like a crown on his head.

The midwife took the baby away with her. She knew a wet nurse, she said, a woman who would understand the needs of such an early infant. That left Ling and the Dane to wash poor Zéphyrine and dress her in the only gown she had kept from her days of glory. She had lost so much blood that there was no weight in her, and her pretty face was white, like marble.

The Dane was white-faced too. "At least you'll have a little brother," he mumbled to Ling when they had done. I had Sebastien once too, she wanted to answer him. But she said nothing.

The next day, they buried Zéphyrine in the old graveyard in Lincoln. Afterward, down in the camp field, the Dane set fire to the wagon he had shared with her, just like the Roms do when somebody dies.

The Dane's Child

THERE WAS SILENCE in the room, except for the whisper of ash falling into the hearth and, sounding from outside, the clean chops of an ax.

"But, what happened to you then, Ling?" I asked. I felt a chill deep in my guts, as if I had swallowed her terrible story instead of hearing it. "What about the baby? You never said any of this before."

"He disappeared," she said in a flat voice. "The Dane, he pays the wet nurse for weeks, but one day he says it is time. He says he will take his child away to be on the road with us, that Kirsten and I will take care of him, as if we were his *petites mamans*. But when he went to her place, the wet nurse was gone away with the baby, and nobody knew where."

"Gone!"

Babies did not go anywhere unless they died, poor things. Mother had lost a boy before Nan was born, and she still mourned that little life, though neither Hugh nor I could remember it.

"You see, he was a very handsome baby," Ling said carefully. "I did not see him after he was born, but people said he was so fine that she must have taken him somewhere to sell him for good money. To people who had no child. But there was not a trace we could find. And after that, the Dane went mad. Truly. For a week or so he was *complètement fou*."

"That was when he sold Belladonna?"

"He sold *all* the horses, Thomas! He was crazy, but clever crazy, like a fox, *n'est-ce pas?* He sent us around to all the villages nearby to ask questions about new babies with white hair like a crown. Then, while we were out of the way, he took men and brought the horses to the fair at Brigg and he sold them. It was a fortunate thing that everyone there remembered Belladonna, and so they could tell me who had bought her. But Canigou and Tournesol and Basil and the others, they were gone, all our dear friends. Gone to work on farms, to be slaves." She ground her teeth.

"And the others? The others in the company? Augustin?"

"They all went south toward London. He told them they would find work in the theaters there; he wrote letters for them and gave them a little of the money he made from the horses. Augustin was keen to try that, but me, I did not believe it would be so easy. We are French, remember!"

She tried a toss of her head, but a sheep would have done it better. I closed my eyes.

"Anyway, I wanted to find Belladonna, so I would not go, not till I found her. But the Dane took Kirsten away with him. He said they would try to get a passage to Denmark from one of the ports in the north. He lost his spirit, I think, when he lost his son. I never saw him after that."

He lost his spirit. Please the Lord that Ling does not lose hers, not now, I prayed.

She straightened herself up and moved away along the bench so that no part of her touched any of me. Zachary grumbled and struggled after her, for the softer lap.

Her eyes were enormous. "Thomas, you think now that I am a monster. That is what I have the most fear of tonight, not the escape, not that at all. But I had to tell you this at last, because you did not know everything.

You think I am like some angel on a horse, and it is not true. I want you to know what is true, what I am. Then you can decide."

"How could I think that you are a monster? Why do you say that?"

"I say it because I have seen your family. So close you are! So happy together even when you are not, and your warm house around you like *this*." She picked up a walnut casing from the floor and held it out to me, tenderly, as if it were one of her trick eggs. Then she threw it into the blaze.

"But there was only my *maman* and me always, and wherever we lived, *n'importe-où*, and then a wagon on the road. And I could not let myself love that baby until I knew he would live, that he would be safe."

"But that was only good sense, after Sebastien."

Ling narrowed her eyes and watched me closely when she spoke again. "And also I could not love him because he killed my mother. There! He did that, even if he was only a baby. And worse, he was the Dane's child. He was more *his* child than he was *my* brother. That was what I felt when my mother died. And he was not safe after all, so I was right not to care about him, you see."

I said nothing.

Poor Ling. It was only a couple of months ago, or less, since all this had happened. In that time she'd lost first her mother, then the horse that was her best friend, then her companions. All the life she knew. Of course she'd had no room in her heart for the baby, when all these things happened the way they did. But why had she not told me this? If not at the beginning, then later?

I had my answer.

"I sing for my supper, Thomas." Her voice was not even a whisper now, but a breath. She was fondling Zachary's ears with her thin fingers, turning them over and back.

"I could talk to you like nobody else I meet in my life. *Bien,* I even said this to you one day. But I sang for *you,* too, Thomas, all along, I sang for you. *He will not want to know that the torches were truly all gone,* I said to myself. All the beautiful *étincelles* stamped into the ground and all the dancing stopped? No, Thomas will not want to know that! I thought you would forget me if I had no more stories. I thought they were my power over you as your . . ." She stopped, and I could hardly breathe in case she would not finish her thought.

"Oh, Thomas, you must know how I love you for being so *passionnant* and so quick, and your tall body like a prince. You see me and you like it, but you do not see this, the picture you make to others. You do not see how it is I feel for you."

There was blood flowing through my veins again, but she rushed on before I could think further, as if she had taken a vow to speak instead of to be silent.

"Until last night I thought that it was best if you did not know all this, if you remembered me as the French girl *sans pareille*, like nobody else. But then I could not sleep, even though Monsieur Harkin gives me his own bed. I wanted to tell you this so that you would know everything in the end. I wanted to be true, not cunning, *pas raseé*. Not with you."

She let Zachary's ears drop and reached to take my hands.

"Thomas, now that you know this, you can think of Ling what you like. Maybe Hélène was a better girl for you? But, anyway, we will both be gone from here tomorrow, Ling and Hélène." She closed her eyes and swallowed before she continued. "I want you to put a stone up for my mother. Now she has only a cross of wood with her name. The man in the *cimetière* will show you where it is, because he will remember me."

There was a flash across her face, whatever it was that *she* remembered. "The cross is there now, but when there is a winter storm, *pouf*. It will fall. Will you do this for me?"

I nodded. There was a lump I couldn't swallow, and so I couldn't speak.

"I have written the words down, Thomas. I do not know how you will do it, because I have no money for a stone, just a silver crown that your mother gave me that day." She lowered her eyes. "I stole her bread and then she gave me the coin. I was so ashamed, Thomas."

I found my voice at last. "Esther gave me this for you."

I opened Father's packet with the silk kerchief inside. This time she smiled. She took her own piece of paper with the words written for her mother, folded it inside the kerchief, and put the packet back in my pocket.

"You keep it for me once more. That makes three times you do this, yes? I will come for it one day. I will find you because I love you, Thomas. If I do not, it will be that I am put into the sky. Then you must look for a star called Hélène."

Before I could speak, the Clock came inside, stamping a warning ahead good and loud to us, as if his boots were the hooves of poor Percival Pell. His arms hugged a clutch of chopped wood.

"We should take our rest," he said. "It will be morning soon. I think we are safe enough now, Thomas. Sleep inside."

He threw some of the timber onto the fire, and the room darkened for a small while until the flames caught again. I told Ling she should lie by the hearth and that I would lie just inside the door. But she came to lie beside me there anyway, when I was settled. She placed her head on my shoulder, her head shorn of its warm scarf of dark hair, and I could feel her breathing, rising and falling, rising and falling. After a while I knew she was asleep.

Paying the Ferryman

CLOUDS HAD GATHERED over the estuary during the night, bunching together to the east like sheep in a pen. That was a good thing, for a bright sun might make harsh work of a horse painted chestnut from walnuts. But Belladonna looked sleek and smooth in the early morning light. If there were patchy parts to her coat, I couldn't see them.

The Clock insisted that Ling take his blanket. She wore it folded across her shoulders instead of the boy's long buttoned velvet jacket that would be known to the constables. She hid that and the tricorn hat deep inside her bag. The Clock had picked out some crabmeat for her, and some bread, and she wrapped the food in a linen handkerchief and put it in the bag too.

The best gift he gave her was the Irish cap made of heather-colored tweed. Ling gave a little whoop when she saw it. She twisted her cropped hair inside the crown and gazed up at us, her dark eyes half hidden under the peak.

"You look like a stable lad from Newmarket," the Clock said. A fiddler had given the cap to him long ago, he told us, in exchange for some little piece of craft he had worked.

We all walked, Ling leading Belladonna. The shore path was not a proper pathway, but sometimes people tracked along that way, and so the tall grasses that pricked like sword tips had been tamed a little. The Clock said nobody would be about before we reached the Winteringham ferry. All the same, we left Zachary behind in the cottage in case he caused more notice than we needed.

"Look," Ling said. She was pointing toward the water, only a little distance from the shore. I saw a creature leaping up and diving down again into the current. A great gray fish. Or was it a whale, perhaps? Jack Proctor often told stories of the things the whaling ships brought into port. This beast carried a fin above the water.

"*Le dauphin,*" Ling said. "I do not know the English word."

The Clock told her that it was a dolphin, a sea animal, bigger than a seal, not as big as a whale. "It likes to play and frolic in the deep water, as a child might in the shallows," he said. "At sea when you are lonely, a dolphin gives you heart."

The Clock had been to sea?

"Ah," Ling said. "But of course *le dauphin* is a prince too, the first prince of France. I saw our *dauphin* once! He was riding in a carriage with his wife and his little babies. My *maman* had the same name as his wife. Marie-Zéphyrine. The *monsieur* told us that. You will see her name on the paper I gave you, Thomas. It is the long word with a latch in the middle."

I stole a look at her. Her face was clear of all that had twisted her up last night. Her shoulders were back, and she picked her way along as quickly and neatly as Belladonna. My feet felt as if I wore shoes made of lead. For the first time in my life, I knew it was better to leave than to stay.

I love you, Thomas.

She had meant those words. I believed that. She hadn't made a song out of them but said them simply, as you say a prayer. She'd said more than I had, for all my passion. Perhaps she knew I needed to hear her words because of all the doubts I carried, like flies around my head.

By going along the sea path, we were able to skip the

village of Winteringham. Down at the ferry slip, all was quiet, though the boat was already tied up and rocking below. It looked sturdy enough, but Ling gave me the bridle to hold and tramped along down to it to check that it was fit for Belladonna. She came back, satisfied.

It was a good notion that we were gathered as a group, even if only Ling was to board the ferry. A lone rider would stand out and lodge in people's heads. The lady's constables along the Humber might set their noses twitching if they were to hear of such a passenger. Even a boy—even one with a chestnut horse. But there was nobody of that kind around, best I could judge.

We watched as a couple of men straggled toward the jetty. Behind them, in the village of Winteringham, a church bell rang. Some other people were coming from that direction now too, one of them on horseback.

The first to arrive were the boatmen. They said nothing, but one of them looked at me and held up three fingers in question. I shook my head and held up one of mine, signaling Ling and the mare.

"Horse aboard is worth another soul's rent," the man said. "More if I had my say." He told us what was owed. It was the Clock who paid the ferryman, though Ling began to go through her breeches pockets in a sudden fluster. She held up a fat silver piece, triumphant, and tried to give it to the Clock, but he waved it away.

"You'll need that," he said. Out in the air, the Clock's

whisper would tax the fairies to hear it. "The boy's mother meant for you to keep that."

"Look there," the ferryman called out, pointing. "There's another beast coming along now, so best aboard, boy, or lose your place, for I'll have only one horse along each way."

That was enough warning. When a couple of men had trooped up the plank, Ling let go of Belladonna's bridle and reached out to shake hands, first with the Clock, then with me. Her hand was small and warm and it pressed into mine.

A hand for a heart, I thought.

Her face was stone, what I could see of it under the cap. I wanted to bend down and kiss it, and the hand too, but that was impossible. My own hands were rough with chill, even the one that held Ling's. Perhaps I held it a little too long, for the ferryman grunted something.

Then Ling led Belladonna up the plank and settled her into the most suitable place at the stern, but facing forward, away from us. When six other passengers were on board, the ferryman held up his hands in a cross to forbid any more. The man with the other horse, a large cob, complained that he traveled every week and deserved to go first, but a man already on board put him down quick enough.

"Ye'll make Brough soon enough, Bert Dodd. This

boy's going farther — ain't you, lad? — and needs the early passage more."

Ling nodded quickly but kept her head down.

A gust of wind whipped at the water around the ferry-boat. There was a shout, and one of the men left ashore threw the mooring ropes across to the boatmen. One hit Belladonna's rump and she bucked a little. She whickered, and Ling put her hand on her neck to soothe her.

"Your fat Charlie, he'd have the boat over were he down here with us, Bert, instead of that dainty dun mare!"

That was the same voice that had spoken before, jeering from the boat below. But the man's last words had farther to travel than his first ones, because the sail had picked up the breeze more quickly than anyone might have hoped. The ferryboat began to tack its way through the channel of deep water that lay between the sand shoals away to left and right.

Ling was standing behind Belladonna now, so we had good sight of her, and as we watched, she raised her arm. I knew when and where I had seen her making that very salute. She'd held up her arm in that same glory way when she'd performed the *capriole* outside the stable yard at Baysgarth.

When Belladonna had flown.

∵ Part Three :~

Ice

WINTER CAME IN soon enough that year, and it grew cold even before my birthday in October.

Whenever I called to the Clock's house, I saw the army of geese that lined the shore, more and more of them each time I came. They came to escape from frozen places, he told me. "People wear animal furs in those parts, but the poor birds cannot, so they come to us for shelter, Thomas, as if they were crickets looking for the hearth."

I wondered if the Clock had ever read Mr. Defoe's account of the wildfowl. He certainly read music, loose pages with spidery marks on them, but I saw no books in his house. One thing that had been said about Henry Harkin, however, was a lie. He never trapped a duck to boil it. That was only a silly story, like many another people tell when they know nothing.

The Clock would never speak of his life before he came to Horkstow. He still spoke little enough, and sometimes I had fears he would return to his old state. But he played his fiddles now when I visited, especially the big one he sat between his knees that sounded like a human soul singing. Nan said she heard him humming and whistling in the yard at home.

Zachary grew into a lean young dog, the color of straw. I could hardly believe that the same animal had once fit across Ling's lap. I wondered if he'd kept that memory, as I had.

The Clock told me about the bits and pieces he kept on his shelf. "I dig for them," he said. "Sometimes on purpose; sometimes I find them when I'm looking for something else. People who were here in these parts long ago have left behind precious things for us."

One day he gave me something for myself. It had come in on the tide, he said, and still had the smell of the sea in it.

I turned the rock over. It was split open so that it made a kind of box with a lid, or, even better, a half-open book. Carved inside was a creature as long as a girl's finger, no more. Its tail was curved like the scroll the tiniest fiddle in the world might have. It had a horse's head but no legs at all.

"What is it, Mr. Harkin?" I asked. I traced its bones. "Did you carve this into the rock yourself?" It was such a fine piece of work!

"It's a sea horse, Thomas, that was trapped long ago in that rock, I don't know how. I did nothing but find it. Those are its bones, made into a fossil forevermore. Isn't it a sweet thing? I thought you'd like to have it."

I kept the sea horse in my bag under the bed, stowed along with the red silk. Nan would love the sea horse, but I felt it should belong to Ling. If she didn't come back by next summer, I'd give it to Nan for her birthday.

If I do not, it will be that I am put into the sky. Then you must look for a star called Hélène.

Most of my time I worked with Stubbs. Although we did copy work in the main now, working at the table in the stone house, Stubbs still insisted we scrub our hands afterward with soap and vinegar, even if we never touched the roan. That beast was only bones now, but the ground was too hard to bury them. Sometimes during those months, the ice on the water barrel was too thick to break. Then we had to take our soap to the beck and wash, even though the skin on our hands felt as if it might peel away afterward, as if the fast water were knives.

There were other days when I was ordered down to the smokehouse after the work, to practice my reading and writing. Stubbs was a patient teacher, and he had advanced me as he said he would. My mastering words suited him too, of course, but it suited me better, as I began to feel the torment in my head clear. Over those long evenings, my splotches and smear script gave way to more workable lines, though these were never beautiful.

His way was to show me how to break up words into bits. "Think of the horse's leg," he said, "all those bones, little and long, that together make a perfect limb. You find the bones of a word, Thomas, and you'll have the whole, by and by."

One day when this jigsaw work of *o*'s and *a*'s and long-tailed letters was going well enough for me, I showed him again the penciled pages in my notebook, where I'd drawn the mouths that did just that, that broke the sounds of words up into shapes. Stubbs slapped his knee. "That's what it is! I hadn't figured it when I saw it first."

He tried to read the sounds and even got some of them right. "You're a clever lad, Thomas," he said. "You look to Nature for your lessons, and I try to do the same."

After that, he had more faith in my eye for the look of a thing. He showed me sketches of horses in groups and asked me where I'd put a tree down, or a shed, so as to set the groups off best. It happened that we agreed on the position each time. One day he showed me a strange drawing he had in a book, done long ago by an Italian called Leonardo. A man with two sets of limbs was fitted into a circle, his arms and legs looking as if they were spokes set into a wheel.

"That's perfect proportion in a human being," he said. "All this time that's what I'm after in a horse."

Look to Ling, then, I wanted to say, who didn't need to be bound into a wheel but was perfect in all her shape. But I knew that of anybody in the world, Stubbs was on the right track for what he searched for. I thought his finished drawings were perfection.

I asked to borrow the book to show the drawing to my father. Father stared at it for longer than I'd seen him look at anything that wasn't made of wood. "So those are the kind of wheels you look at down there, Tom," was all he said. He was good at holding his praise back, but I knew he watched me pick his books over to settle on one for my lessons. We had not fought in an age, he and I, and I supposed that was glory enough for me.

Mostly, Stubbs had me copying so much that I cannot say exactly when the way of reading opened its door to me, though I was not swift going through it, and still today I must take my time with what I take from and put on the page. As with the dead things he treated, Stubbs showed me I need not be afraid of pen and ink or printed matter. It was the best gift he gave me, unless I counted that I owed him Ling.

My mother was like a child, boasting my new skill around, and she pestered Grandfather to send us journals along with the ragman, Fulk. These made poor reading as well as poor smelling after their outing on the ragcart. Poor Nan was a little out of joint because she'd set herself up to be Tom's eyes-on-a-page for always.

Mary Spencer praised me too. She said her near sight was too poor to help Stubbs with his copy work as the nights drew in and the candles ate themselves up.

There were so many words to be written down. Stubbs had not broken with the baronet lady from Baysgarth House after all, nor she with him, but in those months he made few visits and kept his energies to finish his anatomy work. His master drawings were nearly complete for graving by printers, he said, but he needed to work on one more horse. He wanted to check every part once again. "That one will be my dictionary horse, Thomas."

When that last dissection was done, Stubbs was going to travel south to London and then to other places where there were great houses and rich people who bred horses that might be painted for money. That was all I knew. Nothing had been said about any part I might play. I kept my head down and did what I was asked.

If I kept busy by day, I did not think so much about what I lacked. There were certain nights, however, when I went into the yard to stare into the heavens and count what I saw there, as if I were a shepherd making check of his flock.

I knew it was foolish and that Ling had said what she had when it was the worst of times. But I had lost *Tohmah,* the best part of myself. He was in some other place, and I did not know where that was.

Barrow House

I CANNOT REMEMBER when the dreams started. Or dream, for it was always the same one. I stood on the edge of the barrow mounds and watched Ling approach, on Belladonna. She was cloaked, so I couldn't see her face. Nor did she see me, or hear me, even when I shouted a warning to her. Always eager to change themselves, my dream feet now grew roots, so I could do nothing but watch as girl and horse walked into the barrow house and were swallowed up. The earth closed over them like the suckings of a marsh.

Hugh complained about my tossings and my groans, but it was Mary Spencer who saved me. One afternoon I dozed off when I was supposed to be matching a table of notes to the horse map Stubbs had plotted with letters, like a pin cushion. I woke to a shaking and Mary's white face.

"Oh, poor Thomas. Wherever you were, it was no place for a good boy like you to be."

Perhaps if she had not said "good." Perhaps if her voice had not trembled as it did. Certainly if Stubbs had been in the house at the time, I know I would not have turned crybaby. But all I reckoned right then was that Ling had nothing to fear from Mary Spencer, not any longer, and so I spilled out my dream to her. She asked me this and that and I told her more, and in the finish she knew pretty well everything, save the recipe of walnuts that had done the trick, where Ling had headed, and the Rom people she'd had in mind to meet there.

It seemed Mary was still fond of my hands, for she was clutching them when she spoke. "Thomas, I told you your girl would be safe because of this." She tapped the long line in my right palm. "But I cannot believe that you haven't stirred yourself to care about the other poor little one, after all she did for the pair of you."

I flushed so hot it was painful as a burn, but if Mary noticed, she gave me no credit for my guilt.

"It's as plain as the day what that dream is telling you to do, and all the while you're beating it back with your grand notions of your French girl. Does the cloak that hides the girl's face tell you nothing? Barrows indeed! It's to the *place* called Barrow you should take yourself, as soon as you can, and find out what has happened to that orphan girl. I'll fix this matter with George so you'll get time to do that."

Mary didn't dawdle. Two mornings after that promise, Walnuts was saddled for me and I was heading east over the rise, with a bag full of meat and bread and my own bits and pieces. The ground was frozen hard, the cob had a good easy stride, and I didn't bother him. He knew the way, and it seemed no time before we were in Barton. Barrow was four miles farther on, but I thought to make a first stop at Esther's house. Perhaps I'd find her there anyway and hear how she got up every market day to steal what she might, and how she brought Dido inside for warmth now that winter was come so early.

It's a sorry day when you make up fables and lies for yourself, not for others.

The hateful street Esther had brought me to looked no better for its sparkle of frost. I found her house easily, and because somebody had removed the top timbers of the door, I could put my whole head inside to take stock. The bare earth-floored room hadn't been improved since I saw it, but it had new tenants. Two men lay snoring on separate heaps of rags, with Esther's pitcher standing between them. Somehow I doubted there was honey in it.

Those two were good for nothing, so I banged against other doors along the street until I got an answer. A stout women came out of her house to look me up and down before she would say anything. "That Quickfall lass? Has she stolen from you? The way that scrawny sly thing went here and around, I'd lay she's at the bottom of a river now, for her thieving or her cough."

Esther hadn't been seen since the summer, a kinder woman told me. Her husband was a knacker man and he hadn't found the gray mare lying alongside any road either, if that might be any hope to me, she said, for hers was a man who turned over everything going.

Everything that I heard told me Esther had never come back to this place. I remembered there'd been a priest who had given Dido the run of his apple orchard. That scrap was enough to make finding the man easy enough, but he had no news for me either.

I didn't know any road to Barrow other than the one that passed close by the gates of Baysgarth House. These were gaping wide, as if a carriage had just gone through them, or as if nobody cared to deal properly with them anymore. I tipped Walnuts to the right and we trotted up to the gates, where I halted him. He pawed the ground, impatient to seek out his regular stall and his feed of oats inside, no doubt. I stayed him while I thought on what I might do.

When he was teaching first Hugh, and then me, what it was to make a wheel, my father preached us a short lesson about doing proper work. Every man jackstone must be turned over in order to make a wheel perfect. "Did you turn over every man jackstone before you shaved that spoke, Tom?" he'd say. "Did you count everything you should?"

There were jackstones to be turned over at Baysgarth.

I had a bad twinge when we came through the gates, for it seemed that Esther was not far away at all. If I could twist my head like an owl, only one small degree more than it would budge, there would be skinny Ezra and his questions, trying to keep up with my long strides, and after him, gawky Esther, who'd been cheerier than me, and braver too. Esther with her face turned, her face cloaked. Esther with no face at all.

I turned for the stables and dipped my head under the archway, hardly thinking I'd find them, so layabout they'd always been, but I was lucky. The donkey men were out in force, painting the lady's carriage, one on each side, one at the back, though there was surely more paint on the cobbles than on the coachwork. When they saw me, their mouths opened to catch flies, and they laid their brushes down on their pots of blue. I told myself that for all there were three of them, they were lazy louts, and none was higher than a jockey man. I swung myself down from Walnuts and dropped his reins to the ground.

"Don't you know she's hanged, your gypsy robber girl?" jeered one. "By the neck, till she was dead, screeching."

I floored him with a batterknuckles to the jaw and was glad to see he upended his pot of paint over his legs as he went down. But the other two were on me then, and it was elbows and fists in every soft place, mine and theirs, until there was only one of them left standing. We drew apart, heaving, taking in our breaths in sobs.

"Tell me where the other girl is," I said to him. My mouth was swelling with blood, and I spat it out, hoping a tooth wasn't down there in the mix. "She was from the town. Esther was her name, but you likely thought it was Ezra. Did they find her?"

His chest was still going up and down like Jack Proctor's bellows, while mine had eased. I tensed my fists again to show him who was master here.

"The copper head?" he asked. "The boy one?" I nodded. There was only a chance he might know, but I'd beat him anyway if he had nothing to say, for I'd always been sure Ling hadn't told me the half of how this lot had bothered her.

"Barrow," he said. "She ran there; she stayed there. Got herself a place with a clock maker."

The race in my head slowed and stopped, and I closed my eyes. If only I could hear that much said of Ling. "How do you know?" I asked him.

Something like a smile passed over his face.

"Jem Hasp found her there soon enough but got a flea in his ear for his pains, for she'd found herself a right master."

I knew then I wasn't Jem Hasp's only enemy in this place.

"Is he inside?" I tipped my head toward the house.

"Sent packing," the man said, happiest of all to tell me this. He laid his hands down by his side, as if Jem Hasp's end had made us friends. "Gone off south."

I had some vinegar for the donkey men's wounds when I settled myself back on Walnuts and prepared to ride out. "My girl wasn't a gypsy. She was French, from the court there, and so was the white mare."

They stared up at me, stupid.

"She could have killed you anytime. She had a poison dagger, but she said she'd not waste it on the likes of English donkey men."

An Apple a Day

IT WAS EASY to find the clock maker's place, a fine house with windows like clear water and a sundial in the small garden. There was a bellpull and a knocker shaped like a fist, which reminded me of my swelling hands, so I tugged the rope instead, though it probably hurt more to do that.

I could hear light steps on a wooden floor. The door opened, just an inch or so first so that all I saw was a skein of pale cheek, and an eye where the latch was mounted. Then the door was pulled back so wide I thought it must go through the wall.

"Thomas! But look at you!"

But look at *her*. She had a full blue dress on, a white apron over it, and a hat like a little cake on her head. Her hair was tied back in a tiny plait, it had grown so. She was a right girl now. Even her face was plumper.

I cleared my throat. "I'm sorry I didn't come before now, Esther. How are you? You look good."

"More than you do, Thomas Rose, all black-and-blue, but still as lofty as a tree. Come in."

"Is it all right to leave the horse tied there?" I asked.

"He's not the sort would make off with the sundial like some, I'd lay."

She led me down steps and a corridor into the biggest kitchen I had ever seen. On the walls copper pans shone like moons, and on the long table there was a bottle jar stuffed with beech leaves and some kind of long white flower. I could smell apples baking.

"Come right over here and see my Dido now, Thomas." She was pointing through a window as she'd done once before, and I had to smile because I knew what I'd see before I looked, and there she was, a clean gray horse, fine as anybody's, cropping grass at the end of the garden.

"See, she's fat as an elephant from China, and she has her own stall too, right beside his horse in the stable." She bustled about, setting out some bread and cheese. "He'll be down soon for his supper, so you'd better be off before then, in case he thinks you're courting after me or something."

Quickly I stood up and she laughed. "I'm not really eleven, you know, whatever you want to think. Sit down and eat something." Her face settled. "I'm staying here, Thomas. We suit each other, Mr. James Harrison and me. He stood up for me, for all that he's a quiet man. He has the wheezes and so have I, and we're making a study on what we'll do for it."

She rolled an apple across the table to me. "An apple a day is a start, he says." She bit into one and eyed me. "Have you heard from Ling?"

I shook my head. "It's not safe yet. I just don't know anything, Esther."

Well, I wasn't going to make as I'd done with Mary Spencer and sob, that was for sure, and that would likely happen if we continued down that road. "I brought you some things," I said. "But I don't think you need this first lot, with all the good stuff you have here."

Mother's jar had to come back with me again, she'd said, but there were three fat honeycombs inside it for now. I looked around for a bowl to tip them into, but Esther went for a tall pot with a lid and held it while I lifted the combs out with a fork.

"Oh, there's a point to you somewhere, Thomas Rose," she said. She stuck her little finger into a corner of a comb and lifted it to her lips. "Mmm. My master loves honey too, being that he's the sweet man he is. All the same, you should have seen him chase that Jem Hasp halfway back to Barton! He threatened him with his brother in London, who has all the brains, and all the king's navy looking after him."

I told her about the stable boys and she clapped her hands. "Proper bullyboys, they were. They needed a pasting. And they didn't know their backsides from their boots. They couldn't make a horse be nearly human the way Ling did. You must come back and tell me when you hear from her, Thomas Rose, do you hear?"

I slid the other small package across the table to her. She parted the paper and gasped.

"What is it, Thomas?"

"It's a sea horse. The stone is its tomb."

"A sea horse, with no legs! But it's pretty, isn't it?" She stroked its bones, as I had done the first time I held it. "Such a proud little head it has, as if it knew fine tricks once upon a time."

She looked up far too smartly then, for she saw something in my face. "Oh, Thomas, you had this for Ling, didn't you?"

I couldn't say anything. Not yes, no, nor see here. I sat there, the apple tumbling between my hands, left to right. Somewhere in the house a clock chimed, then another. A third. It was a clock maker's house right enough.

Esther parceled the sea horse again. She rummaged through the drawer in the table until she found a piece of twine and tied it around the paper. Then she came around and stood by me, picked up my hand, and slid the packet under it.

"There! You'll take this back, do you hear? You'll keep it for her, for she'll be back along your way one day, I know she will. She was right fond of you, for all that you were nasty to poor Ezra Quickfall. May he rest in peace, the poor soul."

She began to laugh, but it quickly turned into a cough and splutter. I made to clap her on the back, but she shook her head. She mastered the cough in a short while and stood by me, taking in long breaths. "See? Little sea horsey would fair give me the wheezes from his tomb, I'd say. But thank you, anyway, Thomas Rose, for the honey and the decent thought."

I had no more worries for Esther. And that night when I got home, sore though I was, and cross as Mother was to see the battered state of me, I went to bed with no thought of the dream.

It never came back afterward.

Gifts

CHRISTMAS PUT ME in mind of the Dane's child, and I asked Mother if she'd heard anything of a baby with a crown of white hair given to some family in the county for money. But she hadn't, and when she asked for more of the story I told her a little, but without putting Ling into it. I told her Stubbs had heard about it in the town. She shook her head for the bad things people do.

"Pray the Lord the poor scrap hasn't fallen among rogues, Tom."

In the weeks coming up to the feast, I shut myself in Father's shop at night and warned everybody to keep their distance. I needn't have bothered. In that weather, there was no fear of anybody stepping out of our warm kitchen, where the fire blazed, to go across the yard. Not even Nan came. Mother allowed me only one candle each night, so I had to work faster than I wished. Sometimes I lifted my head and caught sight of my great shadow as it sawed and shaped, and I felt sorry for it because it looked so lonely.

If my shadow was lonely, my Christmas gifts pleased everyone.

Stubbs got a fine box of elm wood that I'd fitted out properly. This one was sanded and opened smoothly on its hinges, and I'd made it for him to store his master drawings. When I delivered it, he reddened with pleasure. He gave me a gold guinea in return.

"This is for all your brave work here, Thomas. There's more if you want to come down to London to earn it. You could do good work in the city. Maybe that's where your dangerous little friend headed to on her mare, eh?"

My heart was banging so much, I could only nod and shrug away back to him, like some senseless fellow. Nobody had mentioned Ling in an age. Only I had, and then only to Mary Spencer and Esther. I'd no steer on what Stubbs thought of her now.

But—*London*? Even if there'd been no promise by Ling to return, I wouldn't know what to think about that offer. It was too sudden. I could only give thanks that Stubbs was in one house when he spoke and Father in another, so that I wasn't forced to squint my mind up right away. I muttered something and dipped my head into my bag to look for Mary's gift, hoping Stubbs wouldn't press me.

For her I'd turned a small bowl from a cut of old walnut timber. Its bottom had a buttery yellow swirl, like a smile. I thought she might use it for her eggs, but she told me she would keep it instead for the fine stones and shells she collected on the shore. "If George ever becomes as rich as he should whenever this work is published, then I'll keep my jewels in it, Tom."

At home on Christmas Day, we had our own parade of gifts after church. It seemed everyone thought I was a scholar now, for I now had two new books by Mr. Defoe from Mother and Father, a leather-clad journal from Hugh, wherever he came on it, and a fine swan's feather quill pen from Nan, who'd begged the feather from Grandfather. Perhaps it had come from one of my swans. "And Mr. Stubbs gave me the nib," she said.

I'd made a neat wall box with two shelves and a door to house Father's books and a chestnut box with a small silver lock for Mother's Bible book. Nan had helped me sew two linen cloths inside to line it.

Mother stroked my arm. "Sweet Tom," she said. "The good old letters I had from your father will be safe at last." Father blushed like a girl and she laughed, not only at him but at us, who never went near her Bible book, not even Nan.

Nan wasn't yet too old for the stilts I made for her. I painted one red and one blue and cut a horse's head into each footrest, filling the lines with white. Nan shrieked and climbed up on them to hug me from her great new height.

Hugh got a small folding stool that he could bring fishing. Stubbs had given me the least worn part of the roan's skin, and I'd slung the leather neatly between three stout legs. I made a long willow whistle for Jack Proctor, who'd found himself a stray hound on his way back from Barton one day, much as Stubbs had found Zachary left out on the road.

The Clock's present was the hardest to think of and the hardest to make. But it was worth all the effort to see his face, when the goose and the pig's cheeks and the pudding were eaten to nothing and all our family gifts given out. I swear the poor chap was almost struck back to his silence again when I brought down the oak music stand from our bedroom and showed him how he could keep his music sheets still by closing fast the carved sea horses on either side.

Upstairs, and still uncovered, was a secret piece of craft that was just as fine, I thought, even if I was the only one to say so. I'd begged some iron rods from Jack

Proctor and heated and twisted them into a neat frame that stood on two long straight legs. The piece of walnut I'd been sanding and polishing for weeks slipped easily into the frame. After Christmas, when the carving work was done, I'd figure how I'd find time to bring it to its proper resting place. That was what I'd promised Ling, so long ago.

Her other gift stayed under the bed, collecting dust in its delicate bones.

The Diklo

AFTER CHRISTMAS, on the eve of Twelfth Night, I went with Stubbs to a farm at Elsham, where he was to pick out his last animal.

"I know that place," Father said. "They'll have the broken-winded, the lame, and the halt. The last dregs of horses." He shook his head, disgusted. I didn't tell him it would be the last horse. I didn't want to bring the thought of London closer to my life. I'd have to decide my way soon enough, and Father's thinking on it wouldn't help me any.

It was a day when sleet blew slant from the east, changed its mind, and stopped. Then, just when my nose and cheeks began to feel alive again, back came the shafts of ice. Walnuts snorted all the way, and I guessed his broad nostrils were pierced full of them. I crouched on his rump, behind the saddle, and turned my head against the weather, trying to get shelter from Stubbs's broad back.

The landlords of the livery place at Elsham had no care for how their horses might be protected against the weather, and therefore the people who came to prod and poke the animals had to stand in the yard in the driving sleet and rain. We had to pay our penny to get in too, because the big man at the gate, who was covered head to toe in a dirty canvas cape, opened it only for money. Stubbs dropped two coins into his hand, and the gate swung free.

Once inside, he moved among the sodden horses, where they stood in a huddle. He felt a rump here and a thigh there and stooped now and again to lift a hoof. The animals hung their heads and caught nobody's eye. Wherever they would go next, it would be worse for them, and each one seemed to know that.

I wished I might be by the fire at home, my finger moving across the print in Father's copy of Mr. Defoe's book, tracing those words of false weather. *'Tis not once in a wild duck's age, that they have any long frosts or deep snows.*

There was a sudden noisy helter-skeltering at the gate. "Oi! Thieving gypo! Get him, lads!"

The big man was shouting after a boy who must have slipped in without paying his penny and who was running even now toward the sad clutch of horses in the middle of the yard. None of the stablehands bothered to step out of shelter to go after him, I noticed. Likely they were as poorly treated here as the animals were. But everyone was watching the fugitive, as cats watch a bird. Even Stubbs had straightened himself up at the shout.

The boy was every bit as dark-skinned as Ling had looked the last time I set eyes on her. There was no doubting this was a boy, however. He was smaller than me by a head, but was as broad across his face and body. His dark hair was long and curly, though the rain made wet strings of it, for he had no cap. He wore a dark-red waistcoat and a brighter red scarf tied around his neck, with a patched old tweed jacket topping everything. On this bitter day, he had no boots, only loose soles bound with twine, which slipped and sloshed through the puddles.

He pushed into the middle of the ring and clasped one of the animals, a small black gelding, around the neck. He bent to kiss its muzzle and ran his hands along the jaw and up to the ears. Then he untied it and jumped up, all in one deft move. He leaned forward and said something into the animal's ear. I was near enough to hear the strange words. *"Kushti,* Morgan, *kushti, gry."* Something like that.

The stable lads made their moves then. "Get yourself off that beast, gypo," one of them shouted. But the boy was kneeing the black horse out of the huddle now, drawing his legs up high on its withers, as if he wore invisible stirrups.

"He's mine!" he shouted. "That fat hedge mumper over there took my *gry* while he was grazing along the back of this place less than a quarter moon ago."

He pointed at the big man in the canvas coat. "That's the *gry* diddler, not me, and you know it well, though you're only slaves here. Now, let me fare out of here, lads. Away out of this dirty place."

But Stubbs had the bridle then, and though the boy hit him a blow on the shoulder, he held it fast. "I had my own eye on this one, lad."

"Well, he's not for your pester, mister. He's mine. Get out of my way, *gadjo*s."

Then they were all there surrounding him, the money man, the stablehands, and Stubbs, and the boy was held for sure. I moved closer and saw that the boy's eyes were panicked, like a wild thing trapped. It wasn't just rain that streaked down his cheeks either.

"How much?" I said to the fat man. "For that gelding?"

Stubbs twisted to look at me. "What are you saying, Thomas?"

The big man made slits of his eyes. He'd not be taken for a fool—that was the last thing that would happen here this day. "Ten sovereigns."

"I'll give you a fifth part of that," I said. Two sovereigns was all Stubbs would pay out this day, he'd said, for that should be the going rate for such poor horseflesh.

The man looked from Stubbs to the boy, who said nothing but bit on his own hand as if it were meat, and then he turned back to me. "Show me your money," he said.

"Mr. Stubbs?" I was pleading. "I have more than half of that in my pocket." My fresh guinea was worth a shilling more than a sovereign, it was true.

Stubbs's face was set hard now. He looked back at the horses and pointed at a swaybacked gray whose large rump rose like a hill from the dip in its back. "I'll give you three for the two of them, the black and that poor wreck," he said to the man. "Not a penny more."

There would be no other buyers this bad morning, only gawpers, that was clear. The man spat a great dirty gobbet onto the cobbles. "Give me it, then," he said. He bit harder on my coin than he did on those Stubbs gave him, but all passed and he shoved them into a purse on his belt. He turned to me.

"Don't let that one fool you out of more of your cash, boy. You don't know half the harm the gypos bring with them every time they come by."

Stubbs unhitched the gray, and he, I, and the boy moved toward the gate, every eye there stuck to our backs. When we were outside, the boy pulled his pony over and jumped down. He put his hand out to take mine. Stubbs kept going, but slowly, leading Walnuts.

"I don't know why you did all you did there," the boy said, "but this *gry*'s still mine, you know. *Gry* is a horse, and this one's called Morgan. That means a hare, in your tongue. He was fleet as a hare once, though he's fair trashed now. You're a *gadjo* lad. I'm a Rom lad, and I thank you for what you did. But just because you gave your pester to that fat grunter inside doesn't change it that Morgan is mine."

His black eyes didn't dip once but held mine, the weasel's trick of dazzling a rabbit.

I shrugged. I was no rabbit and hadn't expected more, anyway. But I'd never spoken to a Rom boy before and was curious. "I know," I said. "I could see he was rightly yours. I knew someone once whose horse was taken the same way as that, just like yours. What I did in there was for her."

I cocked my chin toward Stubbs. If he heard me say that, let him make what he would of it, whatever I owed him, whether there'd be London or not. What I'd said to the gypsy was no more than the truth. Thieving a poor person's treasure was the worst of all theft.

The boy had been set to mount his pony, but my little speech jolted him enough to put his leg down again. "Did this pass near here last summer, at the fair in Brigg? Was it a white *gry*?"

First there were all the French words to figure; now there was the trying to keep up with this fellow's riddling talk. Stubbs had mounted Walnuts and gone ahead, leaving the swayback in my hands, but now he stopped and looked back. He gestured to me to catch up with him and turned his head again toward Horkstow.

I took in a long breath before I spoke. "A white mare with a tail the color of barley. That's what my friend Ling always used to say about her Belladonna. That's the one that was stolen."

It was good to say her name. It made a warm feeling in my throat.

The boy hit his forehead. "God's blessing!"

"What did you say?"

"*You, gadjo.* You're him, aren't you? You're the Thomas, the *kopanari* boy, the woodworker? She sent me south to Pappaneskey Tem to scout for you after the feast of the holy child. But then the *gry* diddler stole my Morgan, and I didn't look anymore."

What rubbish was he talking? I wanted to seize him, hold his arms down, make him speak plain, stop him jigging about, his daft duck's feet ever in danger of dancing into a puddle of rain and splashing everything around him with icy water.

"But she said you had to show me the *diklo* first. That way I'd be sure it was you and not some other one who'd spring a trap on her. If you were the right lad, then I could tell you where she is now and where you'll find her, coming soon."

There wasn't a body in the world that could stand more of this. I grabbed the lad and held him, for all that he flushed with anger at being taken and stamped a foot on my boot. "Tell me, what is a cursed *diklo*? What am I to show you?"

The boy had very white teeth when he laughed. "It's right here in front of your eyes!" he said. "Oh, *gadjo* boy, you're not able to guess my meaning any more than you know what the *goorgooritsa* sings from the tall trees. Look. *This* might be called a *diklo*, but only if it were on a *chavvi*, on a girl."

He pulled his red neckerchief loose from his neck and flapped it across my face. It was wet through and smelled of rain and old smoke. "Show me this, then. The *diklo* made of red silk, if you have it."

Pappaneskey Tem

Thomas

    I teach my bon ami *Simeon what he must say to you if he finds you, but I send this letter too for little Nan to read to you. Simeon will tell my story and use my words as best he can. His voice is still sweet, like a bird's. Not a frog's like yours! But let Nan read this too, for she is a clever girl.*

    All this cold winter I am in York, very safe in the little vardo, *the wagon, where my Rom friends live. I am their daughter now, they say, for they have boys only, small ones. But soon it will be time for us to come south* for the spring. I will come to Lincoln with the Roms for the Resurrection feast. It comes in March this year, so very early. After that I will go to London after all, even if my friends do not. A monsieur who came here to look at our animals told me that a new theater with a ring for horses will soon open in that city. He said Belladonna would be a princess there. He said nobody in London will believe a horse can fly like she does, like Pegasus. Perhaps I will meet Augustin and Sylvie and the others there.

Thomas, Belladonna is white again, whiter than ever! And I too, though my hands and face stayed dark for so very long, just like one of dear Monsieur Harkin's violins. Please give him my sincere affections and an embrace too for Zachary dog.

If you have any news of my brave Esther, you must tell it to Simeon. Often I have a dream of her and her poor Dido on the road, and I do not know if this is a good or a bad dream. You had fear for me, Thomas, but I have fear for her. I dream too of the baby, but none of the Roms have heard any stories of him in their travels.

Thomas, we will bring our animals, and all the tin and silver things made here during the cold time, to the space in front of the cathedral of Lincoln on the day after the Resurrection feast. I will be happy only if you can be there. On the morning of the feast, I will go to put hyacinths and jonquils on my mother's grave. It is not important if you cannot make the stone for her, Thomas.

It is so far away for you, I know, and I do not know if you must still do all the terrible work for Monsieur Bluebeard. But the flowers will grow for my maman *every year, and they have the name of her blue eyes.*

Simeon is very excited to go to Pappaneskey Tem. That is the name the Roms call your big flat country between the great river and the big bite of the sea below. Pappans *are what they call the wildfowl, all the gooses and ducks that live there and fly in strings to the marshes and rivers.* Tem *means home place. You did not know that, but neither did I until I came here. They have made all sorts of names for every part of your England.*

I send you my best kisses, Thomas. I embrace you. Simeon promises me he will say these words to you too. I tell him I will ask you if he does! I send you too what I cannot write, what I cannot speak to anybody but you. I have missed you so much all this time.

I will try to understand if you cannot come. If I do not see you, there will be less of me for all the rest of my life, but still I am glad that we two knew each other in this world.

Ton amour, ton Hélène, your Ling

I held Ling's letter in my hand and amused myself watching Simeon try to hop over telling the parts that caused him to turn red as his blessed *diklo*. But I stopped him when not to do so would cause me the same bother.

There was no time to write to her myself and show off my new powers, for the boy had lost so much time in his search that he needed to go north at once, he said. Besides, he feared the reach of the man at Elsham.

I gave him the kerchief and some goose meat in bread from our kitchen and told him there was good news of Esther Quickfall, but none of the baby. I wished him good speed. Then I brought the poor gray sway-back on his last journey, but my heart was singing to the tops of the bare trees, as if all the Clock's fiddles were tuned to it. *Ton amour, ton Hélène, your Ling.*

My Ling.

Soaring

AHEAD OF ME, Lincoln perched on its hill, safe as a magpie's nest in a tree.

For all I knew, all the roads in England led to this city. But the straight paved road that I was on, the one that gave me the weeping blisters, certainly knew where it was going. It hurried along like a wheel. It was my poor feet that were too slow, even in their new boots. Likely my new boots were the problem.

There was also the matter of sleep. Or no sleep, to be correct.

It might be Easter, but because it was March, darkness still fell early, and I'd been almost three days on the road. Everyone told me I'd need luck to meet a carrier because I'd picked the holy days for my journey. The worst of it was that everyone was right. I'd got no lift at all. But I did what Mother asked and stayed the nights in decent rooms and didn't tire myself too much. My feet made the rule on that, anyway.

I passed Good Friday night with Grandfather in Brigg. He grumbled that I'd turned up my nose at the decent trade of gloving and blamed Father for being daft enough to give me a year to try my way with the world, so far from home. The night following, I stayed just off the road, in an inn that kept its ale locked away until Easter morning. All the same, I got precious little sleep on either night.

Closer to, I could see that the people of Lincoln had built towers to bring them even farther into the sky. Not one but three towers, three arrows pointing to heaven. Even I could see this, because the morning was so clear, so new made, with its sky the color of a thrush's egg.

When it looked the right thing to do, I left my straight road and began to follow little crooked ones instead, climbing always, my boots making a racket on the uneven cobbles. At last the way became level and I was on the hill, in the heart of the city.

On every small street, people were out and about and greeting one another. Their Easter clothes were bright and fresh-smelling, especially the women's. Some girls even smiled at me as I passed, and I knew I was no piece of fashion, with my tow hair and the great load that must look like a horse's nosebag wrong way around on my back. Children ran out from doorways, up and down the lanes, ducking and diving. From the lower floors of the tall houses I passed, I could smell roasts as they turned on their spit, the smells of fat geese and legs of mutton.

Suddenly there were the bells, the bells of Easter! All at once! Music spilling out of the towers, giddy bells and others that sounded deep as wells. There must be dozens of bells swinging up there halfway to the sky. Dozens of ringers below too, one on every rope. And I'd been daft enough to ask Jack Proctor how I would find my way to the cathedral. No wonder Jack had laughed.

"Don't you worry. It'll find you, Thomas Rose. Or I'll put it this way: you'll not miss it for long."

I went under a stone archway that brought me right in front of the cathedral, to the wide place where Ling had promised to be on the day following, selling tin stuffs with the Roms.

Up close the cathedral had a wide front like Baysgarth had, only it was many, many times greater and taller. It was made of the same golden stone as the towers, with three archways cut into it, like caves for people to enter. I looked up and saw faces cut into the stone, dozens of them. They put my four friends in the church at Horkstow to shame because they had bodies and long legs to carry them.

Above them again, very high up, were faces that jumped out into the sky like boys jumping into a river. A pig. An old woman's face, twisted. Gargoyles! My neck hurt when I tried to see more.

I thought it best to go inside the cathedral to ask where the graveyard was. It would surely be easier to stop someone where it was quiet, rather than shout my question outside, with all the pealing bells and the children shrieking. I chose the right-hand side and pushed open the door.

And there it was, the stone ceiling, so far above my head that a forest of lime trees from the wold would fit under it and still leave room for rooks to fly above the trees. The stone silk was stretched taut and sleek across ribs of stone.

I knew these ribs. These were the same ones I'd seen that first evening in Stubbs's smokehouse, the bones of the horse. The cathedral had its own ribs, and they curved as a boat's ribs curved, as a horse's ribs did, and a man's too. I felt my own rib cage to be sure of that, but my eyes stayed on the stone sky.

Everything, the ribs, the roof, the pretend windows running along the aisles, everything rested on fat pillars, colored honey and black, shiny and beautiful. They made an avenue, these stone trees that marched along the floor, for miles it seemed, though it could not be.

I wanted to stay here for as long as it would take to work out how this building was put together. How did it stay up without tumbling? Even the giant Samson in the Bible story, who had knocked a temple down, could do nothing to upset this place. I wanted to learn how to make a building as beautiful as this. I wanted that to be my work.

If I could learn that much, then I would know as much as anyone in the world. As much as Stubbs knew about how horses are made. As much as the Clock knew about music. As much as the man Leonardo knew about anything. After all, it was only proportion, and Stubbs said that all you needed for that were eyes and a brain.

A small man wearing black clothes came through a door to the right and hurried up toward the great area in the middle that was blocked by a screen. I went after him. If he had any Easter goodness in him, he would surely tell me where a Papist might be buried.

It would hardly be near here. Unless Ling had spun the best story of her life to someone. Anyway, it was better that poor Zéphyrine should lie somewhere plain and less wonderful. If I tried to plant my gravestone near the cathedral, someone dressed in black would pull it out of the earth and throw it away. The piece that I had made so proudly did not belong here.

This was a place for the masters.

Belle Aimée

THE EARTH WAS so hard and I had no spade. I looked around for the man who'd shown me where Zéphyrine's grave was, but he'd tramped away to eat his wife's Easter dinner, just as he'd said he would.

"I'll show you where she lies, then, but only for the sake of that pretty little one who buried her last summer," he grumbled. "Easter Sunday is no day to ask a man to conduct his ordinary business."

There it was, the simple cross Ling had talked about, two peeling sticks of birch tied together with some black fabric knotted in a bow. It listed backward toward the bare earth, where only a few tough weeds had seeded since winter. *The grumbler must have tended to it,* I thought, but he could do little enough. The graves were as poor as the soil they were laid in. I saw very few proper stones standing.

All I could do was use the birch sticks as best I could to poke two holes open in the ground and fit the iron legs of the cross into them. It must be all in place before Ling appeared. I cursed my laziness for not getting on the road before dawn and began to work.

It was not so bad in the finish. I was able to root the cross firmly into place, twisting it farther down, like a screw into wood. Then I footed the earth back around it, filled the hole, and stamped it to make the whole space smooth. I pulled the weeds and lobbed what stones there were into the distance, beyond the nearby mounds. I thought to do the same with the birch sticks, but instead I tied them together again into their cross and planted it into the grave alongside, which had nothing to mark it.

Zéphyrine lay among the unknown. But she had her own place now.

CI-GÎT
MARIE-ZÉPHYRINE CLAUDEL
COLOMBINE BELLE-AIMÉE
SANS PAREILLE
MÈRE AU GRAND COEUR
À SES TROIS ENFANTS
PARIS 1726–LINCOLN 1757

I could only guess at the words I'd chiseled so carefully into the piece of walnut wood, but I'd laid them out exactly as Ling had written them on her paper.

That was Zéphyrine's name in full on the second line, of course, and so I knew now that Ling must be called Claudel too. *Belle* looked like the first part of Belladonna. *Enfants* looked like "infants." I could make no sense of the rest, except that poor Zéphyrine had made only thirty-one summers in her life, for all that she was born six years after my mother. I had given her the finest letters I could make, crisp and clear like those in a book, with tops and tails on them.

I stood clear of the grave at last and hugged myself. The sky was still clear and high, but it was colder now than it had been earlier. A robin touched down on top of the old cross and looked at me, its head cocked.

She had said the morning, surely? I reached in my pocket for her letter, though I could say it off better than the Rom boy ever could. Morning, it was. I'd heard the cathedral bells again, over and over as I worked, but they'd been silent now for some time. I was sure it was long past noon.

Perhaps something had happened to delay the Roms on their way to Lincoln. It was no matter. There was the fair tomorrow in front of the cathedral. But would the churchmen let Ling and her people set up there? I thought of the man in black whose face had changed when he heard my question. Though he had told me civilly enough where I would find the graveyard, he had waited for me to walk the length of the avenue of pillars, watching until I opened the door and stepped again into the light. He'd reminded me of Julia from Baysgarth.

I thought of all the things I might have done if I'd been about good and early in Lincoln. I could have walked the streets and asked people about the Roms and what they sold when they came. If I'd found a livery stable, I could have asked what happened to horse thieves in this city. There would surely be an assizes after Easter, but I still didn't know whether the city's powers stretched as far as Barton and Horkstow when it came to giving out punishment.

Thomas, Belladonna is white again, whiter than ever!

All I knew was that constables had the longest memories among all classes of men. Jack Proctor said that, and I believed him.

Now I could smell smoke from hundreds of chimneys and could see it too, drifting higher than the steeples, for spring quickly gave way back to winter in these March afternoons.

I took out my day's bread and scattered a little between the graves for the robin. He wasted no time being shy but hopped down and set to, even though my boots were no distance from him. I thought of Nan, who could make a robin in the yard eat from her hand.

Well, if I was going to be here for much longer, I'd make that small bird keep me company, I thought. I prepared a feast for him on my palm, but as I was doing my crumble work, there came the smallest crunch from behind, as if somebody had stepped on a twig.

I turned on the instant, but there was nobody. I stared and squinted, and squinted and stared, but saw nothing. Then I reckoned the winter had been so cold that perhaps twigs cracked their last gasps when spring came. I turned back to my taming of the robin and found my twitching had left a mess of crumbs on the grave. I had to bend and sweep it clean with my hands while the bird pecked away between my fingers.

Then two things happened. The robin rose up like a lark, and straight after, my eyes were blotted out, shut tight, pressed down. I struggled to stand, and strong legs gripped me around my thighs and climbed me, and a laugh blew into my left ear. Warm breath, warm hands that smelled of flowers, fresh flowers. But the hands were so small! How had I not remembered they were so small?

"My Thomas!"

Tohmah.

Fin

I SET HER DOWN behind me, carefully, before I turned.

She was still in breeches, though I couldn't tell if they were the same ones as before. They were a dirty cream that might have washed out from brown. She had a pale striped shirt tucked into a black shiny waistband. A boy's black greatcoat sat on her shoulders, and a black broad-brimmed hat trimmed with white covered her head, perhaps a little too much. I guessed that her hair reached her chin now, from the few lengths that escaped. Her face was as pale as mine must be.

"Thomas, you have grown again! What shall we do about that?"

"Was it you who made that noise? Like a whip crack?"

She nodded. "I was behind that stone. I was silly, like a child. I wanted to see you first before you knew I was there."

She reached her hand to touch the crown of my head, then ran it down my nose, over my lips, my chin. She stroked my cheek and murmured something I did not catch. Then I saw the little basket of daffodils and blue hyacinth flowers she had set down. She lifted it now and held it up for me to sniff the same sweet smell that was on her hands. All I could do, stupid, was point at the gravestone.

"I couldn't work a stone one for you," I said. "But Jack says she'll last, this one. Is it all right, Ling?"

My stomach was bobbing inside as she inspected the piece, bent on one knee. When she read out the words I'd carved, all the air left my lungs.

"*Colombine belle-aimée.* You see, that was the character she loved most to dance, dear Colombine with her tender heart. I thought that was the best to put, because when she was Colombine, my *maman* was happiest and everyone loved her. All the *messieurs* in Paris said she was *sans pareille,* that nobody was like her. And she was mother to three children; you see where you have put this, Thomas? For my mother with the big heart, who is gone. Thank you."

She bowed her head, but I saw the tears anyway.

Cleverer than I was, she had a little tin trowel with her, and now she set to digging holes for the blue and yellow flowers, setting them into the earth. They made a bright band across the neck of the grave.

"Where is Belladonna?" I looked as far as I could see, back to the walls of the graveyard. "And your friends?"

She laughed. "Simeon is well pleased to mind Belladonna for me, never have fear, even though he loves his old horse Morgan still. He told me what you did for him, my brave Thomas. Now he will do anything for you. For all your life long, you will have Simeon as your friend."

She pointed somewhere in the distance, where the light was already changing, thickening into rose. "They have a camp, down by the water. You know it?"

I shook my head. "All I know is the cathedral and here."

"You will come with me and eat with my friends? It is not necessary you go away now?"

Her eyes were huge with the question, and when I saw that, my heart began banging away, as if someone had made a bell and clapper of it. She wanted me to stay. What was I thinking of? Was I afraid to speak after all this time?

I reached into my bag and took out the rock with the sea horse inside. It looked best when it was wet, when all the creature's bones showed clear, but Ling took it and handled it as if it were a piece of the king's porcelain. Just as I had done, and as Esther had, she traced the little beast's remains from head to tail. Her mouth trembled a little.

"This is more precious than what I have for you, Thomas." She reached into the pocket of her greatcoat. "Close your eyes," she ordered. I felt her slipping a ring on my little finger. She giggled as she struggled to get it over my second knuckle. "Now you can look."

It was a plain silver band, smooth, with a sheen like kid leather. There was a tracing of leaves and script woven together across the entire ring.

"Shall I read it for you?"

"No!" I said, outraged. I took the ring off and held it away from my eyes.

"Ton amour, ton Hélène, your Ling."

I kissed her. The robin must have thought we were made into statues, because when we came apart at last, he was shocked into rising again. He came back down to perch on my cross and scolded us for keeping him from his crumbs.

"It's beautiful. You are beautiful."

"But you could read the ring, Thomas!" she said. "French words! And I forgot this, that Simeon told me he thought you read my letter while he spoke."

I nodded. "You told me the truth. Monsieur Stubbs was a good teacher."

She shook her head. "*Mais non,* it was not him, not your Mister *Barbe bleue*! No, Thomas, it was like, what do you call it, what the *castors,* the beavers, make in a river, their little street of branches that lies across the water and stops it?"

"A dam?"

She smiled. "Yes, a dam. That was what you had inside, but now it is gone and you are free to be clever for always. Like a spell is lifted."

I did not argue with her but told her then about Esther, and she clapped her hands with delight. I knew what her next question would be. "My mother has heard no news of the baby, not in Brigg or any of the villages. I'm sorry, Ling."

She made an *O* with her lips, just that. I said nothing.

"Maybe he has found good parents," she said at last. "Maybe he will be happy *à la fin.*"

"Ling, I have something else to tell you. I'm going to London too, to join Stubbs. He left the village last month with Mary, and he swears he will find work for me in the city, with them, or else with somebody they'll find. I'm good for woodcraft and scribing and any task like that, until I can find a different master. My father gives me a year to do this."

I stood her in front of me, took her arm, and pointed it toward the cathedral, which was washed with silver in the late light. "I know what I want now. There, where I am pointing."

Her head burrowed back into my chest as she leaned against me. "I see the big cathedral, Thomas. Do you want to be a priest? I hope not." She twisted around to look up at me, and her eyes were teasing. "I think not."

I blushed. "I want to make buildings. If I can learn that anywhere, it will be in London, I know it."

She wriggled away from me then, lifted her hat off, and spun it on her finger. Her hair was not grown very long yet, but it reached her neck and turned neatly in at either side, glossy black as a fruit. "Bravo, my Thomas," she said. "You will make the stones and bricks obey you to make the beautiful thing. Like so."

She raised her arms above her head, curving them from the elbows, first in, then out. They were not wings, but I thought of wings.

Then she giggled. "That story I told you, Thomas, about my wedding. It was not quite like that how it happened. That big cathedral you like so well, it made me *très*—what is the word?—imaginative. Perhaps I am not a *vicomtesse*. Perhaps I am only an *aubergiste*'s wife. An innkeeper."

I pulled my brow down to make a fierce face, but she pressed it back into place.

"And Monsieur Stubbs?" she asked. "He still cares for me? He would let you entertain such a wicked thief in his house in London?"

I shrugged. "Who knows where I'll stay? I'll work with Stubbs until I find my feet. He says I am welcome with him and Mary, and he knows about the trade I want to learn now, though it is not his own. We are honest with each other. But the anatomy is over forever. It goes into a book to be printed and sold. So there will be no more dead horses, I promise. He says he can paint the best of them alive now because he knows how they breathe and move and think."

Ling snorted.

"All the time I know *that*! And better than he does!"

I remembered something else Stubbs had said to me before he left.

"He said he would put both of us into paintings. I'd be a groom or something plain, but you'd be different, special. A racing jockey in stripes, he thought. Everyone would think it was a boy, but it would be you."

She laughed. "Oh, no, Thomas. No more racing for me, unless it is in the theater. But now, *mon brave*, look how it is that you and I can be in London together! Just the two of us, and all the people and all the places we will see. Imagine that! And you can bring Monsieur Stubbs to see Belladonna and me in the horse ring. Then he will see what must be seen in a horse, and he can paint that if he wishes. My Belladonna will teach him more than any poor dead horse." She stamped her foot. "But he will never have her in his hands again, not for one instant, not unless he makes a gold statue of her."

She slipped her arm through mine and we stepped away from Zéphyrine's grave, so raked and fine now, with its necklace of hyacinths and daffodils.

Belladonna. Sans pareille. Belle aimée.

All these good things.

⌒ Hind Words ⌒

Horkstow is a real and ancient village in North Lincolnshire. The painter George Stubbs spent time there between 1756 and 1758 (there are no exact dates), doing the work described in this book. He engraved his own drawings and published his *Anatomy of the Horse* in 1766. It's still consulted in veterinary science libraries as well as by painters and lovers of art.

There are several other real-life characters in the book, including Mary Spencer and the young baronet John Nelthorpe. John Harrison, the man who discovered how to chart longitude at sea, came from Barrow-upon-Humber. He had a brother, James, who also made clocks.

All other characters are fictional.

Acknowledgments

My thanks to Hawthornden International Retreat for Writers in Scotland for providing space, time, and endless goodwill so that I could finish *Belladonna*.

David Morley's poetry (*The Invisible Kings*) introduced me to the wonderfully descriptive Romani language. I thank him for reading Simeon's words. Claire Defaux scaled and polished my French. Neither is responsible for any errors I may have made.

I am very grateful to Henry Fell of Horkstow for sharing time, footwork, car work, and much valuable information about places and lore in the village and locality.

My thanks, too, to Anthony Nelthorpe of Scawby Hall, Lincolnshire, for providing material on the Nelthorpe family.

Brigg Tourist Information office was most helpful.

To my editors, Mara Bergman and Deborah Noyes Wayshak, and my agents, Sarah Manson and Ann Tobias, I am, as ever, in awe and in debt.